RED MiCE

R BLOOM

Copyright © Racheal Bloom 2016

Racheal Bloom has asserted her right under the Copyright, Designs and Patents Act, 1988 to be identified as the author of this work.

This novel is a work of fiction. Names and characters are the product of the author's imagination and any resemblance to actual persons living or dead is entirely co-incidental. Places, if real, are used fictitiously.

All rights reserved. No part of this publication may be reproduced, stored in a retrieval system, or transmitted, in any form or by any means, electronic, mechanical, photocopying, recording or otherwise without the permission of the author.

Cover Design : SelfPubBookCovers.Com/RLSather
Cover Typography : Jimmy Gibbs.

For my husband, mum and uncle

And for my grandparents

Acknowledgments:

Heartfelt gratitude to the amazing people on this page, I'm indebted. Thank you to my husband, mum and uncle for their love, support and patience.

I'm especially grateful to writers, and others, for answering questions, engaging, and being genuinely lovely folk. Thanks to Rob Dinsdale for his invaluable perception, and for generously giving his time. Thank you to the legendary Ian Rankin for being so kind, inspirational and encouraging. My thanks to Marika Cobbold, Susie Maguire, Alison Bonomi, Oli Munson and Stuart Ross for shedding light, and offering wisdom at various points along the road. Thanks to Vanessa Robertson for 'taking a look' and for her insightful proofing.

Thanks to Dan Cleary for 'kicking my ass', and to 'Commodore' Dan Alonso for talking bars. Thanks to Beverley, sadly no longer here. Thanks to Leigh, Lex, Peter G, Andy S, Diana L, and to my friends on Facebook for support. But most of all thank YOU for reading. I hope you like the story,

Racheal Bloom 2016.

WWW.REDMICE.UK

*I pull in resolution and begin to doubt the equivocation
of the fiend that likes like truth*

Macbeth. Act 5, Scene 5. Shakespeare

*Camera got them images
Camera got them all
Nothing's shocking*

Jane's Addiction, Ted Just Admit It … 1988

Red Mice

1

Jude - Tuesday

Amsterdam

It was Sunday when she called and thirty-six hours later I was sitting in the aisle seat. I strained to see past the other passengers to the sky. The air was grey, the weather wet and stark. I hated flying at the best of times and right now I wanted both feet on the ground. The seatbelt sign flashed a couple of times and the voice-over from the captain assured everyone that we would be able to disembark shortly. I sank deeper into the large black overcoat and found my sunglasses in the front pocket. Sighing, I slid them on. I hadn't seen or heard from Coco since the split six months earlier until, out of the blue, her name lit up caller display.

"Hey baby, how are you?" Coco asked as if it were yesterday.

"I'm okay," I replied, lying. "You?"

"Jude. You know where I am. You know how to find me, if you want to, that is ..."

She was still living in Amsterdam, laughing at life, challenging me the way only she ever had. The opaque offer of a couple of nights to hook up was tempting. Having nothing better to do, I'd succumbed.

Fifteen minutes later I was standing at Schiphol Airport, reflections of colour and chrome bounced off an over polished white tile floor. The language on the signs the only real difference between Schiphol and any handful of Euro-Airports, every one of them impersonal, sprawling and overbearingly fluorescent.

The other passengers moved out of my way as I headed towards the luggage track. A year ago I would have enjoyed the way they parted; now I was just used to it. My size and the way I walked cleared a path through a lot of places. Not that I was intentionally menacing or threatening these days, I was depressed and needed a break. Life wasn't going anywhere fast or anywhere at all. Nothing worked out the way I wanted it to and I wasn't interested in trying to re-balance the apple cart. Welcome to burnout, at age twenty-four. But when *she* rang I took that call.

Being with Coco wasn't marriage. She never stayed in one place long enough, with one man long enough. I remembered the first time I saw her, London two years ago. She'd walked into the bar and ordered a Mojito. I'd nodded at the barman who owned the place, a friend of mine, Jazz. He poured, I paid and we clicked. She had a rooftop flat in South Ken. I stayed, got work around town after hours as a doorman. Turns out she had some contacts in the import export business and one night she introduced me. From then on I took care of supply and demand in the clubs, at first to keep the wages topped up and later because I got hooked on the cash. I scored lines for personal use now and again, and London life ticked by. Coco didn't have a regular job, she travelled a lot, the bills were paid on time and she always had money. I didn't ask questions.

When she said she was moving to Amsterdam I went with her. We spent over a year together, a record for her and for me too. Afterwards there was no contact - until that phone call. I didn't know why she'd called, she wouldn't say. There didn't have to be a reason. That was just Coco.

I turned my collar up against the cold; the Dutch weather was similar to home, unappealing and unpredictable. I grabbed a cab, showed the driver the scrap of paper with the address written on it and awkwardly shuffled backwards into the seat. Waiting. Wondering.

She opened the door looking as artlessly beautiful as ever. A slim figure wrapped in a turquoise silk kimono, she smiled. A large amber necklace hanging from her graceful neck, her long brown-black hair coiled sexily in a knot already half tumbling down.

"Hello sweetheart, long time no see," she said, reaching towards me with her slender arms. I stepped into the embrace, conscious that I didn't want to crush her and suddenly too aware of her lithe strength and the shape of her body through the thin fabric pressing up against me.

I pulled away abruptly, smiling. "You got any coffee in this place?"

Coco stepped back and, holding my hand like an errant child, drew me into the apartment closing the door behind us. I didn't want to break the contact. But I wanted to have a conversation, catch up, chat and talk, the way normal people do. But that wasn't Coco. Or rather it wasn't me and Coco. We never did much talking. She stood and silently undid the Kimono. It slid off her and fell into a silky puddle as I pulled her towards me. That didn't take much effort, she was already there kissing me all over fiercely.

Some time later when it had grown dark, I thought I heard voices. I turned over, waking slowly. The voices died down and there was a silhouette standing by the bed, etched and framed by the light behind.

"You awake baby?" she asked.

I sat up, rubbed my hand across my head, up the back of my neck, stretching. "I'm awake. Still not had that coffee though."

Twenty minutes later I was buying lattes in Rick's. The place was crazy busy, bodies three deep along the bar, but then I didn't expect anything different. The tempo never ceased. Yellow walls and a throbbing bass-line, the transient home of an ongoing flow of people, beer, coffee and smoke. Regulars knew that the booths and tables upstairs were the real chill zone away from the tourist trade. Rick's Café Amsterdam had probably been there when my mother had visited Amsterdam in the seventies, opposite the Bull Dog, everyone knew it, easy to find, even easier to lose yourself in. Chilling, sitting, fifteen minutes turned into three hours. I remembered the past, time spent getting wasted with Coco and now here we were again, upstairs at Rick's. We sat relaxing in each other's company, the familiarity was soothing and I felt myself smile properly for the first time in too long.

"So, what's been happening?" I asked.

She returned the smile, enigmatic and evasive. "A lot has been happening. Six months is a long time."

Never taking her eyes from mine she raised the glass and drank some of the coffee. Then lighting the joint she took a long toke, her beautiful eyes lightened faintly as the smoke hit its target.

"I need a favour actually Jude, there is something you can do for me," Coco said, lowering her voice and passing the rolled up cigarette. I dragged deeply, exhaled, the smoke gently, slowly soaring upward slow-mo, slow smoke motion.

"What would that be?" I asked as I took another hit and passed it back.

The coffee was barely cool enough to drink but Coco drank again, and then replied. I was almost mesmerised by her long lashes, almost, but not quite, lost in the spider black lash fringes as I heard her voice.

"There's something I need you to take back to the UK for me," she said phrasing it less like a request and more like a statement.

"No," I said, the word flat and hard.

Coco looked surprised, then for the first time lowered her eyes. "No, it's nothing like that," she said. "Not drugs," she said softly. 'Just a package, I need someone to take it to a friend there and I don't trust the post, that's all.'

"You don't have friends Coco, remember I know you," I laughed and drank more coffee. The joint tasted even better with coffee. Or did the coffee taste even better with the joint? I didn't know which.

"Please Jude," she touched my hand.

"So, that's why you got me over here," I leant forwards. "Coco it is *always* great to see you, you know that. And you knew when you called that I would come, hell, you probably knew all you had to *do* was call and I would have come, regardless of how it ended. We both know you could have had me back anytime. And look baby here I am." I sighed, placing my hands palm upwards on the table and shrugged. "But life is different these days. I've not done any jobs since …" I lost the words staring into her eyes. The seconds passed and she smiled at me.

The spell broke. I shook my head. "My family live in the UK and I ain't taking anything back with me. Not even for you. If it really is kosher, just use the post." I laughed at her expression. "Forget it baby. Drop it. You don't need it in your life." I stubbed the last remnants of the joint out in the ashtray. I meant it, the answer was no. Whatever it was, this time I wasn't getting involved.

2

Jude - Tuesday / Wednesday

Amsterdam

It didn't take long to pack the little holdall bag. I hadn't unpacked more than my toothbrush and shower gel but when we got back to the apartment I collected them from the glass shelf in the bathroom. They were still damp. I didn't kid myself and there was no point in staying now I knew what Coco wanted. It didn't matter. It was great to see her. She walked in as I was zipping the bag. "What are you doing?"

"Thought I'd head off," I shrugged.

"Hey come on. Don't be that way, stay, you're only here a few nights Jude. We haven't seen one another for a long time. Please," she turned her big eyes towards mine, standing leaning backwards against the sink, shoulders almost resting against the mirror behind.

Now two versions reflected back at me, both her mirror-back and the reality of the front. Maybe I had smoked too much in the café. She was wearing a pair of jeans, a bikini top with a vague, fragile, lacy cardigan over the bra and she looked so beautiful I didn't think I would ever be able to leave again. Lingeringly she touched her collarbone with her fingertips, my eyes followed, next thing my teeth were gently nipping where her fingers had been, tasting the exotic taste of her skin. Losing myself in her I made no mistake - she was a fast, dangerous ride. But I could handle it.

Next morning, surprising both of us Coco made breakfast. She poured coffee and rolled a decent joint, so it was breakfast of sorts.

"Anything you want to do today?" she asked as we smoked.

"Nothing at all," I replied, smiling at her.

"Well before we do nothing I have to go out. I won't be long. Make yourself at home and when I get back then maybe … we could do something," Coco said smiling.

She was still wearing my T-shirt, rumpled and warm and that was all. Her bare legs were maple syrup colour tanned and I could see her nakedness when she moved. She caught my gaze and laughed as she pulled her jeans on, faced the mirror and twisted her hair into a knot. I walked up behind her, a tall dirty-blonde polar bear by comparison, the glass emphasising our differences keenly. Her dark brown eyes stared into light green via our reflections. I watched, and then felt, as she reached one hand backwards, touched my face, stroked the side burns and teased the soft skin just beyond one of the diamond stud earrings I wore, before returning to caress my cheek. She swung round, kissed me full on the mouth, brushed the stubble with her soft lips and pushed her fingers into the nape of my neck where thick dark blonde hair was sheered down to skin. Then she pulled away, smiled, picked up her bag and walked out of the door.

After a long shower I felt awake and more coherent. Suddenly I was hungry. I looked at the clock on the kitchen wall, midday. No wonder I was starving, Coco had left about thirty minutes ago and there was no guarantee what time she'd be back. My stomach growled as I opened the fridge, knowing before I looked what I'd find. I glanced at the bottles of Veuve Cliquot Champagne and Absolut Vodka. Coco didn't buy things that needed eating. I wanted decent food and fresh air. With her pink towel barely wrapped around my waist and droplets of water hitting the floor from my wet hair, I padded across the cool tiles towards the kitchen counter. It was a long black marble covered workspace with stainless steel drawers and cupboards tucked neatly beneath. I needed keys and mine were back in Manchester. The first drawer was full of cutlery. The second contained rolls of cling-film and plastic bags. The third was empty, except for three red mice, our code for 'I love you'. I touched one of the heart shaped mice, the fridge magnets I'd bought the day we'd moved in together. I was surprised that she'd kept them, and smiled at the memories.

Then I tried the corner drawer underneath the kettle, corkscrews, odd candles and a pair of scissors. No spare keys anywhere. I went back to the bedroom, dried off roughly, dressed and called her cell. I was still sitting on the bed wondering why the phone was turned off when she walked back in five minutes later.

"Hi ... I'm back," she called as I heard the door open.

"Good, let's go out. Get some air and some food."

"Mmm, you look hot enough to eat," she replied softly as she came into the bedroom. "I need a quick shower before anything else and then sure ... whatever you want."

I didn't ask her where she'd been or what she'd been doing, as there was no real point. Coco didn't like those kinds of questions and since she herself didn't ask them, she deemed that they weren't important. So I waited, hungry, whilst she showered.

The afternoon blurred, we wandered by the Canals being lovers and tourists, strolling past rows of skinny, tall, crushed together houses by the water, visiting the Van Gogh Museum, eating, drinking and laughing. A nation of bikes lined grey railings as cyclists without helmets zoomed over footbridges. Almost everyone was part of the two-wheeled revolution.

I looked at my watch. It was getting late. Tomorrow morning would come too fast. Coco, her arm linked in mine, saw the shadow cross my brows.

"What?" she asked.

"Nothing," I half smiled.

"What? Tell me," she frowned, mocking me.

"Nah. It's nothing," I replied, not prepared to tell her that I had felt more alive in the past two days than during the past six months and that I wasn't in any hurry to go back home. I put my arm around her waist, pulled her closer and looked away. She didn't ask again. She knew me as well as I knew her.

3

Jude – Thursday

Manchester

Way before I wanted it to, night melted into morning and I was flying home. There hadn't been much time to think in Amsterdam, Coco was like that, or maybe it was Amsterdam that was like that. But together the mix was a heady, smoky, surreal recipe for amnesia. I hadn't wanted to leave but there was nothing there aside from the past and that wasn't going anywhere fast.

Coco was showing signs of boredom after forty-eight hours and that meant she had something or someone on her mind. She was tetchy, edgy, had obviously had enough of my company and I wasn't humiliating myself. So, I had kissed her goodbye and left; gone to Schipol Airport and caught the flight back like I was supposed to do. I had upheld my part of the deal, arrived when called and left when planned. Now all I had to do was forget her and the way she made me feel. Easier said than done. I hadn't managed it during the last six months but hey never say never. I caught a cab and then I was home. That was the easy bit.

The key slid into the lock, I opened the front door and clicked the light on. Despite the midday sun it was dark. I dumped my bag on the leather sofa, didn't bother to unpack. The dishes were still piled in the sink from before I left and the rubbish needed taking out. I opened the curtains wider to let some of the struggling light filter through the fog. The flat was dark and had a bad odour. I didn't do more than sleep here and it wasn't much of a home, although maybe it could have been if things were different. But they weren't. I checked my watch and grabbed my coat, all I wanted to do was score some gear and get wasted. It was Thursday, almost weekend and that was as good a reason to party as any other. I knew just who to score off. That particular friend would be or at least *should* be at work, so that's where I was headed.

4

Rae - The Office, Tuesday

Manchester

The warehouse isn't really that big. It has one office with scarlet painted walls, and one boss very fond of designer labels that collects girlfriends like bees to the honey, and me. I have another life out of this place, a world I'm trying to cook my way into filled with flavour and taste. In that world I'm just 'Rae' and no one cares about the latest sales figures.

But four days a week I keep the boys in the warehouse in line, work the office, stay on top of the deliveries, chase the stock and pick up the boss's dry cleaning. Seven nights a week I study for my cookery degree, look after Scott and deal with my mother. Add the two together and that makes eleven days a week, every week.

Alex's Blackberry goes off again, he's left it on the desk and it's buzzing like a beetle on acid. I glance down at the display, *Sienna calling*. I have no idea who 'Sienna' is but I mentally add her to the pile and wonder how long she will last. I pick up a thousand pounds worth of Prada biker jacket, and drape it over the back of the dark red chair. Alex, my boss, wouldn't know how to ride a motorbike if it fell on him. And that jacket would be as much use on a bike as he would.

I reach over to the printer and remove the hard copy

of the email I have just typed to one of our Chinese suppliers. We need more stock but there are design problems with a couple of pieces of the 'dancing doll' range. Alex ought to go to Beijing in person to sort all this out, we're not getting anywhere by phone. I make a note to investigate flights for him next week. As I bite my fingernail, I notice that the blue polish is mostly gone and remember that I've run out of nail varnish remover.

A gust of cold air surges into the office. Someone has left the door wide open, again. I turn to see a man standing in the doorway. He fills the space, looks around and then slowly strolls in to the warehouse as if he owns it, which I find odd, as I've never seen him before. As the light falls on his face it's clear he is not the Terminator, or Colin Farrell, although he is more than six feet tall and does look like a movie star. He has thick black hair, which falls leisurely to his cheekbones, and dark chocolate coloured eyes. His mouth has been struck by a beauty spot in a facial hit and run, and he's on his mobile phone: "Bye sexy. Be a good girl now. Sending you a big kiss."

I pull my attention away as Alex suddenly bursts into the office. "Christ Rae! Before you send emails to the Chinese suppliers speak to me, you know their English is appalling and they misunderstand everything. I've had them chewing my fucking ear off for the past half hour," Alex's voice cracks with rage as he snatches his Blackberry off the desk, not even checking it as he stuffs it into his back pocket.

I glare at him, "That's impossible. I've only just sent it."

"Whatever. Anything that goes out there goes through me first. Got it?"

Deliberately ignoring Alex I turn away and stare at the

stranger's back, he is flicking through the daily business accounts lying in Alex's in tray. He raises his hand and rubs the back of his neck, as if he can feel my gaze before I even speak.

"Excuse me. Those are private," I step towards the tray.

He turns to me, but Alex answers. "Leave it Rae, go and do something else."

I shake my head, and walk into the warehouse without saying another word. Family friends and business mixed like French dressing. I bite another fingernail and sneak a glance over at the office. They're still in there, talking.

"Hey Rae, how's it going? Alex in a bad mood again?" It's Tom, an old housemate of Alex's who drops in and works in the warehouse whenever he's between jobs. I've known him as long as I've known Alex, which on days like today, feels like too long. He gives me a lopsided grin as I head over to the back wall where he is sitting on a pile of crates. He's wearing dirty jeans with an open face and an even tan.

I shrug and sit down. "You know Alex. How are you?"
"Yeah, good. Seeing Sean later, having a few smokes, the usual," he nods. "You heard we finally got it together?"

"I'm happy for you both."

"Thanks. What about you?"

We've had this conversation before. He's told me about Sean at least three times in the past month, Tom's short-term memory is shot. But today I have some news of my own.

"I just got engaged," I say, testing the phrase out.

"That's fantastic!" Tom's eyes light up.

"Yeah," I reply thinking back.

Less than a week ago I was standing in Paris with Scott

at the base of the Eiffel Tower, when he turned to face me and went very quiet. Then he took my hand in his. His palms felt damp.

"Are you okay?"

"Do you love me?" he asked.

"You know I do. What's wrong?"

"Nothing! Will you marry me?"

I was suffocating under the weight of that stare. A queue was forming. People thought we were waiting to go up the tower. "Okay," I said not knowing what else to say. Scott nodded and we got on with the day.

Scott was a boy in a band when I met him; a guitarist with a blue fender, eating rice and cold baked beans whilst he paid for the instrument he loved more than air. Back then Scott was a poet who wrote songs until three am, fucked me until six am and then slept until noon. We'd met at a gig one night in London and got together. We had no plans, no aim at all, other than getting wasted and having great sex. He had long hair, decent ink and black leather was a lifeline.

But after eighteen months of bad dope, dull parties and losing temp jobs faster than I could get them, I'd had enough. The lifestyle of a groupie wasn't where it was at for me, so I got a grip and moved back home. I started regular work with Alex, enrolled at Uni and straightened out, again. Scott visited, but money was tight. Then two years ago we ditched the train rides and got a place together. The gigs had dried up. The band was dead. One day Scott cut his hair, had a personality transplant and began work as an actuary using his applied mathematics degree.

And now we were engaged. Not that there was a ring yet. Not that it mattered.

"Congrats Rae, you're engaged!" Tom put his arm round my shoulder and squeezed.

"Apparently I am," I blushed.

Tom looked at me. "So, when's the party?"

"What party?"

"What do you mean 'what party'?"

"I hate being the centre of attention."

"We need to have a party!"

I laughed, "No, we don't. I *need* to tell Alex before the grapevine gets to him ... and you know how he feels about people our age coupling up. The teasing will last a month."

"Silly. He'll be happy for you! Go in there and tell him!"

"Can't. There hasn't been the right time yet."

Now wasn't the right time either, the floor shakes as Alex storms into the warehouse. I quickly take the opportunity to leave Tom, and head towards the office to tidy a few things up before I go home.

But just then Movie Star speaks, addressing Alex quietly in his oddly accented voice and looking over at me as if he's judging the Darwin awards. I'm not exactly surprised as I'm quite sure I don't rate as female in his book. My cheeks flush scarlet to match the walls as the corners of his lips twist upwards, but when his eyes meet mine it's as if I am standing there stark naked.

Instinctively I glance down to make sure I've got clothes on and see black cargo pants, urban trainers and a ripped Marilyn Manson t-shirt, the kind of stuff that the women Alex knows wouldn't even do their cleaning in. Not that they do their own cleaning. The work of art recently inked on my left arm - the black day of the dead skull surrounded by flowers - seems to float above my skin. He stares for another second, turns abruptly and follows Alex outside, leaving the delivery door open.

There is a huge draft and it is an extremely heavy steel door. I am still struggling to get it closed when he comes back.

"Glad you came back," I say.

He looks at me, eyebrows raised.

"I can't get this door closed," I supply.

"It's not difficult, even for a woman your size," he replies, cigarette hanging from his lip.

Good god this man is arrogant. I want to say 'fuck off' but instead mutter, 'Thank you' and get away as fast as possible. He follows me, uninvited.

The office is tiny and he has such presence that I feel claustrophobic. An ocean of silence drowns us. Five minutes later his phone buzzes.

"One of your girlfriends?"

The words fall out of my mouth of their own accord. I am horrified. He looks at me squarely as his eyebrows hit the ceiling and I can't tell if he is amused or angry. He is extremely good-looking, handsome in the way that Alex and his friends are, and there is an open, automatic acknowledgement that women and girlfriends are in the plural.

The whole of Facebook would look anorexic by comparison to this guy's list. I shudder at the thought of him and Alex out together, it would be carnage.

"Treat your women well then?" A second later those words follow the first set all by themselves. I shrink into myself and hope I don't say anything else. My skin is burning as he stares at me whilst I continue sorting bills and papers in the deafening embarrassment. Suddenly he speaks.

"So, what about you?"

No one else walked in, he means this me. "I just got engaged," I said.

"Congratulations," he replies.

Silence overcomes us once again. A rush of speech and then silence, it is becoming a pattern like the beat of the waves as they hit the rocks.

And then he is speaking softly and I have to listen hard to catch his voice. He is looking at the floor. "I was married once. We were together five years, married two months. Over. Like that," he clicks his fingers, his face creasing into a frown. He is sitting on the chair opposite me as he stretches out his legs, crossing them at the ankle.

"I adore women," he smiles. "It's relationships which are the problem."

My lips are suddenly glued by his candour. The Tourette's has vanished along with normal conversation skills. It doesn't seem to matter as he starts talking again.

"So, anyway, tell me, what do you do? You can't work here all the time."

"I don't. I'm studying for a degree in cookery."

"You cook?"

"Yeah. It's a habit, I never went to Uni when everyone else did, I was …"

"You were?"

"I was different then, but things change. I want my own restaurant. I've got the business experience to run it. Sounds funny right?" I look at him, waiting for the laughter.

"A good friend of mine is a head chef. What's funny?"

I shrug, "Someone like me, someone who works in a warehouse wanting their own restaurant."

He shakes his head, "Here 'someone who works in a

warehouse' I'll give you his details." He starts flicking through his phone menu, picks up a pen and a post-it from my desk, writes down a number and hands it to me. "Give him a call. He'll help you."

"Thanks that's really nice of you," I say, sliding the note into my back pocket.

It turns out he's lived in London and we know the same places. We're sharing stories on the holes that Scott and the band used to play in, when the door flings open and Alex walks in. The atmosphere smashes. We *feel* it shatter as if it were as tangible as the china figurines on the shelves. Alex stares at us, from one to the other, and back again.

"What are you two talking about?" Alex demands.

Before I could get any words out, Movie Star Cheekbones answers,

"She is telling me about her future ex-husband!"

I grin at him, a full beam. It's not often a man is quicker than me and sharp too. It's definitely time to leave. Alex follows me into the warehouse and I am just getting my things together when I say, "Alex, who's your friend?" nodding towards the office.

At this point the friend comes out, lighting yet another cigarette and Alex says, "Sorry I should have introduced you guys. Jazz this is Rae. Rae this is Jazz."

I smile and say, "Hi Jazz."

And Jazz smiles back.

5

Rae – Wednesday

Manchester

Alex was Elvis reincarnated and bad-boy bad habits oozed from every CK smelling pore. With looks that lit up Blackpool promenade and a smile that knicker elastic couldn't resist, Alex's ability to attract women was as flawless as his stubble. Elvis of the North was not, however, a morning person. His friends were A-Listers, out all night, every night until dawn. Whilst Alex worked as hard as he partied, which surprised some people, he didn't keep regular office hours. Nothing Alex did was regular. It was also a well-known survival skill that no one should ever speak to him before noon. That suited me fine. I could get on without being nagged to death or having my head ripped off.

I wasn't having the greatest start to the day so I'd wandered into work hoping to clear my mind, instead of driving the usual five minutes around the corner. The walk took twenty minutes, and did nothing to calm me. As I passed the silver birch trees choking on the clouds of smog and entered the concrete trading estate, my thoughts were still full of Scott.

This morning I'd been downstairs fifteen minutes and he hadn't spoken to me. Not a 'hello' or a 'good morning.' Not a single kiss, nothing. His nose was so far in the newspaper it was as if I didn't exist. I'd made him a coffee, put it on the table and still nothing. I'd stood at the door, smoking, wondering what thirty years would bring. And then the words were out.

"Scott, are we going to choose a ring anytime soon?"

"Sure. Find one you like and let me know."

"You are joking?" I ground the cigarette into the paving stones. The tobacco split into two gold snakes.

"What's wrong now?" Scott asked, his paper landing with a thud.

"What was the fucking point in asking me to marry you - if you didn't have a ring?" I asked, finally voicing the buzzing in my head.

Scott's skin flushed ruby as he fingered the neck of his shirt collar, tugging it away from his throat before saying, "I'm sorry." His voice sounded trapped like it was stuck somewhere. "I actually do something impulsive for once and you throw it back in my face."

"Throw it back in your face? You asked me to marry you and now you're saying it was on impulse?"

"Rae, for fuck's sake, you know that's not what I meant. Don't twist this. I want to marry you, I didn't come prepared that's all. Go to the jewellers and choose something."

"On my own? You want to me to go to the jewellers to choose my own ring? Does that mean you want me to pay for the fucking thing too?"

"Don't be ridiculous! I have to go. We'll talk about it later," Scott said as he got up, leaving me speechless.

I felt the back of my eyes burn at the memory. It was hard to believe we were supposed to be happier than we'd ever been and looking forwards to spending the rest of our lives together.

As I unlocked the office I took a deep breath and pushed Scott to the back of my mind. We were all relieved that the warehouse was withstanding the recession well. Alex had networked to the bone for thirteen months last year. Strategic phone-calls, drinks, well-timed birthday gifts and hey presto, china figurines were on shiny display in the homes of the rich and famous, gleaming from news stands in the latest issues of 'Hello' and 'OK!'

The photo spreads gave Alex the initial exposure and he hadn't paid for advertising. The website mail order side had really taken off, and the business maintained a steady turnover. He never produced more than a specific number of each design and, city-by-city, people fell under the spell of the dancing dolls as their puppet master worked his magic.

I was checking the post when my boss strolled in, drenching the air in aftershave. He took his Ray Bans off and gently lay them on the desk, clumsily clunked keys and mobile down, grabbed a black coffee, did the 'good mornings' with the boys in the warehouse and then leaned in, his body near mine, his chin over my shoulder, "What's the deal? What's happening?"

He was talkative and smiling. I stepped away and looked at the clock; it was 9 a.m. I suspected his favourite breakfast (gratuitous sex) to be the culprit.

"What have you got for me? What needs my undivided attention? *Who* needs me?" He beamed, again.

"Post needs you," I said, shoving enquiries at him.

As I got back to work I felt, rather than saw, Alex looking at me from under dark hooded eyebrows. I was wearing a cherry red polo neck jumper, a black sleeveless body warmer and black Miss Sixty's jeans tucked into a pair of killer New Rocks (boots). Maybe it wasn't the most conventional office attire, but this wasn't a conventional office and besides, the warehouse was freezing. The heating had broken, again.

Just then both phones rang, we grabbed one each and stared out of the internal window as three customers then two more walked into the showroom. Alex, sitting deep into his blood red chair, finished his call.

"I'm going out for a while," he said, flexing like a cat.

"No! Alex, it's mad out there. You can't leave me on my own, it's not even ten, the boys are out on deliveries, it'll be hell, come on, please."

He held eye contact for a warm second, "You'll be fine. I trust you!"

And then he vanished.

There was one quiet moment when I snatched the chance to sweep the floor and get rid of the foam packaging and cardboard before the next onslaught of customers arrived. The china figurines watched in silence from their glorious showcases.

Morning was a distant memory as six or more hours flew by. Exhausted I sat down, finally finding time for Volvic as Alex returned.

"Hey what are you doing chilling out in my office? You should be working."

"I'm tired."

"What do you mean you're tired?"

"I mean I'm tired. It's been crazy today."

"But you don't do anything. You sit around at your desk all day long and get paid for doing nothing."

"I work here and I study for a full time degree!"

"Not my problem. I'm only concerned with the time you spend here working or rather the time you spend here when you *should* be working for me."

"I work really hard for you. I can't believe you can say that."

He was wearing faded blue jeans and a soft white rumpled cotton shirt with casual open toe big leather sandals. His feet were a nice brown.

"Is it sunny outside? Did you have a good time whilst I was stuck in here working my ass off? You know something Alex? Sometimes you can be such a fucking wanker …"

Just then the door went again and in came Jazz with Ben, one of the drivers.

"They're at it again," said Ben with half a glance, and retreated.

Jazz settled down comfortably in the nearest chair, ready to watch the next round.

"What did you call me?" Alex spat.

"A wanker. Should I spell it for you – W.A …"

"Oh man it is the real thing. Sure sign of love."

That got my attention. Jazz.

"Pardon?"

"Yes you are very much in love with him. I can tell by the way you argue."

"What the fuck are you talking about?" I looked from him to Alex and back again. Alex was staring at the floor as the silence pounded fifty decibels louder in my ears.

"You're in love with him." Jazz said again, leaning forwards and re-crossing his legs.

The guy was serious! I laughed.

"You're insane. No one in their right mind would be in love with him, least of all me, anyway I'm engaged, remember? I don't know why we're having this conversation! His ego doesn't need inflating any further believe me it's bad enough trying to work with him as it is. Do you have any idea what he is like? He's slept with the whole of Manchester, half of Europe and he thinks everything in a fucking skirt is in love with him!" I grabbed my bag.

"I'm out of here before I really do say something I regret," I stormed out of the office, slamming the door so hard I was afraid the glass had cracked.

But I knew, even as I was walking towards the car, that I was going to have to phone Alex to apologise. Not even five minutes had passed and I couldn't believe I had lost my temper. I felt sick. No matter how long our families had known one another as friends, and no matter what I knew about him personally, Alex was still my boss. He paid my wages. So that meant I had no right to talk to him that way.

I left it an hour before dialling his number, dreading it but knowing it was necessary.

"Hi Alex, it's me."

"What do you want Rae?"

"I'm sorry … I'm so sorry I spoke to you that way. I shouldn't have done."

There was silence. "Forget it. See you tomorrow."

He was gracious, he really was, but I'd overstepped a boundary that his own behaviour often made impossible to enforce. Something changed that day, and we both knew it.

6

Rae - Thursday

Manchester

Arguing with Alex didn't help. I was exhausted before I reached university and by the time I got home, Scott was already asleep. Some days my life felt impossible. I stood in the kitchen with a glass of water, wondering why I was trying so hard. Too tired to eat or think, I fed the cats and fell into bed.

The alarm rang a few hours later. I showered as fast as I could, as I didn't want to be late for the early delivery at the showroom. Scott was up by the time I was out the bathroom.

"Rae are you there?" he sounded a mile away.

"Yes?" I was buttoning my jeans as I looked over the top of the stairs. His cropped hair was shot through with silver and he looked so different to who he used to be on stage five years ago. It was as if the other Scott had never existed.

"We've Japanese clients over. I don't need you to cook - I'm taking them out. Don't wait up, I'll sleep in the spare room," he said, which I took as a pointed reference to the fact I'd woken him a lot recently. He picked up his briefcase and left. 'Let's do something together at the weekend' died on my lips as I watched the front door close.

Lately, for some reason being with Scott was hard

work. It wasn't like I didn't want us to be happy, but we just couldn't seem to stay on the same page for longer than a sentence. For a minute I didn't move, all my energy faded. I sighed. I had to get to work, Alex relied on me, and even though we argued we were still a team.

The traffic was quiet and I was there in minutes. As soon as I got in I found a message on the machine. We'd had the delivery, it was still at the airport and the staff were now demanding a huge fee and insisting on a swift removal. I reached for the phone as it was ringing off its cradle and saw the post-it Alex had left stuck to the wall above my desk: "Phone me if you need me. Gone to Marbella."

Predictably I discovered this neat little yellow note *after* I'd taken the second furious call from the freight handlers. They were under contract, I had a boss who would stop my wages for six months if I paid them twice without double-checking and there was no record on the bank statement. Luckily Alex was surgically attached to his mobile.

"Hi Alex."

"Hey doll."

"Sorry to bother you, the delivery is in, but the airport hasn't been paid. It looks like a bank mix up. I wanted to check with you before I pay and send the boys to collect."

"'S okay. 'S no bother."

I could tell by his voice I'd woken him up. "Sorry, call me back when you get chance."

"No, wait, I meant to run through this with you, shipments are to go via Bells. They're in the red book, give Johnny a call. Introduce yourself, tell him I want the stuff at the warehouse by midnight and I'll see him there. Any problems call me back."

"Okay, will do. Bye."

Ten seconds later I got a text. "Thanks." Alex had this new habit of texting when he'd forgotten to say 'thanks.' I couldn't help but smile.

The rest of the day skittered away from me like a child on a sled skimming frosty ground. Time flew recklessly and out of control. Finally things slowed down late afternoon and I was sitting in Alex's chair, checking my email when my cousin walked in. It was a warm day and he looked like an extra from the Godfather.

"Don't you want to take that off?" I said nodding at the heavy overcoat he was wearing.

"Nah, didn't get much sleep last night," he said shoving his fists deeper into thick woollen pockets. Dirty dark thick blonde hair was razored into teasing spikes and his eyes were black saucers, all pupils where the iris should have been. Jude looked young, barely filling his twenty-four years. Usually he had an easy thirty-plus aura, but not today. He caught me looking and in reply slid a pair of sunglasses in place, hiding his give-away-eyes.

"I'm thirsty," I said, taking a couple of coins out my jeans and pushing them towards him. He sloped off to the drinks machine. A minute later he was back, slamming two cokes down on the desk and sitting himself next to the Dell.

I ripped my can open, "Cheers. Well, c'mon who's your favourite girl this week?" It was a game we played, my transparent way of keeping an eye on him as much as he allowed, which lately wasn't much.

"Oh y' know," he said shrugging, snapping the ring pull off noisily, not meeting my eyes even with the shades.

"No," I said. "I don't know."

He poured the bubbles down his throat, "Haven't had time for women lately."

"Why? What's up?"

Just then his phone beeped, and as he stared at the screen the colour from his face flooded out.

"Are you okay?"
He slid the phone into his pocket, coughing, "Yeah, I'm fine. Sorry, what did you say Rae?"

"Who was that?"

"No one. Wrong number."

"Oh really?"

"Yeah."

"You were going to tell me something."

"I don't remember," he shifted and stood up, drinking his coke.

"You know where I am if you get your memory back," I said, knowing better than to push it. "So, who are you seeing?"

"Lisa, you met her, with the fake … (his hands made breast type shapes). Great body! Karen's done with."

"I'm sorry, I really liked Karen."

He shrugged, "I did too. But easy come easy go. I'm seeing a top bird, she's hot for an old chick."

"Old chick? How old?"

"Thirty-four," he laughed loud. "I'm doing pensioners now!"

"Thirty-four is old? I'm almost thirty!" I said, feeling ninety.

"Think that's it. No! How could I forget? Last weekend I met one hot Latino lady! Got her number but not taken her out yet," he rubbed his chin. "But I tell you who I really do fancy …"

"Please tell me you have shares in Durex."

He continued, "A couple of sisters I've had my eye on for a while, Jazz's cousins."

At the unexpected mention of Jazz my stomach spun. His name brought back the memory of that row with Alex, but I knew my cousin and the way his mind worked. One wrong murmur and Jazz and I would be doing the rounds of verbal gymnastics on Manchester's gossip vine.

"Jazz's cousins. Right, they're family so I presume you're doing those two at once? Actually forget it I don't want to know. Where in hell do you find the time?"

He grinned as he shook his head slowly. "There's always time. As for the J-Lo, I've forgotten her name but very sweet girl, unforgettable ass, perfect like peaches," his hands were gesturing unmistakably.

"Enough for fuck's sake!"

He laughed. "How're things with you? How's Scott? You being good?"

"Fine. Everything's fine. You know me, I'm always good," I said.

"Yeah but remember I do know you and you weren't always good!" he said ruffling through my hair as if I were a child.

I ducked, reluctant to tell my cousin anything about Scott and me, and instead I forced a smile. "I've grown up since then. I've been good the whole time I've been with Scott and that's almost five years. Anyway you were still in nappies when I was out and about!"

He shook his head. "I was never in nappies! But I know. Everyone knows. Man, you were wild."

That was a long time ago when I was a kid, and I had freedom to party whenever I wanted after dad vanished. Mum found out about his affair, he didn't bother to keep in touch and she went through a chameleon string of distractions. She was out, so I stayed out. She never let having a daughter interrupt her social life. She wasn't that type of mother. And by the time my young cousin was old enough to be around town I'd learnt discretion as I'd had enough of people voicing noisy opinions on my business.

Jude accepted the silence, and then suddenly broke it, "Where's Alex?"

"On an aeroplane," I replied looking at my wrist.

7

Jude – Thursday

Manchester

Alex hadn't been in the warehouse or the office. Disappointed, I opened the car, sparked up, inhaled and watched as the windows became grey fog. Everyone knew Alex had lived in the showroom for the past year or so. Before then it was impossible to predict where Alex would be from one hour to the next. Now Alex was making real money he could afford to relax, get back in the scene. Stoned, I laughed out loud at the thought of Alex getting back into the scene. Alex just did his own thing and people followed.

Besides, I had been to Amsterdam for forty-eight hours and not told a soul. The only person who knew where I had been was Coco. Business or not, Alex flying some bird out to Marbella for twenty-four hours on a whim to impress her was nothing out of the ordinary.

I stretched and switched the engine on. The black VW chugged into life. I accelerated, surged forwards and then swore as I was forced to slow down. The traffic lights were against me and I wasn't sure where I was headed. Maybe home. Maybe out. But instead I filtered left as the lights turned green, and drove towards my mum's. She should be in, although if not I'd had some family contact so the message would get back that I was still alive. It was good to see Marae. Our mothers were sisters, neither of our dad's had been around so we'd spent time together growing up. The habit had stuck. By the time I hit fifteen we were going to the same clubs. That was when 'Marae' became 'Rae.' She was twenty-one and she'd looked much younger. Whereas I'd looked older, *felt* older, than her. I'd kept an eye on what she was up to, but it worked both ways.

Rae had been the one I'd turned to when it all came crashing down around my ears. Rae and her sanity, far more like a sister than a cousin.

My mind flickered back to that morning in our apartment seven months ago when Coco came out of the bathroom. I'd just got in from work at 8 a.m. She was standing leaning against the white bathroom door, her hair sleep-messy sexy, tumbling around her shoulders. "How the fuck did this happen?" she said as she looked at me.

I had no idea what she was talking about. "What?" I asked as I went to the fridge and poured orange juice, one for me and one for her, the same as usual.

"This," she repeated, jabbing a white plastic stick in the air.

"I'm pregnant," she said shaking her head. "I'm on the pill and I'm fucking pregnant."

The words jolted through me as if a bolt of electricity had surged up from the floor where I was standing and right then I felt my whole world light up. I went over to her, wrapped my arms around her waist, my hands spanning her stomach thinking our lives were about to change. "I love you," I whispered softly, my mouth against her ear.

She shrugged me off, stepping away quickly as if I was diseased and looked at me. "No way," she said. "No fucking way."

"No way?" I stared at her.

"No fucking way," she repeated and then turned, leaving me standing alone in the kitchen with two glasses of juice and a loud bang as the bathroom door slammed shut behind her. I stood in the silence until I heard the shower.

I started smoking twenty-four seven to numb it, doing lines when the smoke didn't help, paid for by jobs I shouldn't have done for people I wished I hadn't met.

Big things were happening around me. I saw my life spiral out of control. One of the gang suffered an accident so with him in hospital I moved up the food chain. A job was going down that couldn't be interrupted, a large amount of gear was being brought into the country and then divided up, to be sent out to various interested parties. It was down to me to make sure the deal went ahead smoothly, stay in touch with the right people, ensure none of the smaller buyers got cold feet and remind them of what they had to lose if they changed their minds. To keep our backs covered I'd lined up secondary contacts and arranged a decoy cargo at a different port the same night in case the police got wind. I even worked out I'd a talent for it.

But right in the middle of it all the girlfriend of the injured man got frightened and started shouting her mouth off about what she knew. Someone was sent in to keep her quiet. Permanently.

I wasn't into that level of violence. And somewhere in the back of my head I realised I was slipping.

I argued like bitter-hell with Coco about the baby but she wouldn't hear it. There was no negotiation. She went out a lot; we hardly saw one another and then a couple of weeks later she booked herself into a clinic. That was it. End of.

The truth was that if it wasn't for Rae I'd still be adrift in Amsterdam, mourning what might have been, or worse. After Coco had the abortion I'd phoned her. The very next day she'd caught a flight and she was there. Rae, the family pragmatist knew I would never leave on my own. She said she wanted me where she could keep an eye on me. I didn't care to argue. She'd packed my things whilst I had sat stoned, and never once said afterwards that I was pathetic or I told you so. Rae had warned me that Coco wasn't the settling down type and that a woman like her wasn't going to fall into motherhood with any grace or ease. But I'd loved her.

I was on the verge of telling Rae I'd seen her when that text message had come through. It was clearly a wrong number. But all the same that had taken my mind right off track. The moment was gone so I'd chatted some shit and left.

Sitting at the lights I switched on the phone again and looked at the text. "*You have something of mine. We need to meet. I will be in touch.*"

And that was all. There was no name and no other details. I'd never seen the number before in my life. The lights changed and unable to shake the cold water running down my spine, I drove off.

I pulled up at my mum's ten minutes later, saw her shape through the glass and felt her smile before I even saw her face.

She opened the door and reached for me, hugging me tight. "Hi stranger!"

"Hi," I grinned at her, "Something smells great!" Mum's house always smelt like home.

"I'm glad you're here Jude," she said, her black dress swishing noisily against her bony frame as she walked.

"Yeah?" I replied as I shrugged my coat off, leaving it on the stairs.

"Yes, Rae gave me one of her new recipes the other day, it's fabulous and we can't decide if it is just us, or if Rae is in fact a genius!" she laughed.

"We?" I asked, as I headed into the kitchen through the white hallway, past the plants and the bookcases.

The kitchen table was covered with dark crumbs but I didn't see more than that as I was knocked into the wall by tumbling legs and arms, a child doing a great impersonation of a black Labrador.

"Zara!" I swung her up into a ferocious hug.

"Hahaa!"

"You're getting heavy!" I said, smiling at her.

"I'm not!" she said, her whole face pouting as I put her down.

"Must be all that cake. Did you leave any for me?"

"Sticky chocolate and pear," Mum handed me a plate with a generous slab.

I took a large bite, "God. That's amazing!"

"Don't speak with your mouth full," Zara interrupted.

"Guess what? I'm going to Jenna's party tomorrow, and sleeping over."

"Who's Jenna?"

"My best friend from school. It's her birthday," Zara said, her fingers slowly creeping towards my cake, long thick black hair falling forwards, blue eyes holding mine trying to distract me from the thievery.

Alex's baby sister was going to be a heartbreaker one day. I smiled and put my hand on top of hers. She pulled away, grinning, caught out.

Mum looked over, "I picked her up from school. Alex is going to collect her on his way home. He's taking you for pizza isn't he?"

Zara nodded, clumps of cake stuck to her fingers. She took the dishcloth from the draining board and tried to wipe her hands.

"You're better off washing those properly Z," I said.

"Okay," Zara nodded and skipped off to the downstairs bathroom.

"Alex is going to have a job picking her up, he's on his way back from Marbella," I said quietly.

"Marbella?" Mum shook her head. "Typical Alex. If he's not back I'll take her. She's no trouble."

"Where's Auntie Beth?" I asked, pouring a glass of water as Zara came back in.

"At a health spa with Rae's mum for two nights, they found a great deal on the net."

Zara began cleaning the table, slopping puddles between the plates.

"How come you didn't go?" I asked, drinking.

She laughed, rescuing the table from Zara's exuberant efforts. "A health spa? Jude! You know I love my sister and I love Beth *like* a sister but I can't spend forty-eight hours listening to those two without a bottle of wine or a cigarette!"

I laughed too and stood up. "Okay I'm outta here." I bent down and kissed Zara on the top of the head. "You be good tomorrow at Jenna's."

She smiled, "I will."

"See you soon?" Mum asked. I slid into my coat at the door.

"See you soon," I replied nodding, feeling the urge for a cigarette of my own that I couldn't smoke in front of Zara or my mum. I had just enough gear left for one small one. It would have to be enough.

8

Rae, one week later – Wednesday

Manchester

It had been exactly one week and a day since I'd met Jazz and I couldn't stop thinking about how I'd behaved. Since Alex rarely mixed business with pleasure and as I was never invited to socialise outside of family events, it was unlikely that Jazz and I would cross paths again. But the truth was I needed to fix things. The memory of being abusive to my boss and slamming the door hard enough to break crept back into my mind, again. I didn't want that to be anyone's lasting impression of me, especially if I was hoping for a work placement with a friend of theirs' who just happened to be one of the city's Head Chefs. 'Crazy' wasn't the character reference I'd been aiming for.

Jude had been out on the tiles. One of the boys had mentioned something about Jude "really going for it" plus Alex had been grumbling about wanting to speak to him and not being able to get hold of him. But that was all. I hadn't seen or heard from Jude either since our disjointed chat. Seconds later my mobile rang, flashing my cousin's number. I smiled. Think of the devil and he calls …

"Hey! What's up?" I flicked him onto loudspeaker.

"What do you want with your falafel? Hummus or tahini?"

"Queen Street?"

"Yep!"
"Thanks, hummus *and* tahini please!"
"Is Alex in? Am I buying for both of you?"
"Just me. He's got a lunch date in town."
"See you in five."
"Love you!"

The deli on Queen Street was an old style delicatessen graced with an irony canopy outside, and a long slim counter inside. With every 'delicacy' you could dream of from salt beef to roll-mops and no room for more than a queue of eight people in the shop at any one time, it was one of South Manchester's best. Queen Street was always busy, the food fresh, the portions plentiful. And it had been made the general rule that whoever was passing and had been paid recently, bought lunch.

Ten minutes later Jude appeared with colourful bulging fat pitta breads for each of us. I felt my throat tighten. Jude's cheeks were hollow, his skin sallow, and he was still wearing that coat. Whatever partying he was doing looked like *it* was doing *him* lately. But if he was interested in food, that was a good sign. We sat down and Jude gave me a thin smile as he unwrapped his pitta. I tried not to look as worried as I felt.

"How much do I owe you?"
"Nah, don't be silly."
"In that case an angel must have sent you."
"The angel of empty stomachs?"

"You're the angel of Pitta and Falafel!" I joked, swallowing hard. "No, actually I was thinking about you when you rang."
His eyebrows rose whilst he continued eating.
"I was wondering if you were okay."
"Sure I'm okay. What do you mean?"

"I'm not being heavy, you just seem to be on a mission lately. Is anything up?"

"Up? No, not at all," Jude lowered his eyes, and shrugged. "Been having a good time, a bit of fun."

"Are you sure you can handle this much fun?"

"Of course I'm sure but thanks anyway babe," smirking Jude pulled out a pack of cigarettes. He flicked the box lid up so I could see a line of neatly rolled joints stacked in an empty Marlboro packet. "Chill out Rae, you want one?" he laughed tugging a white stick out of the row and gently rolling it between his fingers before putting it up against his nostrils to inhale the scent.

"No thanks. But it's not just weed is it? I wasn't born yesterday. You look like shit at the minute."

"I have a smoke at night. Since when does that make me a fucking addict?"

"That's not what I'm saying."

"Right. What are you saying?"

"Maybe you need to give it a rest for a bit that's all. Do other things."

Jude put the joint down and pulled out a wrap of paper the size of a razor blade, slid tight under the flap of the cigarette packet. He opened it, stuck his finger in white powder and licked it, offering the wrap. "I do other things! Here, have some, seriously babe, this stuff is sick! It'll do you good!"

I shook my head, "Not what I meant!"

"Lighten up Rae, there was a time you'd have known what the fuck you were turning down," he glared at me. The food lay forgotten on the desk.

"You're right. I'm the last person who can tell you what to do. I worry about you, that's all. Old habits, can't help it," I said, my hand on his arm.

"It's really no big deal. I do a bit of stuff here and there, have a couple of pills at the weekend with the guys on the door to pass the time and I smoke. That's it. You know the score, no worries, got it all under control. Seriously." Jude shrugged, re-wrapped the powder and closed the packet sliding it all back into his large pockets.

There wasn't much else to say. His ears were shut. It wasn't like I hadn't been there myself but I knew Jude wouldn't listen, for one thing I was a 'chick' so I wasn't 'expected' to handle it whereas it was 'different' for him. The problem was that as long as he felt he had a choice, in his mind he didn't *have* a 'problem.' Reality hadn't reached him and I was worried about how long, and how much gear, it would take before that happened. I decided to ask Alex to keep an eye on him. He looked up to Alex. Alex could talk sense into him.

Jude picked up his pitta in silence and ate another few mouthfuls before he gave up and slung the rest in the bin.

The silence lasted a strong minute. "Jude ... I'm sorry. Come over for dinner later? Please?"

"I'm good. Got stuff in."

"Anytime, you know that."

He nodded.

And then before I could stop myself the words fell out, "So, have you seen Jazz recently?"

"Oh yeah?"

"Is he okay?"

"Pardon?"

"I ... wondered how he was."

"How he was?"

"He ... seemed nice."

"Nice?"

"Yes. Nice! Fuck! Is there a parrot in here?"

"Jazz isn't nice, Jazz is like me but older."
"Look, if you see him, just tell him hi. From me."
"Since when do you say 'hi' to Jazz?"
"What's with the inquisition?"

Jude looked at me, eyes narrow. "No inquisition. I'm asking why you want to say hi to Jazz? I didn't even think you knew him."

"I don't know him ... Look the truth is I lost it with Alex in front of him. Right after I found out that Jazz's friend is Head Chef at Malmaison and he'd said he would put in a good word. That's all. You know how much I need a decent placement. Forget it." I stood up, trying to squeeze past him, I needed to go and wash my hands. Feeling guilty for mouthing off was one thing, social suicide, another entirely.

Jude began flicking his phone. "There you go!" he said triumphantly.

"There I go what?" Suddenly lunch turned into rocks. My stomach hurt.

He showed me the screen: "You said stay away from your family, well my family likes you. Remember Rae?"

Before I even caught a breath Jazz's name lit up the screen. Jude grabbed his phone.

"Hello," he laughed. "I'm good and you? Yeah – what does it mean? My cousin for your cousins! Yes I know it's two for one ... But mine is ... Exactly!"

I couldn't believe my ears! Jude was trading me as part exchange for the couple of models he was interested in. I swung at him, my hand thudding into solid muscle and bone, bouncing off, hurting me more than him. I lunged, aiming for the phone but I wasn't anywhere near tall enough.

He deflected, grinning from ear to ear as I tried to grab

him. It was futile. I looked around the office for something to silence him with, or even better kill him, but there were no sharp objects. Awash with horror I stood shock still as Jude relentlessly held the handset away from his ear, deliberately pointing it out in the room on speakerphone with the volume up. Thank God we were the only ones in the office.

"She has a fiancé," Jazz said.

"Since when does that matter to you?"

Jazz laughed, "True. What's her number?"

Jude actually gave him my number whilst I was too stunned to react.

"Now your cousins, yeah! Both! I need a good session!" Jude reached past me and grabbed *my* pen to write down the two numbers he had traded me for. Smiling with what distinctly looked like a glossy veneer of victory, he ended the call.

"Fucking hell Jude! How could you do that to me?" I shoved my hands into my pockets tightly.

"So you can sort things out with him, I thought that's what you wanted. Now you can."

"But not like that. He'll think I want to sleep with him! You know I can't do that. I don't even *want* to do that. He treats women like shit, plus I am engaged! I'm happy! Call him back."

"He doesn't treat women like shit, for fuck's sake. He loves women! Get over yourself!" Jude shoved me out of his way and sat down in Alex's chair, reclining and resting his legs on the desk.

"Me get over myself? Whatever! At least you got what you wanted! You got your two numbers. Two more girls you have to have or the world stops. Not everyone is like you and anyway it's not as if he's going to call. Why would he? He probably can't even remember who I am."

"Jesus Rae! When did you get so uptight? You wanted to speak to him, now you can. I was doing you a favour. Trust me he'll phone. He always phones."

Right then the door swung wide open and Alex walked in.

"Who phones? What's going on?" Alex started to ask but was quickly distracted when he saw who was talking. Jude sprang out of the chair and slapped Alex on the shoulder.

"Hey man!" Alex said grinning.

"He-hey!" Jude said when Alex had stopped hitting him on the back long enough to allow speech.

"Good to see you what's new?" Alex asked.

"He's an asshole but that's nothing new," I muttered, still furious.

Jude glared at me, "She's got time of the month, ignore her. I'm good, how's it going?"

Alex threw a curious glance in my direction but I didn't reply, and he hit Jude on the back again, "Good, do you want to go for a drink later in the week, maybe Friday? Hooking up with the boys in town. Usual crew you, me, Jazz, Giggsy, couple of others. Interested? Or are you working all weekend?"

Jude lit up, "No, I'm not working this weekend."

I guessed he was remembering the last time. So was I, remembering hearing about it anyway. I shook my head at the pair of them. Here I was with two key players from Manchester's A-List and one was my cousin. It was insane that a small group set the social standards by which the entire city failed. Alex and Jude reflected one another, wearing almost identical outfits, their only differences being hair colour, taste in drugs and income.

Their plan was simple, meet at the Hilton Cloud Friday night at ten. The bar was literally in the clouds on the twenty-third floor of the Hilton Hotel, jutting out from the side of the building, like a glass ledge (or green-house) with ceiling to floor windows. The vertigo from the view added adrenalin to the alcohol rush. It was trendy, townie and full of too-old Taylor Swift and One Direction fans. Scott and I completely avoided the place.

After Jude left, Alex sat in the office, chewing a pencil and sketching new designs. He caught me staring through the internal window, he looked away but I saw the smile. He looked different when he was drawing, softer. I was tempted to go in and ask him to talk to Jude but he was clearly preoccupied and I didn't want to disturb him.

About an hour later he stuck his head into the showroom. "Rae?"

I was chatting to a customer, "Yes?"

"When you're free."

I laughed at his expression. "Give me a sec.'"

"Sure. Thanks."

I finished dealing with the customer and then went into the office.

"How are we doing in Amsterdam?" Alex asked.

Alex had branched out and was now selling the dancing doll range to selected franchises in European Cities, whilst he still had control over the exclusivity of the UK collection. I picked up the hard copies I had run off the system. I had Brussels in my hand, knowing that if he wanted Amsterdam he'd want those figures too.

"Here you are," I said handing him the documents.

"Thanks doll. So, how are we doing? Are they selling okay? What about Brussels?" he asked, crossing his legs and leaning back into his chair as he scanned the figures.

I handed him the Belgian report, "Like you don't know how we're doing down to the last Euro."

"Sure I know, but I want to hear you tell me," Alex replied.

I quoted the figures at him.

"It sounds better when you say it," Alex said.

"You know exactly how well they're doing every single time before you ask and you also know that they're waiting for the next delivery," I perched on the edge of his desk. "So are Marbella and Paris for that matter, all waiting for the next delivery. Europe loves you."

"Rae! Seriously, have you seen the figures? Look at this! We're up by 500% on this time last year and we're in the middle of a recession," Alex said, a broad smile spreading across his face when he realised how much money he was making. He flicked backwards and forwards between the reports. "I think I'm going to have to take a little trip to see the CEO's. I've not been since the initial meetings."

"The design issues need sorting first. I've booked your flight for the end of next week. It's in your diary, look."

He nodded, "Thanks. That's perfect."

"How about the week after to meet with the Euro CEO's?"

"Great. The sooner the better."

He was in a good mood and now seemed like the right time to talk to him. "Alex I need your help with something. Well, actually, specifically, with Jude."

"Sure. What's up with Jude?" he swivelled on the chair, leaning forwards.

Just then Zara, Alex's little sister came running in through the warehouse. She pushed the door to the office wide open and beamed at us.

"Hi Zara," I said, smiling despite her timing.

Alex looked at me, "Catch up later, yeah?"

"Sure, no worries."

Zara's thick hair was tangled, her skirt twisted, both knees dirty and scraped. She looked like she'd spent the day climbing trees rather than in a classroom. She grinned at Alex. "Daddy said I could come and see you. I've got a kitten! He's gorgeous!"

Alex laughed, "Does mummy know about that?"

"No but daddy said she would love it. Rae you have to come and see him," she said as she sat down on Alex's knee and spun round to talk to him, her face animated and light.

"I will, as soon as I can, I promise," I replied, as the door slammed shut.

Back in the showroom I faced an ongoing stream of customers. But I couldn't stop worrying about how much food I had to prepare for cookery tonight, my mind sautéing as I chatted and sold. There wasn't chance to even attempt to talk to Alex again.

Later, as I was leaving my phone buzzed, I picked the thing up off the desk so Alex wouldn't mistake it as his going *again* and dropped it into my pocket. I remembered the text when I was in the car. I tapped the little message as I drove off, expecting to see Scott's name followed by the usual request to sort dinner out. Scott's priority was always his stomach. But as the text opened, I realised it wasn't from Scott and saw instead that it was from an unknown number.

"Rae I thought you had a fiancé. Naughty. Text back! Jazz."

I stalled the engine. Sitting at the T-Junction I restarted the car. That was the one thing I had consoled myself with after Jude 'helping' me with the consequences of my outburst at work. It was also the one thing I was certain of. I wouldn't have to prove to Jazz that I wasn't a psycho for the way I spoke to Alex, because there was no way Jazz would get in touch.

But he had. And that took me so totally by surprise that I completely ignored his instruction to text back and drove to Sainsbury's instead. Now that I had my chance to fix things I suddenly had no idea what to say to him.

As I got home with bulging bags and managed to get the key in the door I was glad my fiancé was working late. After a two hour wait I finally gave Jazz his text back.

"Hi, I haven't been naughty! Friends?"

Beep beep.

Impertinent text. Immediate reply.

"You can be naughty. I even want to say: 'Be naughty.' But I don't dare. Yes, friends. Let's go for a drink. Talk soon."

The little keyboard on the Blackberry felt as if it had been dipped in olive oil as my fingers slid across it. Damn it! I shouldn't have picked up on his word 'naughty.' And damn Jude for putting me in this situation. I took a deep breath. I could handle Jazz. I'd been around Alex my whole life and exposure to him was the best education in managing males with excessive testosterone that anyone needed.

"No one is going to be naughty! But a drink would be lovely."

Beep beep. "Tomorrow evening."

God he was fast. I was choking at work and had a presentation for Uni to deal with, and although I wanted that placement badly there weren't enough hours in the day. "I'm really sorry, I can't. How about next week?"

No reply. I chewed a nail. Clearly Jazz had far better things to do than go for a drink with the 'crazy person who worked in a warehouse.' But after fifteen minutes of waiting I couldn't stop myself: "Hey. Attention deficit! ☺ Will you have changed your mind by then?"

Beep beep. "You are very cheeky. When?"

"Next week, anytime after May 5th."

Another ten minutes of silence passed. That was it. I wasn't texting him again, that in- person apology would have to wait until hell froze over.

"Hi I'm home." Scott's voice rang out.

"I'm in here," I said, just as my mobile bleeped and Jazz sent his last text:

"No problem. Keep in touch. X"

9

Rae - Saturday May 1st

Manchester

It was Saturday, the morning after Alex, Jude and Manchester's big night out. Not that I had gone but I hadn't been able to forget about it happening. Jude was a permanent worry and I was nauseas with anxiety about the looming presentation. Unable to sleep I'd been downstairs, studying since six, when Scott appeared in the kitchen just before nine. With the radio on low and the door shut, I hadn't heard him get up.

"I'm going out," he said, running his hand through his hair.

"Oh …"

"I know it's early but …"

"Will you be back for lunch?"

"No. I'm seeing Matt at the gym for squash. His wife's sister is visiting for the week. We'll grab something there and head straight to the game afterwards."

"United? You got extra tickets?"

Scott nodded, "Yeah. They've never been. Should be a good one."

"That must have been planned quite in advance."

Scott shrugged, "Rose wanted to go to a game."

"Who is Rose?" I felt my mouth go dry.

Scott narrowed his eyes. "I just said, Matt's wife's

sister."

"No, you didn't say. But … Whatever."

"What's the problem? You never want to go to a game." Scott squared his shoulders. "It's getting late, Rae."

"Fine. See you later." I said looking at the cupboard, swallowing hard.

Scott's words stung but I didn't want another row. The phone started ringing. Scott passed it to me and left. He didn't look back.

I sighed as I answered the call. "Hello."

"Morning Rae, you do realise it's Zara's 8th birthday this weekend?"

"Crap! Thanks Mum, I'd completely forgotten. I haven't even had the time to drop in and see her new kitten."

"Beth just phoned, they're having a party for her tomorrow afternoon."

"I'll sort it," I said, planning to nip out to get her a fast card and a little present. I began looking around for my keys whilst my mother was still speaking.

"You'll bake her a birthday cake."

I didn't answer.

"Rae?"

"Why not. It's not like I have anything else to do," I replied, knowing that the sarcasm wouldn't register. She never thought I had anything to do.

"That's lovely darling, I said you would. Speak to you later."

I put the phone down, and opened the larder to see if I needed anything. The shelves were crammed but it didn't help. I washed my hands, looking at the kitchen clock. I had no idea what time Scott would be back and I hadn't heard a single word from Jazz since our texts. I wasn't going to be the one to get in touch with him first. I didn't have time to breathe until 'presentation day' and yet here I was baking birthday cakes. But Alex's family were my extended family. I didn't mind making the effort. It was just a question of timing. And the assumption from my mother that I would automatically drop everything; which was *exactly* what I had done. I sighed, again.

"Hi, Auntie Beth? It's me Rae, are you home?" I asked.
"Hi darling, sure. Come over!" she replied.
"Okay, see you soon."
Within ten minutes I was pulling up the driveway of Alex's parent's house and parking behind his mother's silver jeep. As I struggled to get out of the car with the iced sugar-pink number eight, the white double-doors of the house opened wide, and Zara waved. I stopped swiftly, slid the cake on to the backseat, and stood awkwardly in front of the car door.

"Hi Zara! Can you tell your …"

"Rae! Have you come to see my kitten?" Zara shouted as she ran off.

A moment later Auntie Beth appeared. Her dark hair drew attention to a barely-there painted face with pretty eyes and sharp lips. Everything about Auntie Beth was subtly sculpted. She was a woman who, like the late Joan Rivers, believed cosmetic enhancements were a 'natural' part of the ageing process.

As a result she looked fifteen years younger than she actually was. Wearing a figure defining plum vest, snug midnight navy jeans and a pair of studded cowboy boots, she rushed over and hugged me tight, peering through the car window over my shoulder. "Wow! Darling! That is gorgeous!"

"For tomorrow," I said smiling.

"Thank you," Auntie Beth said, holding both of my hands as we kissed cheeks.

"Rae lovely to see you," Uncle Sam patted me on the back less than a minute later.

"Come in, I'll put this away," Auntie Beth insisted.

"Yes come in," Uncle Sam said putting his arm around my shoulders. His black hair had turned dark grey. I wondered if Alex's would do the same one-day.

Uncle Sam was tall, easily around six feet. He bent his head towards my ear, "Your mother and Lola are having a planning meeting. How much planning does it take?" He shrugged, not waiting for an answer. "Twenty kids arrive, get fed, and leave. Our role is to prevent them destroying the house."

"Maybe they're discussing escape routes for the adults?"

His mouth crinkled into a smile. "Talking of which, Marae, you can't disappear without saying hello. She knows you're here." His tone hit my conscience.

"So that's a bad thing, then, if I leave?" I dug my toe in the ground as guilt curved through me and I thought of my work lying on the table at home.

"She's your mother. Five minutes, that's all," Uncle Sam replied.

I relented, allowing him to walk me in to the house through the large open hallway. The floor was polished and wooden, fresh pink roses sat in two small vases on the rectangular mahogany table along the wall. Tiffany lamps stood in each corner as photographs in gold frames glinted in the sunlight. This was a family home, full of happy memories. Throughout the decades laughter had been frozen and captured, but the life reflected on these white painted walls was real and vibrant.

"Rae! How are you?" Auntie Lola breezed toward me like a force nine from the kitchen, holding a tea towel in one hand and a cup of coffee in the other. She hugged me, "I've just seen the cake, looks fantastic sweetheart! Hope it didn't take you long."

"Isn't she fabulous?" Auntie Beth beamed. "Zara will love it, it'll make her day. Would you like a drink? Stay for something to eat!"

"I can't, I've too much work to do, but thank you," I replied.

"Rae! This is Princess!" Zara appeared, holding a wriggling black kitten with blue eyes to match hers.

"Here!" she said, offering her to me.

"Princess?" I asked as I took her, "Isn't that a girl's name? I thought 'she' was a he?"

Uncle Sam raised his eyebrows, "Yes. So did we and apparently not."

Princess gazed up at me. Her black fur stuck out at angles on her tiny head and framed her face, with longer silver pieces sprouting from her ears. She began motor-purring and head-butting my chin softly, before snuggling against my chest. I could feel her little heartbeat. It was hard to believe that my cats were ever this small. "She's lovely," I said as I gave her back to Zara.

"Miranda, your daughter's here," Uncle Sam said loudly toward the open-plan dining area.

"I thought I heard her. Hi darling," my mother arose from a black leather couch like an extra from I Claudius, Roman, deadly and imperial.

I took a deep breath. Her Jimmy Choos clipped the floor as she staccatoed toward me, beanpole thin and wearing more labels than House of Fraser.

"Hi Mum," I said going for the hug. It was brief and to the side so I wouldn't smudge the mannequin-perfect make up. She smelt of Dior's 'Poison' and her perfectly ironed blood red hair, hung in silk sheets on either side of her shoulders. She looked like she'd just stepped out of Vidal Sassoon, I caught myself. It was Saturday. Of course she had.

"Goodness darling, what are you wearing?" she asked, looking me up and down.

But it wasn't only my clothes that concerned her. I knew she was scanning for fresh tattoos. As her worse fears were confirmed her nose became more pinched. She remained silent until her gaze settled on my feet. "We need to go shopping."

"No, we don't," I replied.

"Don't you own any actual shoes?"

I looked down at my twelve-hole, metallic silver-on-black custom-sprayed Docs and took another deep breath. "I'm going to have to go now, sorry Mum. I've got tons to do," I said, my voice sounding colder than I intended. "Tell Zara I wish her happy birthday."

"Marae …"

I heard my mother call as I let myself out the front door. I wasn't getting into an argument about my choice in wardrobe. Or tattoos. Or how it was my body so that meant I could do (and wear) whatever I liked. We'd been there before so often there was a script. And it wasn't worth re-visiting because neither of us had changed our position.

As for shoes, unless they cost six month's wages and had a heel capable of first-degree murder, my mother didn't consider footwear. Anything less wasn't deserving of the description 'shoe' and certainly didn't belong on her feet, or mine, by extension.

10

Jude one week later - Tuesday May 4th

Manchester

Something dragged me from sleep. Yawning, I looked around the room for the source of the noise. But it was too early to be in the land of the living, the day needed to wait. I closed my eyes, sinking. A minute later I heard it again. My body resisted and my head hurt, badly.

I stumbled, stood up and tried to work out where the sound was coming from. It was a phone, but I couldn't see it. The room was chaos. Light streaming in from between the gap in the dirty curtains highlighted every misdemeanour.

Mixed underwear strewn over the floor, coffee cups, glasses sticky with last night's booze, cigarette ends and crumbling piles of ash trying to escape from the overflowing ashtray. CD's were half stacked and falling everywhere, disc cases had been used to snort skinny lines of white candy. As I saw the powdered remnants scattered over the small stereo I licked my finger and stuck it into the coke, the buzz stirring me. Next to the discs were burnt strips of foil and a couple of dirty syringes. Someone had used needles. It hadn't been me. I would have remembered, or at least I fucking hoped I would. I wasn't sure anymore.

Then I heard snoring. I looked down and saw two naked girls half-wrapped in a duvet on the floor. They were out cold but I thought they'd left last night. As the memories of their bodies flooded in I scratched my head and realised I had no idea what either of their names were. After I threw up, I called the cab.

The taxi arrived and the girls were out within ten minutes, avoiding eye contact. One had mumbled about meeting later, the other agreeing, all of us knowing that wouldn't happen. I'd stood politely as the taxi left. As I went back inside an odd feeling flared. The flat was an empty, dirty shell and I wasn't much different.

I stood in the shower until I could face breathing.

As I got dried, and dressed I felt the bile rise in my throat a second time. My head was throbbing as I grabbed a plastic bag and started collecting debris. I opened the windows, allowing some of the grey smoke-smog to dissolve. Five minutes later I knocked something into the dining table with the Dyson, and realised it was my phone.

There was one missed call that was 'number with-held' and one new text message. The message was from the same wrong number that had text the day I returned from Amsterdam. My mouth went dry as I tapped the screen and read: "*The time is right.*"

I felt a chill as I dialled the voicemail and listened to the new message. A man's voice, European, metallic and distorted. "*You will receive instructions on this phone later today. I want what is mine. That is all. You will not be harmed.*"

I didn't have anything of anyone's. But someone thought I did.

All the air rushed out of my lungs. This had to be Coco's fault. I'd said no when she asked me to bring something back and now someone was leaving 'let's play cluedo' messages on my answer-phone. I was going to kill her! She must have planted something whilst I was with her in Amsterdam. There wasn't another explanation. Paranoia ripped through me.

I needed to clear my mind, focus, and stop jumping to conclusions.

But suspicion insisted that wasn't a wrong number. Not twice. The message was meant for me. I pulled open the wardrobe door, shoving the jackets aside, dragging out the navy little holdall bag I'd used to go to Amsterdam. It was an Addidas rucksack, nothing special. Kneeling, I roughly turned it upside down, shaking it hard. Razors and tissues from the bottom of the main sack fell out. Empty.

The zip pocket at the front ... I yanked the zipper open pulling out a packet of condoms, moisturiser and a toothbrush. Nothing. I tipped the whole fucking bag upside down again and shook it harder. Still nothing. I was wrong. Relief soothed the edges as I recognised I was strung out. Sickly I realised all this drama was down to me. The call was a genuine mistake. Reaching for a cigarette, I sparked up, inhaling in silence.

A moment passed before I remembered the compartment that ran around the side of the bag and into the lining. Time stretched as I located the tiny, snug zip and pulled the cord down. I slid my hand into the forgotten pocket.

Something small and soft fell into the centre of my palm, a black velvet bag with a drawstring tie. I felt my heart thudding in my throat. Swallowing hard, I tipped the contents out and saw more than a dozen, glittering, sparkling stones. Diamonds.

These diamonds weren't the average size seen on rings. These were much bigger. I reached for my mobile and dialled the number that had left the text message. It didn't connect. The phone was switched off. I felt like I was being suffocated, air coming in short shallow gasps, as I tried to think.

It was a miracle they were still in the rucksack. The state I had been in since seeing Coco anything could have happened, fuck, I could have left the front door unlocked, had squatters move in and been oblivious. I wouldn't have noticed if the fucking rucksack had been stolen. There'd been so many girls back here in the past couple of weeks, I'd recognise less than half if I saw them in a line up.

I was shaking. My palm was damp and the stones felt cold and solid against my skin. I slipped the gems securely into the pouch. Then not knowing what else to do, I tucked them back into the lining. It wasn't as if I could just phone the police, dial 999 and say: 'Excuse me officer, anyone lost a bag of diamonds?' The police and me didn't mix. As the shock slowly vanished, anger hit hard. How the fuck could she do this to me? My temples throbbed. I needed air and I needed a drink.

I grabbed the keys and left, locking the door self-consciously. The flat wasn't great but it was in Castlefield, a 'designer' re-developed part of Manchester at the edge of the city, a cool place to live and near to where I worked. I was a barman five nights and looked after the doors at a dance club two weekends a month. I made enough to get by and the job came with girls, cheap weed, pills and powder. Most days that was all that mattered.

I walked along the purpose built pathways down by the canal, past the converted Victorian Cotton Mills full of rich twenty something's, the shape of the buildings the only visible testament to their unholy past. By contrast the water slapped dark green and gelatinous against the brickwork. I headed over the white metal pedestrian bridge by the local radio station and into Duke's. The barman came straight over, spiky hair, Balearic tan and fake smile.

"Hi, what can I get you? Usual?"

"Whisky. Large."

"Not Guinness today?"

"Just the whisky, no ice," I said as if I were talking to the dead.

He took the hint, lowered his eyes and moved briskly, pouring the amber liquid into the barrel shaped glass.

"Four-seventy please," he said.

I took a handful of coins from my jacket, sifted the change and handed five over. "Keep it," I told him and downed the drink. I couldn't get past how many thousands of pounds worth of diamonds in that rucksack. The amount of stone-cold cash sitting in the flat blew my mind. Outside, fuelled by whisky resolve I dialled Coco's cell. It rang twice then switched to voicemail.

"Hi, you can't reach me. You know what to do."

I laughed at the irony. I could never reach her and now was no exception. I called her apartment but there was no answer. I sent her a text. "Call me." No response. I hit redial and got voicemail again. I left her a message.

"Coco, it's me. Fucking get in touch ASAP."

The last thing I wanted to do was wait for her to get back to me. But there was no other choice. I stared into the canal. The water reflected shifting, rippling, versions of me.

I'd taken a lot of risks in Amsterdam; jobs that I could have gone down for in a heartbeat and although we never talked about it, in the back of my mind I'd always thought with the connections she had that she did stuff too. But I had never personally moved any amount of drugs worth the kind of money in that one bag of ice. I had no idea what the fuck she was into. She'd hit the big time if that was a pay off. Or maybe she was using the gems as currency for God knows what … But whatever she was into was none of my business. I wanted those stones gone.

I was straight now. That part of my life was over. I couldn't go backwards.

My brain was skipping like an iPod on shuffle all the way back to the flat. I opened the door amid a sickening rush of anxiety. Two fast lines of coke would quell it. I thought of the emergency wrap I kept on the shelf in the cupboard in the kitchen. Seconds later I was staring at it, knowing once I opened the paper within one single minute I'd feel better.

My thoughts were full of the diamonds in the bedroom and Coco …

Fists clenched, I took a deep breath, stopping myself touching the coke. I shut the cupboard door. The flat looked as disgusting as any other day. The beginnings of a tidy-up showed in the bedroom, it would be easy to lose the effort and let it go. But instead I slipped my jacket off and pushed my sleeves up. At least cleaning would help take my mind off needing to score and waiting for the phone to ring. As I wet a cloth and started wiping the kitchen tops, I laughed at myself. Nothing would take my mind off scoring except doing it. And no matter how much I wanted to take the edge off, I needed to be straight to decide what to do about the increasingly heavy diamond deposit. Bitterly I got on with the cleaning.

Hours later I stood still. There were three black plastic bags of accumulated rubbish. Every surface had been scrubbed, every glass washed and what couldn't be cleaned had been thrown out. The flat smelt less like decaying fruit and more like a hospital. I checked my watch, it was after 6 p.m. and I'd not heard a thing from either Coco or the mystery European. I dialled Coco again and listened to the click of her voice on the answer-phone. Before it had finished playing out I was switching off. No point.

My stomach reminded me that I hadn't eaten all day. Craving normality I suddenly wanted cupboards filled with breakfast cereal, a fridge with milk that wasn't sour and a loaf of fresh bread to eat. Lately when I called the Chinese takeaway they asked if I wanted 'Lemon Chicken' or 'Beef Satay.' It wasn't funny anymore. I used to be a good cook, I wasn't anywhere near Rae's standard but I would always cook for Coco. Ignoring the memories I snatched my keys, dumping the rubbish into the large communal bins on the way out. Tesco was the nearest supermarket.

It didn't take long to fill a shopping trolley. I felt raw and off balance, because despite worrying about the diamonds I was aware that this was the most 'normal' day I'd had in months. The extra anxiety didn't go anywhere near soothing the coke come-down and in a detached way, it bothered me how I could feel normal with a ton of stolen ice lurking in a rucksack. Deep down, like an undercurrent on the seabed, I was seriously concerned about Coco. She wouldn't blank my calls. It wasn't like her. As I emptied the trolley's contents onto the conveyor belt, I smiled at the pretty blonde girl at the checkout. Her eyes were pale green, and she had a sprinkle of dark freckles across her nose. The corners of her mouth tilted when she looked at me.

"What time do you finish?" I asked.

She laughed, "I've got a boyfriend."

"Give me your number anyway. He won't mind if you don't tell him."

Just then my thigh rudely vibrated. My mobile was buzzing with a text.

"Be at the Quays, 2 a.m. Bring what is mine."
My mouth went instant Sahara desert-dry, I text back.

"Whereabouts? The Quays is a very big place."

From miles away I saw the girl pack the bags as I managed two items with arms of concrete. The longest minute in the decade passed before I received the next message. "Exchange Quay. Fitting."

The girl said something. I didn't hear a word. I stared at her, trying to concentrate. "Sorry?"

"How do you want to pay?" she asked.

I handed her my bankcard, she shook her head and inserted it into the pad. Somehow I punched the pin number in. I wanted more time. "Tomorrow."

"No negotiation. Either you come to us or we find you and take what is ours. Your choice."

Where the fucking hell was Coco? I shoved that question out my mind and hit the keys: "Tonight. 2 a.m. Exchange Quay."

The shopping was paid for and the girl had packed it all. I re-loaded it into the trolley.

"Hey, don't forget your card!" she shouted as I was leaving.

Mechanically I turned, took the card and walked to the car, lifted the bags into the boot and left. At home I parked and started carrying the bags to the flat, brain in overdrive, getting stuck on one thing after another. I needed provisions for tonight and backup wouldn't be a bad thing. I dialled a number. "Hi, it's me, I'm at home. Are you busy?"

Thirty minutes later I heard a soft knock on the front door. I opened it to Jazz wearing a black leather jacket and black trousers. He practically melted into the shadows behind the doorframe.

"Come in. I have a problem."

Jazz raised his eyebrows as I led him inside the flat. "Jesus Jude, have you bought a cleaning company or something?"

I didn't answer as he followed me into the bedroom. I sat down on the bed and tipped the contents of the velvet bag onto the black duvet cover.

"That's some problem," Jazz whistled, a low hiss from his teeth.

"Listen, whatever you're thinking, it's worse. They aren't mine."

"Whose are they? What the fuck are you doing with them?"

"I went over to see Coco a couple of weeks ago, I think she planted them on me."

"You think she planted them? Or you know?"

"They didn't get here by themselves."

"Yeah, but are you sure she dropped them on you?"

"She asked me to bring something back, I said no. Then I start getting messages saying someone wants their stuff ... I find these and Coco is nowhere," I tapped open my inbox and showed him the text messages.

"Is that shit for real?"

"What do you mean?"

"A set up? I don't know, man, it looks like a trap to me," Jazz said, his hands shoved into his pockets. "What if they're fake and she's got the solids? My guess is she's lifted them knowing who would come looking and she's given your contact details."

"No. That's evil," I said, shaking my head.

"Or, maybe someone was watching her and she needed to get them out?" Jazz shrugged. "All I'm saying is if it *was* her then she's dumped them on you for a reason."

"It has to be her. Nothing else adds up."

Jazz laughed. "Yeah you're probably right. But my money's on her giving them your head on a block and now you've got some fucker watching you."

I hadn't thought that I was being watched.

"Fuck. Look, I don't know what she's into but she wouldn't set me up for nothing and as far as I know she's got *no* reason. I don't get it. This is heavy shit."

"Fuck her. If these are genuine do you have any idea how much money's here? C'mon man, it's Christmas! I'll help you find a buyer," Jazz said still staring at the stones.

"Hell no! I'm not into this kind of shit! I'm going to give them their property back," I said slowly, holding up one of the stones to the light turning it over between thumb and forefingers, drawn to the glowing fire. "This looks real enough to me."

"Are you sure you don't want me to ask around?" Jazz nodded his head towards the gems.

I slid the stone back into the pouch with the rest. "No thanks, I'm getting rid. End of. You in?"

"Of course, if that's what you want. Call them."

Jazz stood quietly whilst I dialled the number that had sent the text. The phone rang four times and the same metallic voice I'd heard on the voicemail picked up.

"You got my message. We will be there as arranged to complete the deal at two a.m. exchange Quay." The line went dead.

I looked at Jazz, "Well?"

He nodded, "Real enough to burn. I'm out of here. Don't do anything stupid in the meantime. No heroics! See you later."

"Laters." I said, and tried Coco's number again. Futile.

11

Jude 1.30 a.m. - May 5th

Manchester

The doorbell wasn't working but Jazz wouldn't have used it anyway. At 1.30 a.m. like a caffeinated-cat, I heard the first touch of his knuckles on the wood. I was up from the sofa and at the door before the second knock, opening it. The hallway was lit by the outside blur of security lights.

"Are you high?" Jazz asked outright looking at me.

"No man, not at all," I shook my head. "Have you got everything?"

Jazz smiled, his teeth reflecting the soft light. "Yes, I have what we need."

"Then let's go," I said jangling my keys.

"Slow down," he said walking past me into the little flat. He opened his jacket and I saw two guns tucked into the waistband of his jeans. He handed one to me.

"Have you got the stuff?" he asked.

"Yeah, I got the stuff." I said, sliding the piece in my inside pocket, against my ribs.

Jazz turned, grabbing two tumblers off the side. He poured two shots of whisky, handed one to me and downed one himself. As he finished the drink he took a pair of black leather gloves out of his back pocket, pulling them on, "You're out of practice."

"It's just a fucking drop," I replied, but I reached into a drawer for a pair and did the same. In silence we left the apartment. The air had a steely edge, as night blades skimmed our faces.

Jazz's jeep was at the back of the flat, and by the time I had clicked my seatbelt, his foot was down and we took off. Adrenalin surged through me but Jazz might as well have been on his way to pick up a date. As cool as ever, only his focus on the drive revealed any concentration.

As we reached Salford Quays Jazz slowed down. "Stick to the plan, you hear?" he said.

I nodded, "I'm going to hand these over and get the fuck out." I checked the velvet pouch in my pocket next to the gun, and patted it.

The clock on the dashboard was a light orange colour 01.55 a.m.

"We're going to be a bit early," Jazz said, his hands resting on the wheel as he navigated the way through the traffic lights and business park maze.

Each Quay had its own name, some were bigger some were smaller but essentially they were the same. The Quays were at the east end of the Manchester Ship Canal, built on the old docks, land that had since been regenerated by vast sums of cash. Queen Victoria had opened the docks at the end of the nineteenth century and they'd been in use until the early 1980's. After that the area disintegrated into neglect and vandalism, until the cash injection revived it. Now tall glass offices stood by the water, a place where high finance lived during the daytime and where the even greater financial winners held balconied apartments in the residential Quays.

It was a dark night, thick clouds and no stars. The phosphorous glow of the street lamps lent a sense of timelessness. The area was deserted.

"Look," I pointed at a silver BMW. A single car was parked along the side of an office block. The building was black, and empty, standing stark and tall. Jazz drove slowly.

"That block is barrier protected, it's private land, we can't get in without a pass card or the code," he said.

"Come on, let's get it over with. Stop here, you've got my back." I replied, fingering the gun, conscious of the diamonds in my front pocket.

"Are you sure you want to do this?" Jazz said shaking his head. "You're going to be wide open, vulnerable. You know what I'm saying?"

"Just stop the fucking thing!" I hit the dash with my hand.

Shoulders hunched and muttering under his breath Jazz drove to the barrier, which was as close as he could get to the office complex. I was going to have to walk to the BMW parked about four hundred yards in front of the building.

"I should have brought binoculars," Jazz said drumming his fingers.

"When did you turn into an old woman for fuck's sake?" I exhaled at him.

I didn't wait for his response, and jumped out of the jeep leaving him cursing. I could hear the engine running, a low reassuring growl behind me as I walked across the cold concrete. Unbidden, the thought slithered into my head that someone should have acknowledged us arrive, maybe with a flicker of lights or at least a lowered window. I wasn't expecting a welcoming committee but this was too quiet. I dismissed the paranoia and walked faster, the cool night air flooding my veins with vivid memories of Coco. I needed to see her again. I needed answers.

As I got nearer to the BMW, I could see that the windows were fully blacked out. I reached the car and it was silent. I withdrew the gun, and pointed it low as I opened the car door.

Dead.

There was a man dead, slumped over the steering wheel. The realisation gunned through me and I started to shake. Fuck. I had to keep it together. He wasn't supposed to be dead. I grabbed him by the shoulder and pulled him back to make sure. Dead. Bullet hole in the skull shot at point blank range. Thick smears of blood on the seat behind the head where it had leaked, no brains splattered, clean. He couldn't have been shot here I repeated this to myself, as I flushed hot then cold. No broken windows and no shattered glass meant no shootout.

I took a fast look in the car past the body. The glove compartment was open spillage on the floor, I wanted to see if there was any clue but couldn't. Nothing stood out. I'd seen enough. I slammed the door hard and ran to the jeep. I nearly wrenched the handle off and threw myself into the seat. "Drive! We need to get the fuck out of here."

"Dead?" Jazz asked.

"What? How the fuck do you know?"

"Been around longer than you. Man, you should see your face!" Jazz laughed and thumped his hand on the wheel as the car reared forwards and we took off.

My head was spinning. Jazz's voice brought me back.

"Jude, you all right?"

There was a few minutes silence whilst I tried to think.

"Pull over," I said suddenly.

Something in my tone made Jazz stop. He pulled in by the kerb. We were out of the Quays and back on the main road. I jumped out and for the second time in twenty-four hours threw up.

"Better?" Jazz asked.

"Yeah, sorry," I replied shaking my head. But I didn't feel better at all.

"This is going to get complicated," he said into the stillness.

I had no reply. I was all out of words.

"Get rid of the gloves," Jazz added.

12

Rae - Wednesday May 5th

Manchester

After I dropped the cake off for Zara on Saturday, I clicked my heels and Wednesday May 5th Presentation Day arrived. The morning of the annual post grad conference at Manchester University appeared as I was feeling lost and overwhelmed. Like Dorothy in the Wizard of Oz, I wanted to find my way home too. But first I had to discover where home was. I knew that I didn't want to work at the warehouse forever, but I didn't feel good enough for anywhere else. Today was the date when all first year students needed to submit original findings to pass the year. And this was my turn to be counted.

It was also time to check the handouts and correct the very last version of the paper. I'd written a 12,500 word piece as well as a 2,500 one highlighting the main thrust of the thesis, focussing on restaurants and their nutritional responsibility. I had to present the shorter one and somehow impress a lecture theatre full of professors and experienced doctoral students with an elusive ingredient, 'intellect.' The actual cooking and the practical side of the degree, which I'd done the week before was fine, fun even. But that was because I hadn't had to talk to anyone.

I was panic-stricken. They were all blue blood intellectuals and someone like me with no academic history had no right to be with people like that. I was a fraud and after today everyone in that lecture theatre would know the truth, which was that I didn't belong.

The plan was to present the paper to an open floor. Anyone in the room could query any aspect relating to the argument or the research. I just knew they were going to ask piercingly clever things that I couldn't answer. Because, instead of studying, I'd been far more interested in who was wearing what (or who) last weekend and if Alex had actually done half of what everyone had been teasing him about. I had to get a grip.

But time stops for no man, woman or germ. I couldn't stop sneezing and my throat was burning up. There was no way I was going to be able to make it through the twenty minute talk deadline with just the one box of tissues. Scott had picked this week to visit his family down in Surrey, and long after the door had closed behind him all that had been left unsaid lingered in the air.

My phone buzzed with a text. I automatically assumed it was Scott.

'Get in there and nail it! Good luck doll!'

It was from Alex. I was touched. He always said he didn't 'give a shit' about what I was doing when I wasn't in work. I was replying 'thank you' when the house phone rang. Number withheld. I picked up. "Scott?"

"No darling, it's me ringing to wish you luck. What time are you presenting?" The pitch of my mother's voice indicated that she was on espresso number four.

"Thanks. I thought it was Scott. It's at three."

"Hasn't he called?"

"No."

"I'm sure he's just busy with his family. He'll call you later."

"Yeah. How are you?"

"I'm fine, but you sound awful, look after that cold. Hope it goes well."

We finished the call and I blew my nose, again. It was nice of her to phone. She made an effort when having a daughter fitted into her social calendar of golfing, health spas and lunching parties. She really did try in her own way, but I couldn't stand to be in the same room as her for longer than five minutes.

Her disapproval was tangible. She wanted a daughter who reflected her, who wore the same clothes she did, like her friend's daughters. She needed someone to be proud of, to display at events. My mother needed a daughter who achieved things, so people could tell her how great she was for having such a great daughter. But she should be used to reality by now, and so should I.

I was fourteen, sitting in registration at school, waiting for my tick. When everyone headed to assembly I sneaked into the girls' toilets, painted my face, got changed and slipped out to meet Zack, my first boyfriend. He was nineteen and I was drunk with love, besotted. Everything was perfect until he found out I'd lied about my age and dumped me. I caught the bus home to an empty house, crying.

There was nothing to eat and the house was cold. Mum was out. I cried all night and she turned up just before it was time for me to go to school next day. Usually when I needed money I took it out of her purse, she wasn't mean. She bought me clothes but there was never any food in the house. She was always on a diet. That's how it was.

But that was then and this was now. I dragged myself out the past and got my folders together. For the fiftieth time checked I had everything I needed, handouts, papers and most important of all, tissues.

"Well done, excellent, really great first paper Rae. The depth of research, the ideas … it was all there, fabulous," Rick, my supervisor squinted over his smudged glasses and handed me a warm glass of white wine, his arm brushing around my shoulders in a sideways hug. His breath stunk of stale garlic and he leaned in far too close.

"Thanks," I sneezed again wishing I could slap him. I felt so rough, my throat was closing and my skin was clammy. I had no idea how I had just got through the past hour. I needed to go home to be ill, in private.

"Yes, yes, come along ask away," Rick said turning, waving expansively at a group of young looking twenty-something's. I left the wine on the windowsill.

The students were coming toward me with polite enquiring expressions. We had relocated to the post grad centre now that the afternoon presentations were finished and our last responsibility was to answer undergraduate questions. My head was pounding as a ginger haired girl open and closed her mouth like a Koi fish. I didn't hear a word.

"Sorry, you will have to excuse me, I really need to leave," I said, my voice breaking.

She drifted off back to her super-intelligent friends. At their age I'd have been wasted or at work, in truth, more likely, both.

I watched her go and thanked the universe that it was over. I was going to get this degree and I was going to open my own restaurant. One day.

I grabbed my bag and my folders and left the building, pushing glass doors wide into the late afternoon sun. My head pounded as I found the car, and headed straight out of town through Rusholme, where each and every building was a restaurant or food market. With the car windows open, and the pungent fragrance hovering in the air like a cloud of spice, I drove home.

The cats purred, happy as I dumped my bags on the wooden floor in the hallway and struggled to get past tails and legs. Upstairs I stripped off and stood in the shower. Ten minutes later, wrapped in pyjamas and slumber socks with a mug of Lemsip and sucking on a throat lozenge, I padded wearily into the lounge, flopping down on to our big charcoal grey sofa.

I woke up with a start. A phone was ringing. I looked around, it was my Blackberry flashing and buzzing.

"Hello," my voice a thin whisper.

"Hey there."

"Oh God. Jazz!" I coughed.

He laughed. "Yes, it's me. We're meant to be going for that drink tonight. How are you doing?"

"I'm okay," I whimpered.

"Yeah? Are you sure?"

"I've got a bit of a cold," I replied making the understatement of the century.

"I can hear. Sounds more than a bit. No worries babe, we'll do this another time."

"Sure. I understand you don't want to catch any bugs, I don't blame you," I said hoarsely.

"I'm not afraid of bugs. But it's not fair on you. Leave it, we'll go when you're feeling better," Jazz said.

"Whatever," I said.

"Rae listen to me, do you have any ginger and lemon or do you need someone to drop some off for you?"

"What? No, I've got ginger and lemon."

"Fine. Go into your kitchen, grate some raw ginger and squeeze fresh lemon juice, add some honey and hot water into a cup. Make it now, take it upstairs with you, go to bed and stay there until morning. Drink plenty of liquids and I'll call you tomorrow. Feel better soon baby, okay?"

"Okay. Bye then," I said really too crap to tell him I didn't need to be told what to drink and that I could look after myself. But it was nice that he was bothered about the cold getting better and he sounded like Jude in the way he spoke to me. He sounded like *family*. He said nice things even though he said them the wrong way and he was bossy.

And although his English was funny he had a cute accent, even if he *was* an asshole and dated four hundred women at once. I closed the long crème curtains across the French windows, then shut the door behind me to keep the cats out and made my way into the kitchen.

I took the lemon out of the fridge, grated the ginger as I waited for the kettle to boil and stirred in the honey. I knew that would be the last I saw or heard of him but I really had wanted to prove I wasn't an idiot. I took a sip and the water scalded my top lip bringing tears to my eyes.

Bloody hell! What the fuck was the matter with me?

I was never bothered about people's opinions of me. I couldn't care less. But I had to set the record straight so I didn't mess up my chance of a placement. After speaking to my boss like 'that' in public, I was on dangerous ground. Manchester was a small world. Everyone knew everyone, especially where Alex was concerned, and one wrong word from Jazz to his friend at Malmaison would screw up my reputation before I'd even set foot in a restaurant. Fine if I wanted to stay working in a warehouse for the rest of my life but not if I wanted to move on. Jazz had given me his friend's details so easily that it did make me wonder for a second why Alex hadn't done that. It wasn't like he didn't have the contacts.

My head hurt. I took my boiling mug of lemon and ginger and climbed wearily up the stairs, scanning the inbox on my mobile, there were no new messages. Then I called the BT answer-phone lady, no missed calls or new messages there either. Scott hadn't rung to wish me luck. And then I realised I didn't care anymore. If he could go away when he knew how much this meant to me and I was full of the worst stinking cold, after the endless band practices I had sat through and all those meals I had cooked for his clients, he could get biblical with his mother for all I cared! That's if he was even at his mother's.

I stared at the photograph of Scott on my phone as I sat down on our bed. He stared back, revealing nothing. I thought back to when it had been taken in Paris, only a few weeks ago. The truth was that I was worried he had been seeing someone else. He'd already admitted he'd proposed without meaning to, and that made sense if he was on the rebound from an affair. We hardly talked, hardly saw one another and I couldn't even remember the last time we had sex. I sighed, switched the phones off, and sipped the hot drink, which tasted of nothing at all. I was exhausted and seven o'clock in the evening seemed like bedtime.

13

Jude - Thursday May 6th

Manchester

It felt late. I spun the divers watch round on my wrist as my eyes focussed, almost two in the afternoon and I'd fallen asleep at dawn. It was now thirty-six hours after the aborted diamond drop and I was looking over my shoulder so often I was getting a crick in my neck. I still hadn't worked out what to do next. My mind was stuck on the fact it had to have been Coco who planted the ice on me. I was livid with her.

But after finding the dead man in the car at the Quays, I was worried. That scene hadn't looked like a heat of the moment argument. It was too clean. Coco hadn't been in touch. She didn't pick up her mobile and I wasn't leaving messages in case someone was collecting on her behalf. I had no idea what her connection was to any of this. It gnawed away at my guts and the situation wasn't any better in daylight.

Jazz poked his head around the door. "You're awake at last then?"

"Yep," I nodded at Jazz, "I'm taking a shower then we need to talk."

"Talking won't change a thing my friend," Jazz said as philosophical as ever. Nothing seemed to stir Jazz or nothing that showed on the outside, he was always immaculate. Jazz had bunked down on the sofa bed last night, which I knew without looking would now be tidy and neatly put away. He left no trace of himself wherever he went. Jazz was like smoke.

By the time I'd got dressed several ideas had bubbled through the treacle. I was about to share them with Jazz when I heard him on the phone and caught the last bit of his chat. He was arranging to meet someone, "I don't know. I have things to do first. I'll call you when I'm finished." He ended the call and turned to me. "Well?"

"We need to speak to Alex. Since the dolls took off me and him don't talk business but you two go way back."

Jazz shook his head, "Nah leave Alex out of it, the days of cheap girls and poker games in the upstairs bar are long gone my friend! Anyway this sounds too big for the kind of shit Alex was into back then."

"The upstairs club! That was what, four, five, years ago now?"

Alex could get anything you wanted, *whatever* you wanted. He was no angel but his family thought he was a good boy and Alex liked it that way. Alex kept family and business apart in a clean split. When we'd partied in London everyone hung at Jazz's. ('Jazz' was also the name of the place). He had captured an attitude and poured it in. The coolest bands played and the hottest chicks came to dance.

It was a while before I knew Jazz owned the place. One Saturday a month there was a private pole-dancing club upstairs and an after-hours casino, where big names played for big stakes. After I met Coco and stayed South, Jazz and I became tight. Soon we developed a habit that I'd get his property back when gambling debts failed, keep an eye on the guests, help certain people stay out of the club and remind them to stay away. I had my own thing going on too. But I didn't run dealers in his club. No one did. Jazz had a reputation to protect. There'd been trouble when someone had got it wrong but luckily we'd been there that night, both Alex and me. We'd had to pull Jazz off him. That kid was barely breathing but no one tried it again.

"Man, is it four years?" Jazz shook his head. "It's gone so fast. Listen, let's get back to the present shit we're currently in!" He clipped me on the side of the head, laughing.

I caught his hand, "Enough! I'll sort it. If you hear anything …"

"Sure. But you know how it is, a lot of people suddenly lose their voices at once," Jazz stood up to leave. "Look man, you can't leave that here indefinitely," he pointed in the direction of the wardrobe where the rucksack was hiding.

"Yeah, I know," I scratched my head.

"Do you want me to take care of them?"

"No it's my problem, I'll deal with it. Thanks a lot for the back up the other night but I'm good. I've got a few loose ends to chase," I said slipping into a thick black sweater.

"Okay. Keep them safe. We don't want any unwanted visitors getting hold of them," Jazz replied.

I nodded, "I'm on it. So, what are you up to? You never need sleep do you?" I was looking rough and I knew it, the mirror told me I was grey around the jaw line. And my skin felt like cold porridge.

Jazz, slightly paler than usual but his Med' tan gleamed beneath the surface. He shrugged, "I can sleep when I'm dead. Right now I've got things to do. We'll check back with each other later all right?"

"I thought so, it's gotta be a chick. 'Things to do'!" I repeated laughing at the code we shared for women.

As I led Jazz to the door, I suddenly felt as if I were remembering something from an age ago. I caught Jazz on the arm and using someone else's voice I heard myself ask, "Have you seen my cousin?"

"No, and I'm not going to be seeing her. Too busy!" Jazz shook his head, smiling, as he turned to leave.

"She's my family, Jazz."

"So, she's your family!" Jazz shrugged.

"So, you know the score. See you later," I said, gently punching him on the arm. He waved backwards, as he left. I stood and watched him walk into the dull air.

Jazz wouldn't lie to me and Rae wasn't his type. Still, I felt responsible, Rae was blood, it was my job to look after her and instead I had given Jazz her phone number. I was bombed when I did it and I knew she wanted to see him about his chef friend. Yet I didn't want Jazz going anywhere near her. But if he hadn't called by now then he wasn't going to do, and as he had said he wouldn't there was no point in upsetting Rae by reminding her. Right now I had other, more urgent, things on my mind.

"Thanks for your help, that's great," I shook hands with the corporate navy suited man twice my age as he showed me out of the small room and guided me towards the exit. I made my way outside as the stones were being securely locked into a safety deposit box in the depths of the bank's vault.

For the first time in forty-eight hours I forced my shoulders down, breathed deeply and rubbed my brow, glad that was done. Now all I had to do was decide where

I was going to stash the key. One thing was for sure, I wasn't carrying it on me and I wasn't leaving it in the apartment. I smiled as the idea came.

An hour later I was back walking the city streets. The air between the buildings in Manchester city centre was warm and grey with pollution. Smog covered the early summer freshness, glints of sunshine shattered the clouds and glanced off the white pillars of the old library making the city seem more Roman than Victorian. Opposite the library a limousine rolled up outside The Midland Hotel's timeless redbrick grandeur. There was a flurry of doormen and attendants. Someone famous had arrived. I wondered if Alex knew who it was, or if he'd had a call to meet later. These days his friends filled every edition of the celebrity magazines. His was a different world to the one we had shared.

I felt lost momentarily, as if the past had never been a part of me and I was watching our friendship from behind glass. I dismissed the sensation and reached for a cigarette, catching site of the cuffs on my leather jacket. It was almost time for a shopping spree, but I didn't have the cash. One whisky at the Grapes and then I was going to begin the search for Coco in earnest. Finding Coco was essential.

Minutes later, walking through Albert Square, reality hit like a truck! Coco was God knows where and I was going for whisky? There was a man dead and although I didn't want to admit it, deep down I was point-blank terrified that someone believed my name was on the trigger. Since I couldn't prove otherwise it was only a matter of time before *that* someone was going to come for their diamonds.

When that happened I was going to be in big shit. I had to get out of here. And fast.

I turned and ran down Cross Street all the way to the car park at the Ramada hotel by the gravy coloured river Irwell. I pushed the ticket in the machine, dropped the coins in the slot and chased down the concrete stairs two at a time. I launched myself into the Golf, started the engine and drove back to the flat, packing even as I flew through my mental checklist, toiletries, jeans, smarts, shirts, underwear and trainers.

I grabbed my phone and charger, checked my wallet, took one last look around and left, double locking the door behind me.

I glanced at my watch, ninety seconds. And laughed, congratulating myself on the speed with which I could reduce my life to essentials and throw them into a space weighing less than forty kilos. As I made my way back down to the car I made a call.

"Hi Mum, it's me."

"Jude! Where have you been?"

"Sorry. I know I said I'd be round."

"Are you all right darling?"

"Yeah but I have to go away for a few days."

"I'm here if you need me."

"Thanks, I'll be in touch."

I sighed. I was grateful. She never said she was disappointed that I wasn't working nine to five and when I was younger she baled me out more times than I could remember. I was the reason dad left.

But then, dad was a bully and an alcoholic. That night he'd gone for her was no different to any other except that time I'd decked *him*. He left the next day. Topic closed but some scars never healed in full.

I dropped the rucksack in the boot and headed to the airport. This needed sorting and the starting point was Amsterdam, so that's where I was going. I had to see Coco. I was going to talk to her in person and if she wasn't there then I would find someone who could tell me where she was. People didn't just evaporate.

14

Rae - Thursday May 6th

Manchester

I was ill. My throat had closed. My head felt like a throbbing football, hot sweats and cold shivers were killing me. It was awful. Every two hours I sipped at the lemon and ginger tea. At about 9pm I sent Alex a text to warn him that I would not be in for work. He sent a swift reply saying he'd 'speak to me in the morning get some rest.'

The last time I looked at the clock was 3am. This meant I did eventually fall asleep and would have carried on sleeping had I not been rudely disturbed by a repetitive, loud, high-pitched noise. Something heavy was weighing me down. I woke up to see Tiara standing on my chest, pitifully mewling into my face.

"Meow," shouted Minx from her position on my legs.

I started coughing and Tiara tumbled off me. I stood gently, very relieved that my head felt human. As I padded my way into the bathroom to clean my teeth Minx wandered around my legs and Tiara nibbled my feet. Then I caught sight of the time – 10.30 a.m.

Downstairs I fed the cats, opened the back door and sat on the kitchen counter swinging my legs in the fresh breeze, drinking orange juice. My throat was working and I'd stopped coughing. I punched Alex's number and waited, the red symbol flashed, the call would not connect. This was the third time of trying and if this failed I was sending a text. Just then it clicked.

"Hi, Alex, it's me, Rae," I said to my boss, sneezing.

"How are you doing? Is everything okay?" Alex replied, breaking up so he sounded slightly Darlek.

"I'm definitely better than I was, but I could really do with a day to get over this cold," I said, hoping he heard me.

"No worries, we're not that busy, get well, see you tomorrow," Alex replied.

"Thanks, see you tomorrow."

There was no need for a conversation. Alex was into minimal disclosure from me and polite niceties weren't something he indulged in.

I jumped down and put the kettle on, feeling relieved. I'd been exhausted lately and I never took sick days. In truth, Alex had never had a phone call from me saying I wasn't going in. And he'd been fine about it so I wasn't going to feel bad. It wasn't like I was healthy and taking advantage. My head pounded agreement. I needed time-out.

The house felt peaceful with Scott away. I glanced around the living room, worried I'd have to spend the day catching up with housework but everywhere was clean enough and comfortably tidy.

Downstairs flowed, our walls were painted in easy neutral tones to reflect the light, and we'd stained the floorboards dark mahogany. Or rather I had. It had been a tough job. Scott wasn't into DIY, he'd preferred to make helpful remarks and let me get on with the actual work. The floor matched the dark shelved bookcases stacked with music, which lined the walls.

Between Scott's musician past and my own obsession with live gigs we had a decent collection. My passion for all things Jane's Addiction and NIN reflected throughout. But there were little known indie bands like Urusei Yatsura, along with some rare and obscure early editions from now infamous bands like the Red Hot Chili Peppers, and valuable old blues and Motown collectibles. I just couldn't remember the last time Scott or I had listened to any music together.

Music was something we always 'did' when we'd started seeing each other and that continued when we'd moved in together. We had a ritual when we came home from work, we'd slam the vinyl on, get a drink and then simply sit and talk to one another.

'Our sounds define us,' Scott used to say.

I would always say it was the other way around.

Annoyed, I realised that Scott hadn't replied to my texts. I picked the phone up about to call him and ask why, but instead I took a deep breath, staring out of the huge kitchen window at the blooming flowers and cherry blossom trees. The cats were outside and summer was starting early. I put the phone down calmly on the kitchen worktop. It wasn't worth arguing any more. He didn't want to speak to me or he'd have called.

After a shower I sat on the bed gazing at the cornflower blue walls I'd painted last year. My mind wandered. I was feeling guilty, I knew I should do some university work and not waste the opportunity but my life was non-stop, all of the time. I was a mouse running on a wheel.

Instinctively I picked up my mobile to call Jazz and thank him for being considerate yesterday. Then I thought the better of it. There was no point, he'd had a get-out clause handed to him on a plate and I didn't want to listen to him finding an excuse of his own not to follow through on our 'let's be friends' date.

I chewed on my fingernails. If he thought I was a nut job, then after spending more time together the chances were I might only convince him further. I couldn't hide my personality and guys like him and girls like me weren't going to get on together with any ease. I stretched, it was 11.27a.m and I had the whole day to myself to do absolutely nothing other than relax. The thought was overwhelming.

On the way downstairs my mobile started ringing.

"Hello?"

"Hi, how are you doing?" Jazz asked.

"Oh. Hi. I'm okay… Glad you called," my mind spun.

"Yeah? Why is that?"

"I nearly called you actually. I wanted to thank you for yesterday."

"Thank me for what?"

"You were really kind, thanks," I could feel myself blushing.

"Kind, how?"

"Just kind. Nice. Thanks. You know … to me. When you phoned." I coughed.

"You're thanking me for calling you? You were ill. Of course I'd call. Anyway it's good to hear you sound better. So, what are you doing?"

"Pardon?"

"What are you up to?"

"When?"

"Today."

"Sneezing, but otherwise nothing. Why?"

"Well, I'm in the area, and since you're better, why don't we go for that drink later?"

I inhaled loudly and coughed.

"If you want to," said Jazz into the silence.

"That's a really nice idea. Are you going to tell Alex? If I'm well enough to go out I should probably be back at work."

"No of course not. I don't want to get you into any trouble," Jazz replied.

"Okay, what time?" I asked.

"I don't know exactly. I've got things to do, so I'll call you later when I'm finished."

"Bye until later then," I said grinning at the carpet.

The call ended, and I sat on the stairs. My legs were heavy, and suddenly I felt very confused. We'd said we would be friends and I really wanted to fix things so I could take the placement with Nico the head chef without worrying about what Jazz might say about me. Where was the problem?

Because, my sane self scolded, ten minutes earlier I'd decided not to call him myself, had thought I could make things worse if I did see him and, now, I'd apparently said I would go out for a drink with him. Which meant that Jazz thought I took sick days and lied to my boss, as well as not being able to control my temper. Brilliant. My head felt hot and a small insistent pounding began in my temples. I couldn't get out of it now without looking like even more of a muppet.

I sighed, knowing that I needed to make a decent impression. Yet I had no idea what I was going to talk to him about. I had a relationship with food that involved eating it as well as cooking it, and the closest I would ever get to owning a pair of Manola Blahniks was laughing at my mum's credit card bill. It was no wonder Alex never invited me to socialise, we lived on different planets. But here was I, trying to change that, in one evening with a guy who under all normal circumstances, I would categorically avoid.

The day passed slowly. I was crushing on the hottest not-quite-a-villain on T.V, 'Lucas Hood' in Alan Ball's 'Banshee,' when the phone rang. It was almost six o'clock.

"Hi," Jazz said.

"Hi. Did you get everything done?"

"Sure, all taken care of. Have you eaten?"

"No."

"Great. Let's go for a meal, we can sit and chat."

"Eat? I thought we were just going for a drink!"

"Do you argue with everything?"

"What do you mean? Oh. No. No. Of course not. That … that … sounds lovely," I said, taking a deep breath.

"Good. Are your neighbours going to mind if I come and pick you up?"

"Pardon?" I spluttered.

"Are you sure you are okay with me coming to your house?" Jazz said quite clearly.

"I don't understand."

"Your fiancé?"

"Why on earth would that be a problem?"

"Fine. In that case I need directions, where do you live?"

"Where are you?"

"In town. Tell me where you live, I'll call when I get near and then you can direct me, okay? My sat nav is rubbish."

"It's easy. Head out towards the airport and get off the motorway at the next junction."

"See you soon."

By the time he called back and reached South Manchester I had taken another shower, my hair was rebelling like an angry teen and I was still naked. I stared at the pile of rejected clothes on the bed. What did women like me wear to go out for meals with men like him? I wanted to look friendly, professional and be taken seriously. But my nose was bright red, which matched my ear, due to having to hold the damn mobile as the speakerphone sounded weird and cave-like. As I peered at my reflection, I swallowed hard. Liquid eyeliner was supposed to be defining, not Mortician.

No matter what I tried on I felt like Rob Zombie in drag.

I finally settled on a black cotton dress that had tiny buttons all the way down the bodice, a tight waist and a high Victorian collar, vintage gothic. Lace sleeves and a lace piece across the cleavage, Scott called it Miss Haversham's funeral dress but I loved it. It was so easy to wear and with a pair of solid DM boots I was good to go pretty much anywhere.

Eventually the doorbell rang. I made my way downstairs and opened the door. No one was there. Then I looked down and crouching at a very awkward angle, was Jazz. Minx, the one cat who was incredibly fussy who she shared herself with was now lying on her back, fluffy tummy bared and purring so loudly even I could hear her.

She had all four paws waving in the air then grabbed Jazz's wrist and brazenly leaned upwards to nuzzle him, rubbing her little face around his hand. I was shocked, Minx never trusted anyone.

"I see you've met Minx. You'll have to excuse her, she doesn't usually do things like that."

"I love animals," he replied straightening up, uncoiling like a python.

Wearing a black suit and a black shirt open at the collar, he smiled.

I couldn't quite remember him being this glossy. It was as if he had stepped out of the pages of an Ikea catalogue, "Perfect Man Self-Assembly-Unit. Display by window."

My knees trembled as I walked into the house.

"Would you like a drink before we go?" I offered loudly with my back to him, several minutes later when I finally remembered my manners and got re-acquainted with my vocal chords.

"No I'm fine. Where would you like to eat? Anywhere in particular?" he asked wandering into the kitchen. He had been into the lounge and the dining room already and without invitation. *He* wasn't shy. That much was clear.

"What kind of food do you like?" I answered staring at the floor. I was going to have to snap out of this bout of social awkwardness quickly otherwise I'd have neck cramp all evening.

"Sea food," he said shortly. "What do you like?"

Blushing, as the thought of Jazz eating sea food instantly sent my mind somewhere sexual, I was horrified at myself, and couldn't say a word.

"I'll choose if you have no preferences," he said, as I remained silent.

Suddenly his face appeared near mine.

He laughed as I jumped. "Marae, I don't bite. Well, not unless you ask very nicely, so relax," he said gently.

"Bite? God! I'll just get my things," I said muttering.

"Hurry up, there's a good girl," he said as he spanked me across the buttocks, with exactly the right amount of pressure to sting and leave a warm glow.

No one had ever done that to me. I was speechless for a second and felt my mouth drop open.

"What the hell do you think you're doing? And don't call me a 'good girl' you patronising git!"

He strolled casually into the hall to pick up his keys, laughing loudly. "You take life way too seriously Marae. Let's go, we'll have fun, I promise," Jazz said, holding my front door open as he waited for me to catch up.

I stood in silence, feeling odd, like I was floating above the surface of who I really was. Unable to shake it off I picked up my bag and followed.

15

Jude - Thursday May 6th

Amsterdam

The flight to Amsterdam was scheduled to leave on time and I knew the times of the shuttles like barmen knew cocktails. They hadn't altered over the past six months. Fifty-four minutes to the next plane and the gate would close in nine. I jammed the car in the nearest space in the foul stinking car park, locking it as I ran towards the filthy stained lift. As I zoomed straight up to Manchester Airport's navy blue and steel coloured departure lounge, I looked at my watch, knowing already that I had six minutes. When the flight number was called seconds later, I walked over with everyone else, got inline and queued, boarding pass at the ready.

We were airborne and landing after the second whisky and dry. At Schiphol I walked past the luggage snake, lurching and slithering as it rolled emptily and lazily around and around on its rubber circuit. As the suitcases started being thrown onto the track people swarmed thickly like bluebottles feasting on decaying flesh.

Fifty minutes later, in a dark and silent hallway, I stood outside Coco's apartment. The door showed no signs of forced entry. I knocked once and rang her bell. Nothing.

I waited another minute, listening, but the air was dead. No sounds at all to say she was home or on her way to letting me in, I had remembered my keys this time and unlocked swiftly. The door opened easily and I went in quietly, uncertain what I'd find. I dropped my rucksack on the tiled kitchen floor and looked around.

The sink was empty and the draining board looked clean. I wandered into the bathroom as disappointment seeped in like concrete. She wasn't here and there was nothing good implied by her absence, the layer of dusty silence was too thick. In her bedroom I found myself slowly drawn to her dressing table by the Chanel perfume she always wore, Coco, her namesake. I turned the solid pink glass bottle over in my hand absorbing the smell as it clung to my touch.

She hadn't taken the perfume with her. That was strange. I opened her bedside drawer to see bulging make up bags, nail polishes and the accoutrements of being female. I pulled open the slatted wooden doors to her wardrobe, and saw coats, dresses, tops, skirts, all stacked and crammed against one another. I pushed through hangers like wire fish hooks, holding impossible weight on that slim rod, and was faced with towers of shoes in boxes.

I didn't know her clothes like I used to but there was almost her whole wardrobe in here. Coco never travelled light. This was fucked up. I felt my throat closing in the stuffy heat and stale perfume. I had to get some air.

Sitting in Rick's staring into a cup of darkness, I swirled a spoon around a black coffee and tried to clear my mind as the jukebox pumped Bon Jovi into the weed soaked atmosphere. Two blonde girls drinking beer, smoking and laughing with one another, gave me a slow smile. I averted my eyes, and when I looked back they were standing in front of me holding out a piece of paper with a number written on it.

"Call us!" one of the girls laughed, leaving the paper on the table.

I shook my head as my sandwich arrived, and concentrated on eating. I left as soon as I was done, walking briskly back to the flat.

Starting with the bathroom I began methodically opening cabinets. Lines of toiletries gleamed from behind the mirror. How much stuff did a woman need? Coco had always seemed to be low maintenance, but the effort was well hidden. I couldn't help being pleased that there was no sign of any regular male presence but I needed something to grasp onto, some evidence of where she was. I wanted something more tangible than this perfectly tidy, vacant shell.

I shoved my hands deep into my pockets to stop myself lighting another cigarette, and stared out of the window. The kitchen and the lounge were the only rooms that I hadn't searched. My jacket vibrated with a text, breaking my thoughts. I opened the message from Jazz.

"How is it going?"

"Fine. You heard anything?" I replied suddenly feeling ridiculous. There was no reason to let Jazz know I was standing alone in Coco's flat.

"Got nothing here, sorry man."

"Nothing from me either. How is your date?"

"☺ Sexy!"

"Keep focussed! Joking. Enjoy yourselves!" Someone should be having fun, I thought as I walked into the kitchen then back out into the lounge.

The lounge was an open space with one black leather couch, four stainless steel chairs and a table. It was clean, minimalist and decorated with a few select beautiful things – delicate vases, simple pictures in silver frames. Bizarrely I could feel Coco's presence here more than in the bedroom. Abruptly, I strode into the bathroom, turned the shower on and stripped off. I stepped under the water and closed my eyes, it ran over my face and powered down my aching body. I needed her. I wanted to hold her close, fuck her hard, take my mind away and make me forget. Even for a little while.

Waking up the next morning in Coco's bed alone was worse than falling asleep without her. A grey loneliness as vast as the silence seeped into the daylight. The sheets wrapped around me smelt of her, a stark reminder of how empty my life was since she and I split.

Sighing, I padded into the kitchen, put the kettle on and opened the cupboard. There was just one jar of instant coffee. I was going to have to go shopping for basics if I was staying.

But realistically, there was nothing to keep me here. From the minute I'd arrived and found this place empty, somewhere past the anger and the worry, deep inside my heart I really thought Coco would have left me something, *anything*, which would help me find her. At the very least I believed there would be some indication of where she'd gone or when she'd be back. She knew I'd find the diamonds and sooner or later I'd come looking for her.

I didn't expect her to be sitting here drinking tea waiting politely, but the alternative was that she really had fucked me over. Plant the ice, leave me in it up to my nose and then disappear? It didn't make sense. So despite how angry I was, until I saw her with my own eyes and verified that she was in one piece, I was prepared to give her a chance to explain.

I picked up the list I'd written last night and stared at the names I'd ticked off. Not one of her contacts had heard from her. Those I'd called didn't seem concerned, she often went off on business and stayed out of touch, and as everyone said, of all people I should know that. But the disappointment was sickening. Coco didn't have best friends; she wasn't that type of person. Yet she always had people to party with. And those kinds of people didn't share a lot of personal information. I tipped some granules into a light china mug painted with lilac flowers as the kettle reached its climax.

Hiding behind the coffee jar, near the dried out peanut butter and runny mustard was the navy blue plastic biscuit barrel I'd bought last year. It could fit one small tube of biscuits in. Back when we were together Coco wouldn't have had biscuits in the house, not unless I had bought them, but I reached for it anyway and flicked open the catch out of habit. It was empty, except for a folded white square of paper. It looked like a wrap of coke, left over from a night of fun.

I tipped it out into my hand, tempted. The paper fluttered down like a dying butterfly. I opened the neat folds. No drugs but an address in handwriting I half recognised, black ink hand-printed capitals and somewhere in the back of my mind I scrambled to work out where I had seen that type of print before. It wasn't Coco's messy script but I couldn't remember where.

I fucking had something! "21 Ramblas. Barcelona."

I folded the paper back up and dropped it back into the biscuit barrel, slotting it back into its place in the cupboard with the secret intact. 21 Ramblas. I didn't need the paper. I wasn't going to forget that.

16

Jude - Friday May 7th

Barcelona

I packed my rucksack and took a cab back to Schipol. The next flight to Barcelona was that afternoon. I printed the ticket, walked across the flat square concourse and took a seat by the large windows. The diamonds were safe in Manchester but why she dropped them on me was the one conversation Coco and I needed to have in person. I didn't even want to know whose they were; just how she came by them would be good enough.

My mobile buzzed with a text: "Jude, are you okay?"

I touched the number and dialled. "Hi Mum, I'm fine. How are you?"

"Hi darling! I'm fine thanks. Are you okay? Where are you?"

"I'm good, think I'm going to Barcelona later."

"Will you be there long?"

"No, it's just a quick visit, I'll be home before the weekend is over."

"Oh, okay. Have a good time! Don't forget to eat. Come for dinner when you get back!"

"Thanks Mum, dinner sounds good, see you Sunday night."

I was desperate for coffee. And the coffee places sold food. I wandered inevitably to the main plastic food bar, shuffling coins in my pocket as a girl wrapped a tuna sub in serviettes and slid it into a tight paper bag. She tried to stand it up against the coffee, but a thick bread torpedo leaning on Styrofoam was never going to last. I caught the bag as it toppled towards the floor. The girl flushed pink, embarrassed, trying to apologise. She was young, and pretty, blushing to the roots of her light blonde hair.

Sitting at one of the orange and brown plastic tables I began to chew the airport tasting food.

The plane landed on time. I had booked into a cheap hotel from the same Internet café I'd used in Amsterdam to get the flight. The hotel was on Ramblas, the main street. Not that I'd been to Barcelona before but I knew there wouldn't be any difficulty finding the Ramblas. Jazz had been countless times and so had Alex. But it was Rae who loved Barcelona, she'd been on a hen night for a long weekend last year and fell in love with the place, we'd heard about it non-stop. I'd suggested she go back, get a job and leave Manchester behind, start afresh.

A smile flickered at the memory of Rae coming home brimming with an excitement for life that I hadn't ever seen her show. But she was with Scott and he wasn't the type to pack up and move. The guy was nearer ninety than thirty! Alex seemed twenty years younger and he was almost a decade older than Scott. I had no idea what Rae saw in him. I found it hard to believe he had ever been to a party let alone played in a band. I remembered talking to mum, suggesting that someone should have a word, mention that he should take Rae out, make her laugh once in a while. Mum had said absolutely not. But I couldn't help myself, and the one time I had stepped in, Rae went postal. Then, both my mum and Alex told me to stay out of it. Alex said he didn't need his workforce 'getting upset.' Mum insisted that 'Rae needed Scott's stability' and that I was no expert on relationships and should take my own advice on 'putting the effort in.'

I stood waiting for a taxi as thoughts of Rae drifted away. Here I was, different airport same scene.

The hotel on the Ramblas was dingy, cheap, and smeared with grime. A fluorescent light blinked on and off, like a remnant from an old seventies horror flick as I walked towards the reception desk in the narrow hallway. Green plastic linoleum lined the walls, and a man with dark lank hair sat watching a T.V. He didn't turn his head. Seconds later I rang the bell at the desk. He finally looked away from the screen.

"I'm booked in," I showed him the printed receipt from the web.

He nodded at the paper, swivelled towards a computer and clicked at the dirty keyboard. Without raising his eyes he handed over the room key.

"First floor. No lift." His accent was hard to place, more South African than Spanish.

As I pushed through the doorway and climbed the stairs to the first floor, I felt my skin crawl. But he didn't pay me any attention and the one thing I wanted to be right now was invisible. The greasy walls, the yellow lighting and age-old smoke-stench assured me that nothing was given much attention.

I dumped my bag and glanced around the bedroom, once-white paint on the walls, and no carpet. The bathroom was one per floor at the end of the hall; in here was a sink, a single wardrobe and a single bed. It was all I needed. The thumping bass-line thudding through the thin walls from the club next door was a free unwelcome bonus.

17

Rae - Thursday May 6th

Manchester

Jazz slid his black iPod into the dock and music filled the car. Half a minute into the track I realised it was a Perfect Circle. A band I loved, but not a band I'd have associated with him, dark Indie rock bursting with addiction.

"Good band," I said.

"I don't usually like this type of thing, but I saw them live recently and I loved them."

I smiled at the note of surprise in his voice and was glad that I'd read him right. Somehow that was reassuring. The windows of the car were changing colour in the top corners as the light ebbed away. His profile, set against the glass as dusk was beginning to fall, looked less movie-star and more athletic. He was like a European footballer, sleek, polished and professionally handsome.

"Where are we going?"

"I thought the Lowry would be nice."

"The Lowry?" I stopped myself squeaking, and coughed. "That would be lovely. It's always busy though. I doubt we are going to get in." Anxiously I glanced down at my dress and Doc Martin boots and hoped that the Lowry wouldn't object to my less-than-conventional attire.

Jazz replied, "We'll be fine."

As we arrived outside the hotel a statuesque powder blue Rolls Royce, more like a stage coach than a car, drew to a halt right in front of us and on cue a cluster of paparazzi appeared, showering a slim female figure with white star bursts as she unfolded feet first from the car. I didn't want to snap my neck but that tiny female looked remarkably like Lady Gaga without the guise of an eccentric wardrobe.

A steel mast rose upwards from the concrete, the flags waved in the grey sky and despite their famous guest, two out of three cashmere doormen nodded in unison as Jazz slid his window down. I blinked. The nearest coat was holding my door open. I re-arranged the cream lace shawl across my shoulders, a slow blush creeping to my ears and higher.

"Ma'am. Have a nice evening."

Jazz handed the keys to the doorman, and appeared by my side. I trotted up the shallow concrete steps to the lobby in silence, still blushing, feeling awkward, as the doors were held open by another one of the three. He bent his head near Jazz, Jazz leaned back, a smile spread across his face, his hand on the doorman's shoulder. I wanted to leave. Instead I counted to ten, slowly. The doorman looked over at me, nodded and laughed to his friend. With great effort I walked away from them both towards a display cabinet, trying to think peaceful thoughts about the cats, a strategy achieving nothing calming at all. The cabinet glittered with modern, abstract, art. On a second look, I realised they were decorative shapes of animals, made with gems, looking almost like jewellery.

A few minutes later I felt Jazz's presence behind me and a light touch on the small of my back. "You like

Swarovski pets? Expensive taste, maybe I'll buy you one another day."

"Why would you buy me one?" I asked.

"No reason. Sorry about the delay let's go. Our table's waiting."

I saw his reflection in the cabinet, and before I turned round, before I could stop myself, "Why ask me where I wanted to eat if you'd booked prior?"

Jazz shrugged, "I didn't book, the hotel manager is a friend of mine, when we arrived we got a table."

"Oh. I see." I shifted my weight onto my right foot.

Jazz didn't reply. I crunched into the glass of each stair as we made our way up to the restaurant, the heels on my boots the only dialogue.

A figure created from chicken wire, dressed in designer clothes swung from the ceiling of the upper level. The hand seemed oddly twisted and appeared to reach out towards me. I was about to mention what a great piece of work it was, when I stopped myself. He'd probably seen it three times this week already.

A white tablecloth rested in thick waxy folds against my knees as two glasses of water gathered condensation adjacent to the immaculate silver cutlery. The water beading on the glass, the sole sign of warmth, as the atmosphere between Jazz and I had frozen.

"I'd have thought you knew that by heart," I said as Jazz picked up his menu.

"Pardon?" His eyes narrowed.

"Since you're here all the time ..."

"How do you mean?"

"And it's not as if the women you date eat anyway! You wouldn't find them attractive if they weighed more than paper."

"Marae, have I offended you in some way?" Jazz's eyebrows lifted to the middle of his forehead, and joined.

"Guys like you and Alex offend me all the time!"

"By doing what?"

"The way you treat women, like we're a game to be played and you're always the winners," I laughed into the silence, my eyes catching his.

"I thought it was you who wanted to be friends." Jazz spoke quietly and kept his gaze on mine. He didn't laugh.

"Well, if I'm being honest, I actually wanted to convince you that I deserved the placement with Nico."

Jazz inhaled so sharply the air whistled. "So, in reality to you and your cousin *I'm* some kind of a game?"

"God no. Not at all! But I may as well kiss the placement goodbye."

"Who gives a fuck about your placement! You're saying you want revenge for the women we date? That's ridiculous!"

"No! Nothing like that! And for your information *I* do! I give a big fuck about my placement!"

"Clearly, it's all you care about!"

"That's not fair at all. We got on really well when we met at the office didn't we? I mean, I don't usually talk to people the way I talked to you! Jude gave you my number to help, that's all. Look, I really need that placement, and you were so kind to even suggest it …"

"No big deal. I don't understand why Alex didn't do it for you …" Jazz interrupted me.

"No, I don't know why he didn't either. But then there was that row so I figured I'd screwed it up."

"What row?"

"What row? How many rows have I had in front of

you?"

"Oh. I see. That row, now I get it. So, you thought you'd blown your placement when you lost your temper?"

I nodded, cheeks scalding.

"And," Jazz continued, "You're here because you think I would try to ruin your reputation professionally over an argument you had with Alex?"

I felt my skin flush a colour that they hadn't even invented a name for. "It's not unthinkable. You're friends with them both. Anyway Alex has probably told Nico and that's why he didn't suggest it before now, because he knows I'd fuck it up."

"Alex would test the patience of Mother Theresa and for your information my dear, we don't move in the same circles." Jazz's mouth was set in a firm thin line. "But that doesn't change the fact you have a very small view of me."

The waiter arrived, thrusting two square empty white dishes toward us. Seconds later a waitress appeared with a voluptuous bread basket.

"Tomato or olive?" she asked, metal tongues plucking a bun bursting with chunks of black glossy kalamata olives and dropping it centre stage on Jazz's tiny plate.

Jazz looked up and smiled directly at her. She glanced at me swiftly, before inclining her head towards him, and whispered something only he could hear.

"Great idea," Jazz's voice sounded soft, "I will be in touch."

The girl looked over at me again, and smiled. I was in no mood to return the grace.

After a moment of silence Jazz spoke, "The lady wants both tomato and olive, and can you also bring her a couple of slices of walnut loaf and pumpkin rye. Thank you Natalie."

I stared at him. He did know the menu.

"Excuse me madam."

"Thank you." I muttered and moved backwards whilst another waiter deposited ribbons of sushi salmon, dressed with stalks of lilac lavender. The rush of joy I felt at seeing lavender with fresh salmon filled me with delight. It was a genius touch. Aesthetically, the delicate pink flesh of the fish decorated with tiny purple lilac flowers looked divine, whilst the aroma subtly seduced my taste buds.

Despite the urge to leave and get a taxi home as fast as possible, I wanted to know what other delights this Chef had created. As I worried about how I was going to get through an hour with Jazz without any further clashes, let alone an evening, the extra bread arrived, along with small silver rounds of butter on coin sized trays.

"Everything okay Sir?" The waiter asked, lighting the candle in the centre of the table, glancing at our uneaten food.

"Perfect," Jazz waved a hand. The waiter nodded and retreated.

"This is amazing," I gestured at the plate and suddenly found myself reaching for his hand. "Jazz, look, I am sorry. I would really like to get to know you. I wouldn't be here otherwise. Placement or not."

Jazz dabbed his mouth with his serviette and picked up the cold white wine, resting in the steel cooler. He topped up my glass and then his own. "Of course not, no one would make that mistake," he smiled. "Let's start again?"

"I'd like that, thanks," I took a mouthful of the salmon. It was delicious. "Actually, can I ask you something?" I bit my lip, holding my fork tight. "How well do you know the waitress?"

Jazz raised dark eyebrows, "Relax, Marae, I'm here with you, and you're the most engaging woman I've met in a very long time."

I felt my stomach flip, "All we have done is argue and I haven't even convinced you why I deserve my placement with Nico!"

His hand was on mine, warm and dry. "Try your wine! Forget the placement, it's yours," Jazz said, his eyes smiling as he tipped the glass against his lips and drank slowly, visibly savouring each mouthful. "Cloudy Bay is good this year."

"Cloudy Bay?" I said, kicking myself that I hadn't noticed. "Goes beautifully with the fish."

Jazz nodded. "You know you are going to stay here with me tonight. The question is are we going to argue whilst I persuade you with indecent quantities of alcohol, or are you going to surrender right now?"

"No fucking way!" I almost choked. "Neither! Get a grip Jazz!"

Jazz burst out laughing. "Truly, I don't resort to getting women drunk, I'm joking."

"It's not that! Do you ask every woman to sleep with you?"

He leant forward, warm hand on mine, eyes dancing with candle light, "Baby, believe me, they usually ask me!"

18

Rae – Thursday May 6th

Manchester

Asparagus mousse followed the sushi, and somewhere, in a gentle pause between the main course of lamb, and the cleansing elderflower sorbet, I finally stopped trying so hard and started enjoying myself. Jazz wasn't making assumptions based on my tattoos or my hair colour, instead he listened and talked, and more astonishingly, he laughed. From within a similar bubble of a dark sense of humour, we both found life very funny.

"I heard that he'd fallen off the stage and completely broken his leg. But he was so wasted he didn't actually know until afterwards. How did he find out?"

Jazz grinned, "When he was having sex with two of the dancers, he suddenly stopped and said, 'Fuck! My leg!' – one of them obliged …"

I burst out laughing. "No."

Jazz nodded. "Seriously, I know one of the girls, it's true."

Later, after the meal and the drinks and the coffee, dusk faded and night fell thick and heavy. As navy sky fused into inky water I stood looking out over the river, the classical sound of the Lowry's pianist playing in the lounge bar behind. Jazz turned to me, and touched my cheek, his fingers stroking the side of my face. "Let's go upstairs," he said, as gently as butterfly wings. "It will be fun. Trust me." His eyes met mine.

I shook my head and stepped away, it wasn't him I didn't trust, it was me. And right now I didn't trust myself to speak. A few moments later I found my voice. "I can't."

Jazz smiled, "You can. You can do whatever you want." He said reaching out and holding my hand, his thumb playing with the inside of my palm.

"No, really. I can't."

"If you're sure?"

"I'm sure."

"No problem. I'll take you home."

"Thanks," I pulled my hand away and wrapped my arms across my body.

This wasn't me. I was engaged to someone. Scott didn't deserve it and I couldn't do it. But as awful as it was, equal to the worry about Scott, was the ever-present anxiety that the Lowry hotel was where all the players stayed. The place was awash with visiting pop stars, literally.

Someone looking suspiciously like Noel Gallagher was relaxing in the bar area. I was fairly sure I'd seen Lady Gaga floating in the ether somewhere and the England team had moved in en masse during the last world cup. I didn't belong here. There were at least half a dozen incredibly beautiful, famous females in that room. I was standing on a balcony with a man so handsome that he could choose anyone and yet he was asking me if I wanted to stay. It was all too much.

Jazz shrugged, and with a smile that betrayed absolutely nothing he walked slowly to the doormen at the exit. We waited in silence as they brought the car. Jazz stood fingering his cigarette packet, turning the lighter over and over. I turned to speak and found the words wouldn't come.

That silence between us grew on the drive home and as we reached the curb outside my house, I rummaged in my bag for the keys.

"Thank you for tonight," I said, holding the cold metal tight.

"Thank you for your company," he said, both of us breaking the fragile stillness at once. "I had a lovely evening, you really made me laugh. Thanks."

"Me too, thank you. You're not how I thought you'd be."

"You either. I hardly dare ask, but does that mean you'd like to go out again?"

He looked at me, his head tilted in question and then I was brushing the back of my hand down the side of his face against the slow forming stubble, and somehow I was pulling his face toward mine, kissing him. He turned the engine off, locked the car and followed me inside the house. I closed the door behind us and turned to face him. He took the step towards me and cupped his hands to my face, his tongue sliding into my mouth as my hands were finding their way around his body, running down his back. And then I was tugging his jacket off, opening his shirt and he was kissing me. His mouth on my neck, biting the skin and making me catch my breath until he stopped and tore open my dress. The buttons on the soft fabric yielded instantly, my skin craving his touch as he was pushing bra straps down, his lips against my collar bone, kissing every place as his fingers were sliding into my panties, finding me hot, wet and aching.

19

Rae – Saturday May 8th

Manchester

The shape next to me mumbled before rolling over, wrapping me in his warmth and an all-encompassing 'the-world-can't-touch-us' sense of safety. Jazz. He pushed his chin straight into my shoulder with a murmur as I smiled in the sleepy sexy silence.

It was weekend and it felt like it. This was the second morning I had woken up like this. My head hurt due to almost the whole bottle of Bollinger that I had drank all by myself last night. Jazz had done unspeakable things to me, and I had to stop myself giggling out loud at the memories. I loved every minute of being with him, and I was living for now, not tomorrow or next week. I didn't want to think about anything else. The part of me I'd suppressed had broken free, in one mega explosion. I had tried so hard to make it work with Scott but it just didn't. It was over and I would tell him as soon as he got home.

The second before kissing Jazz in the car, and right before anything else, I knew for certain that I wasn't *in* love with Scott any longer. Kissing Jazz just proved it. The rest had followed. I'd thought the 'being in love' with Scott part didn't matter, that it would all magically work itself out and be okay. But it wasn't. And the denial that I wanted more, needed more, had been going on for so long that I was dead inside. My breath caught as a small tear escaped and crawled slowly down my cheek. I didn't want to cry. I was happy. But I couldn't marry Scott because it was an easier option than dealing with what either of us really felt.

After Scott, being with Jazz was like being brutally dunked in a bucket of ice water. It took a few minutes to get over the shock but afterwards all senses were alive and tingling with electricity.

"You awake baby?" Jazz nuzzled with his teeth, grazing the skin at the base of my neck, nibbling my earlobe as he asked.

I wriggled out of his embrace, and in reply slid along the length of his muscular torso and those perfectly defined abs to dive even lower under the duvet. I wanted to lose myself in him and take advantage of his warm, rich nakedness, kissing and teasing with my lips, tongue.

My eyes were open and I was exactly where I wanted to be, selfish, guilty as charged. But the guilt wasn't there. Stronger than any other feeling and soaring above all else was a sense of pure, exhilarating, freedom.

Jazz had his hand in my hair stroking my head and as silently as possible was refusing to relinquish control even though his body told a different story and his back was arching, even as his breath was coming in shorter and shorter gasps. We were evenly matched and there was a connection between us that didn't need words.

I was lost all right, and not sure I ever wanted to find the way back. So was Jazz currently, lost, as his hands clenched tighter in my hair and I won the battle. Delighted, I smiled, satisfied at the taste of victory.

20

Rae – Monday May 10th

Manchester

The alarm went off at the usual time. The sun blasted through the curtains like floodlights at Old Trafford. I stretched and yawned, listening to Minx yowling. Tiara, patient as ever was sitting on the end of the bed, waiting for her telepathy to wake me.

Suddenly I woke up properly. I had work today and Scott was due back. The thought of seeing Scott sent my stomach spiralling. But I was going to sort it out. It was time to have *those* chats and mentally I had scheduled those chats for *this* evening.

The blissful cloud of oblivion that was 'being with Jazz' had evaporated sickeningly fast. We had eaten together and then as the hours merged spent the time in bed. Afterwards, instead of sleeping he had slid into his leather jacket, and looking like sex, he'd kissed me softly before vanishing into the darkness.

We made no exact plans when to see one another again. He'd said he would be in touch and I was drunkenly happy to see how things evolved. Jazz and I had only just begun. Things would be different after Scott came home. That phrase "after Scott came home" sent chills into me, signalling everything was set to change. My life this past five days had been borrowed from an alternate reality and now I had to return to earth.

The tangible expiry of our time together was somehow mirrored in Jazz and I felt him take a step out of my world and back into his, whatever his world was. I still knew so little about him.

Thinking about him again I chided myself, it was time to stop staring vacantly at the ceiling. Conjuring energy I didn't feel I pulled the duvet back briskly got up and stumbled into the bathroom. The shower was on full, and I was just about to submerge myself in water when the phone rang without revealing a number, it was 8 a.m.

"Hello?"

"Hi darling," said Auntie Lola, Jude's mum. "Sorry to call so early, can you meet for a cup of coffee? Before you go to work?"

"Sure, twenty minutes. Carmelli's?"

"Thank you."

As I fed the cats, I prayed that the house was tidy. Scott would be home later and I knew that I might not have the time to get back before he arrived.

I had to be totally sure there were no traces of Jazz. Jazz, just the thought of him and I had butterflies dancing in my stomach. I had to wipe this ridiculous grin off my face. What about Scott? I felt physically ill about breaking up with him but I was going to speak to him tonight, make dinner and talk. My mind was made up. No going back.

The air had that early morning sensibility, life was loud, full of birdsong and glorious 'almost summer' smells of freshness. A heaven sent world of sensuality surrounded me. The feel of the breeze on my skin had my heart singing as the sun lifted my soul.

I saw Auntie Lola's car parked in the tiny gravel square at the back of the bakery. Carmelli's sold fresh bagels baked through the night, and their coffee shop was open twenty-four hours. This was the teen home-run after the late show at the cinema, the place to go for munchies after an all-nighter at the clubs, and the taste of joy when lovers woke at 3 a.m. with nothing to eat in anyone's cupboards. Carmelli's saved us all.

Auntie Lola was sitting by one of the stainless steel lightweight tables, her long legs elegantly awkward. She saw me and started waving.

"Hello, thank you darling. How are you?" she asked as she stood up and enveloped me in a massive hug. The strength of her grip and the fierceness of the perfume cloud did nothing to hide her skeletal frame. I could feel too easily how thin she had become.

"Is everything all right?" I asked, realising how stupid that question was. Of course it wasn't 'all' 'right' as we wouldn't be here, meeting before 8.30 a.m.

Lola smiled at one of the young Israelis behind the counter, "Two latte's and two bagels please, one plain, one with lox. Thanks."

This was our usual order in times of emotional crisis.

"Okay what's he done this time?" I asked as I negotiated taking my jacket off, and sliding between table, chair and wall, arranging myself in such a way that wouldn't knock into Lola's flamingo legs.

She lowered her Jackie O sunglasses and I could see how fragile she looked. She smiled faintly.

Lola had become a mother to Jude at barely sixteen. Mum's sister and the baby of the family whose life hadn't worked out how either she, or they, had pictured it. I loved Lola. She was far more like an older sister to me than an auntie.

"I'm worried about him Rae."

"Why?"

She hesitated before replying. Looking down at the white saucer she played with the shiny metal spoon and dropped a sugar cube into her milky coffee, slowly stirring as if she were searching for the words.

"I can't say why, it's just a feeling. I know he has done some things in the past but he's changed, he's different now and this isn't like him. Not anymore," she said, her eyes finally meeting mine.

"Let's start at the beginning. What's wrong?"

Auntie Lola was talking in riddles. I knew Jude was doing far more partying than I thought he could handle, but it didn't seem like it was that which was upsetting her.

"I'm worried, he doesn't sound right. It's … as if he's involved in something. Do you know anything?" she said, fingering her packet of cigarettes absently, taking them out of the black and silver D.G bag and then dropping them back. It was no smoking in Carmelli's.

"What makes you think he's into anything?"

"I know my son," Lola replied.

I stayed silent for a moment, then, thinking out loud. "I don't know what he's up to these days but he is over all that. Honestly." I touched her hand and tried to comfort her, she felt cold.

Lola smiled, "Okay. So I'm being a silly over protective Jewish mother, I get it. I should let him grow up already?" Her smile slipped. "I realise what I sound like Rae, but when was the last time you heard from him?"

"A couple of weeks ago," I replied shifting in my chair, feeling bad. I had been that wrapped up I hadn't spoken to Jude in a while. Though, when I thought hard, Jazz had mentioned seeing him the other night.

"Rae, he's in Barcelona. I know he's a big boy and he's supposed to be able to take care of himself but I'm concerned about him, he has no one with him and he sounded ... odd," she left the word hanging.

"Odd how? What's he doing in Barcelona?" I asked surprised. Jazz hadn't mentioned that. "He'll be with a girl surely?"

"Maybe," She shrugged. "I don't know, he didn't say. I expected him for dinner last night but I haven't heard from him since Friday morning. I know it's only a couple of days but he promised to keep in touch and ..."

"Today's Monday. Don't worry he'll be fine, I promise." I said, looking at my watch. It was after nine and I had to be in work. I hugged her tight and grabbed the bagel, eating a giant mouthful. "Gorgeous! I'll phone you tonight. You know what he's like. He needs his space," I said swallowing. "Am really sorry, I have to go."

"Thank you darling," she leant towards me and hugged me back strongly. She hadn't touched her bagel, just drained her coffee and sat for a moment or two longer, as if deciding which had the greatest pull, nicotine or food.

As I ran to the car and jumped in I looked back in my rear view mirror and saw her leaving, pausing to light the cigarette. Nicotine won.

I flew round the corner to work and parked, sitting in the stillness for a moment. I was meant to be in before Alex but as he was rarely in before lunch, I wasn't worried. I wasn't overly worried about Jude either, if anything was wrong, he would have been in touch. Everyone needed time out.

I was struggling with the door, my greasy fingers failing to get the keys in the unforgiving pad lock when a voice behind me said: "I'll do it," and removed the keys from my salmon smelling grip. Alex was icily early.

"Sorry I'm a bit late," I began.

"Save it," he said rudely, Police sunglasses fixed to the perfect tan. Mouth sneering.

In silence the keys slid into place. The padlock fell into his hand, the door swung open and he was at the alarm keypad before I had even got both feet in the showroom.

Alex was in a hell of a mood this morning. I could feel it. As quietly as I could I went into the scarlet office, put my bag down and feeling sick threw the rest of the bagel in the bin. It was going to be one of those days if he was in this early and was this Prince of Darkness-like. The boys weren't in the warehouse yet and the office was empty except for Alex. I didn't count since I was trying so hard to be invisible.

Flicking through post and paper notes at rapid speed Alex abruptly changed direction, slammed the pile down onto the desk and then turned to face me. He pulled the shades down, deliberately folded them and placed them side by side with his keys and his mobile. When my glance caught his I saw something dead behind his eyes.

"Do you want a coffee?" I asked quietly, not really wanting to speak.

"Have you seen Jazz recently?" Alex asked.

"Jazz?" I repeated.

"Yeah. Jazz. About so high, you know, you met him here, with me. Your cousin gave him your number," Alex said.

"I don't know what you're talking about," I said, flushing bright pink.

Alex laughed, a harsh sound without humour, "Sure you know what I'm talking about."

"He's your friend. Have you seen him lately?" I replied and turned my back to him. My face was going to give it away if he kept looking at me like that, like he was stripping layers of skin until he could see down to the bone.

"You don't know what you're getting into," Alex said.

"How would you know what Jazz is into anyway?" I asked playing for time as my mind went spinning.

"I know everything, me. I thought you knew that. Your cousin told me all about it, all about your little crush. Well? You planning on seeing him?" Alex said leaning forwards, his face jutting towards mine, bullying me with his tone.

I was silent for a whole second. I was going to kill Jude.

And then I felt myself snap.

"What business is it of yours? How dare you stick your nose in? It has got nothing to do with you who I see or what I do, and why can't I see him – why aren't I good enough?"

"So go on then! Do what you want, see him, *do* him. Just don't come crying to me when he breaks your life in two and dumps you," Alex replied.

"As if I would ever come crying to you! Like I have ever come crying to you about anything! What the fuck is it to you what I do? I don't ask you what you're doing or who with. It's up to me what I do with anyone."

"You're sleeping with him? I don't believe it. You've been screwing him haven't you?" Alex's jaw went slack with shock. "You wouldn't be reacting like this otherwise."

I stopped. He was right. I'd given it away and Alex had his confirmation from me.

"So what if I am," I said, my eyes never leaving his.

"I can't believe it. I never thought you would do that. You have no idea what he is like. You're engaged for fuck sake. You have your life sorted. He's not for you, and your fucking cousin should have seen to it," Alex said standing with his legs resting against the desk, his fists clenched and down by his sides. He was pale, his face flickering with anger.

"Just what has any of this got to do with you?" I asked softly.

He stared at me in silence for a second and then he spoke, irises changing from winter skies to summer oceans in a heartbeat. "Nothing. It has absolutely nothing to do with me. Except I know what he's been doing and who with and I also have to work with you and I don't want this shit when I come into work in the morning. I know what he does to women. Whatever, I thought you were better than that. Do what you want," Alex replied picking his shades up and sliding them back into place.

There was no way forward with this conversation. But the question flew from my lips anyway. "So you're saying he has a girlfriend?"

Alex laughed, long and hard, an empty hollow sound. "One girlfriend?"

"I didn't know," I said hoarse, in that second dismissing every single thing I had guessed about Jazz.

"Okay so you didn't know. Now you know. Get rid," said Alex.

"It's not that easy," I could feel the tears welling up.

"What do you mean 'it's not that easy'? Fuck. You're not in love with him?" Alex ripped his shades off and suddenly his eyes were piercing holes right into me.

"What do you care? What's it to do with you?" I squeaked.

"Christ. You are in love with him. Look Rae, he's not for you. He's a player. For crying out loud he's worse than me, he doesn't care about the women he fucks. What? Did you think that it was going to be different with you? He went through a dozen different girls last month in two weeks flat when we were in London. Two a day, if he was bored at lunchtime, threesomes after a show, fuck man I lost track. The younger the better but if they're married that's even sweeter, no strings no come back," he paused to get his breath whilst I stood looking at the floor silently willing it to open and claim me.

I was listening but hardly believing my ears and yet somehow I knew it was all true, every last word. Slowly Alex continued his lesson, spacing each word evenly.

"He – does - not - give - a – shit - Rae. Got it? He's one of the guys I hang with but there are some things you don't do. You're as good as family and Jazz had no right to go near you … Not unless he was serious," Alex finally stopped speaking.

I wasn't listening. I was thinking of how Jazz had been kind enough to help me get my placement and that even though I hadn't wanted to like him, I did. But more than anything I trusted him. The connection we shared was special. I would have known if he hadn't meant any of it. I'd have felt it in the sex we'd had, in the really intimate things we had done together. I couldn't be completely wrong about him. I couldn't. This *was* different.

Alex stepped forward and hugged me close. "Look doll, I should have said something sooner, I am sorry Rae. I just thought you had more sense. For fuck's sake don't ruin your life over him."

A mobile went off briefly shattering the numbness surrounding me.

"It's not mine this time," Alex said passing my phone to me.

I held it out as the caller display lit Jazz's name.

"Do you want me to speak to him?"

I shook my head. I couldn't pick up the call though, not when my world had just been hit by a nuclear holocaust. And yet there was light too, from the one direction I could never have predicted in a million years. Alex, the tart with a heart, was playing my knight in shining armour. What a stupid fucking mess.

21

Jude – Friday / Sunday May 9th

Barcelona

Number 21 Ramblas, my Coco-lead was a bar with a flat above, fifteen minutes walk from the greasy hotel. It was midnight, and the bar was busy. But the alley running alongside the building was layered in darkness, streetlight merging to gloom as rubbish bins lined the wall.

Between the refuse I spotted an iron fire escape. As quietly as possible, I swung up to the bottom rung, several feet off the floor and glanced towards the roof. The staircase led up to the front door. I started climbing.

The metal staircase was tucked tightly against the wall, and it moved each time I moved, swaying with my body weight. I didn't like heights. Minutes later I was over the iron railings. I landed on a balcony, my back flat against the bricks, breathing fast, trying to ignore the ground below. The flat was in darkness and the door was tight. I scanned the room. The light from the windows was plenty enough to get a good look, and it was a hole, a dirty studio flat. The bedroom, sitting room and kitchen were all in the same space. Coco wasn't here. There was no way she'd stay in a place like this. I shut the door, climbed down and put Plan B into action.

Making my way through the bar towards the cash register, I took a stool near the end of the optics, away from the lines of people queuing and lit a cigarette, beneath the no smoking sign. A girl pouring cocktails looked over, frowned and forced a smile that didn't reach her eyes. She nodded in the direction of a barman with black hair, serving a continuous stream of beer, saying something I couldn't hear. He glanced up at me once. Seconds later a third man, Asian, pallid complexion, and distinctive tattoos inked up his forearms came over.

"What do you want?"

"A friend of mine is missing."

"Who is your friend?"

I showed him the photo of Coco on my phone.

"Never seen her."

I saw the recognition skim across his eyes. "You're lying. Where the fuck is she?"

"No idea."

"When did you last see her?"

"I can't help."

"The hell you can't. When was she here?"

He shrugged, already pulling away, "Erik may know something. Come back Sunday night. I'll speak to him."

I leant forwards, my hands on the bar, right fist clenching.

"You tell Erik I want to speak to him myself."

I was sitting by the water's edge on one of Barcelona's City beaches, waiting. Time had been crawling since Friday and I was ready to break doors down. I was here to find Coco and with no leads, almost every hour on the hour I had considered taking that flat apart. The truth was I didn't want to start a fucking war when I was here alone, for the sake of forty-eight hours, but enough was enough. Tonight I would get what I came for – answers.

The day was scorching hot and the white sun stung like needles. A group of half naked girls playing volleyball in the sparkling blue water did nothing to distract me from clock-watching. Young boys wandered through the tourists selling cans from ice bags, offering trinkets and bracelets with fizzy pop, as beach attendants opened sun umbrellas above white plastic tables. Google said that this whole area was reclaimed for the 1992 Olympics, before then it was industrial wasteland. Only I couldn't tell the difference between this beach and any other.

Someone took two chairs and set them down in the nearby sand. I glanced up as the umbrella fanned out like an airborne jellyfish and seconds later a man with mud coloured dreadlocks reaching to his waist settled in. The digital sign stuck on a pole in the middle of the concrete boulevard displayed the temperature at 41 degrees C, solid heat. As the minutes passed a stream of uncomfortable visitors approached. He was a dealer.

Trust me to find where to score without even trying. I pushed the shades back in place, firmly. I hadn't had any gear since the day I found the ice and I was sorely tempted. I lit another cigarette, and ignored the roaring in my skull.

The sun pierced my skin with fierce rays at 4:45pm. Finally evening was here. I nodded at dreadlocks and then got up slowly and started the walk back to the grim hotel room. It was impossible to move fast in this heat. As I stood my back pocket started vibrating.

I took the phone out and looked at the display. It held one simple word, 'call'.

"Yeah?"

"I hear that you have been looking for me. You murder my man, you have my belongings and you save me the trouble of even flying to your country to collect." He laughed. "I like you already Mr Jude." The voice sounded robotic – distorted.

"Who is this?"

"Someone who, let's say as a result of your recent action, has a gap that needs filling."

"Hang on a fucking minute. Where's Coco?" I was scouting around for somewhere quiet and not too populated to have the conversation. There was nowhere to go.

"You killed my man. You have twenty-four hours to consider how to repay me or you take the vacancy yourself. Am I making myself clear?"

"What vacancy? What are you talking about? I found him like that. I've no fucking idea who took him out, you can't pin that on me. I was returning your fucking goods. What have you done to Coco?" I was sweating cold despite the heat.

"Coco is not in any danger. However, the man you shot was hand picked to carry out a job. A job that needs completing. Therefore Mr Jude I'm very generously suggesting that you take his place."

"I told you, I didn't kill anyone, the guy was dead when I got there. I'm not fucking doing anything for you."

"There is a debt to clear."

"You can have your stuff back."

"Do you have them with you?"

"No of course not …"

"No gems no deal. You have twenty-four hours."

"Motherfucker! You can't do this!" But I was yelling at an empty connection. The call was over. I turned round and saw a young couple staring at me. I needed to leave. I had to get out of here. Get to the airport. Panic flooding, bile rising in my throat, head thudding … I couldn't think through the red fog. I had to get away.

Instead I slowed my footsteps down. And stood, hands on thighs, bent forward. I felt like I'd been kicked in the stomach as realisation sank in. There was no point in running, they knew who I was. They'd find me wherever I went. People like that always did. Right now that maniac thought I'd killed his delivery boy to keep his ice, and in return he owned me.

I hadn't killed anyone. But if I didn't, who did? Whoever did the hit had left me in it, unless I proved otherwise. That nauseating worry I'd been hiding from since the day I found the guy at the Quays had just materialised.

I glanced at my watch, barely 5:00 p.m. maybe it was possible to get back to Manchester, get the diamonds and be back here within twenty-four hours. If Erik was even fucking based here. If that was even Erik who had fucking called.

I wished Jazz were around to bounce ideas off. I flicked through my phone on instinct, in seconds I had Jazz's number all ready to go but instead I stopped. I shoved the phone back into my pocket. Something deep inside me clicked. It was tangible. In that moment I knew I was not going to phone Jazz, ring Alex or run away. I'd survived in Amsterdam without them. Coco was my problem. Jazz had been great at the Quays but I could have, and should have handled it myself. If I hadn't been so wasted recently I might have behaved differently. Coco had got me into this, whatever this was, but I was going to get myself out of it. Then I was going to find her and get to the fucking bottom of everything.

The heat sweltered claustrophobically. I needed a shower and the only choice I had was the dirty hotel.

Flights out of Barcelona were fully booked. I would have to wait until morning to try and get a standby seat on a plane to Manchester, with no guarantee of getting back here. My gut twisted. There were flights out of Perpignan, France but I needed to get over there, which meant a train as I didn't bring my driving license, and timing was sticky. It was too unreliable. I had been sat in an Internet café for the past couple of hours and the heat of the day had barely faltered.

The air was humid-hot and the pavements were teaming with life. The night trade on the Ramblas was in full flow and Barcelona trembled to the sound of Euros exchanging hands. Africans, Europeans, people of all denominations ran and walked up and down the busiest street in the city. The human traffic never ceased. Birds in cages, calendars, street tattoos, porn, magazines and DVD's as well as children's toys were on show. I could buy a game for Zara, Alex's little sister along with adult top shelf dress up outfits, sexy maids and cut away nurses clothes, from the same stall, wrapped in the same cellophane.

Everything was for sale and the streets were oozing at the seams. Young lovers stopped to pause and kiss, an old Indian man, his head wrapped in a turban sat with his bong and pipes, smoking and talking to anyone who would listen.

I was becoming accustomed to the night pace; it was different to the day. I made my way down towards the harbour. Number 21 was towards the end of the street away from the city and towards the footbridge.

Inside I became part of the crush. The place was heaving with people, crammed with sweaty tanned figures as Salsa music bounced from the condensation dripping walls. The crowded bar was noisy and smoky, the air suffocated by bodies pumping to the beat. Three barmen were tossing glasses, pouring cocktails, and serving. I watched them taking money like magicians, whilst sliding quarts of lime into bottles, Mexican style.

As the Chinese man saw me he averted his eyes and slid a beer along the bar, still serving and turning his back toward me as he spoke, "Erik's not here."

Moving fast I pushed past the queue of people and headed him off as he got to the till at the end, slamming one hand against the wall, my knuckles near his head, he was a full six inches shorter than me. "Call him. Now!"

"I can't contact him. Please. Erik takes care of business himself."

I clenched my fist down by my side, avoiding his body with great effort. I looked into his face. He was haunted big time, fear sprayed all over him, eyes flickering. I took the nearest bottle, stood up and made my way out of 21 into the night air. I'd kept my temper twice. And I had nothing to show for it. No information and no Coco.

Girls were everywhere, skimpily dressed, girls with their boyfriends, brown arms draped around one another. I never saw half as many people during the daytime. At night Barcelona opened up like an orchid attracting bees. The whole of the Ramblas became one market stall. Casually I walked toward the flat at the back, knowing there was no opportunity to get up to the door unspotted. I stood for a second, deciding if it was worth being seen or not, and shrugged. It wasn't like they didn't know I was here.

A minute later I was climbing the metal staircase. It was easier this time, as I remembered where to swing my weight. Another minute and I was breaking the window next to the door. Slowly I lowered my hand through the glass, and reached for the handle. There were no alarm sirens and one glance down the fire escape assured that no one from the bar was chasing me.

I was in. Unwashed dishes filled the sink and covered the stained coffee table; the room stank of debris and stale smoke. I looked around. This place wasn't used regularly and it was nothing more than a bolthole, for late shifts and drugs. I could smell the stuff, more than that; I could feel it, hanging in the air. There was no evidence of Coco. On instinct I started searching through the cupboards, plates, broken crockery. Nothing out of the ordinary. But something caught my eye, one clean space on a kitchen unit. I pulled open the drawer beneath and found velvet boxes. I knew without looking what I had found. Antique scales. The type of scales old school dealers used for weighing drugs. Or gems. No one I knew used them anymore. It didn't matter, it was time to leave. Coco wasn't here and I couldn't picture her ever having been here.

Back at the hotel there was no porter and the hallway was in darkness. I wasn't doing jobs for anyone. I was not getting involved in whatever shit was happening here. I was going back to Manchester in the morning to get the fucking diamonds. My mind whirred. Erik knew where Coco was. So, when I got back with the stones I would force it out of someone one way or another. Because wherever the fuck Erik had hidden her, I was going to find her.

22

Jude – Monday May 10th

Barcelona

My phone was buzzing. I woke up, eyelids sticking in the oppressive heat. I sat on the edge of the bed, feet on the floor, thoughts stagnating as I reached over to the little wooden side cabinet scored with cigarette burns and picked up my mobile. There was a text from another new number that I didn't recognise: *I'm having fun*.

That was it, nothing more. The words sent a chill down my spine. I had slept heavily for five hours. I stood up to grab my towel and make my way down to the bathroom as I heard the phone again. Incoming … Air caught in the back of my throat as I flicked open the message and saw the word ***Incentive*** beneath a photograph of a girl.

Rae. It was a photograph of Marae, blindfolded and tied to a chair. What the fuck? I stared at her legs attached to chair legs, at her arms pulled back tight together. Her wrists were handcuffed. Frantic I dialled her number. Rae's phone rang out - no one picked up. I rang back again and again, but nothing. Nothing at all.

Seconds later another text flew in. "Check your email."

As fast as I could I clicked onto the web on my phone. One new email in my hotmail account, from Mr ABC. I opened the mail. More photos.

Another email flew in, with the same name, Mr ABC. The email was an electronic plane ticket in my name, trying to focus I read the details. There was a flight number, followed by a hotel address and a man's name. I looked at the address and the plane ticket. It didn't make any sense. The flight was for today. To Antwerp.

My mobile was ringing. "Yes," the word sounded hoarse, heavy.

"Hi man, it's me, Jazz, is everything okay?"

"What?" I replied.

"I've not heard from you for a few days, are you sure everything's okay? Have you sorted that little problem yet?" Jazz laughed.

I was so far from speaking that I felt under water, submerged. "Jazz, sorry, can't talk. I'll call you."

I dialled the number on the message, spitting, "What the fuck are you playing at? Who is that girl?"

"I warned you that there would be a price to pay for my colleague's life. Your sister has not been harmed for now. Be at the airport, catch the flight and go to your hotel. Do not contact anyone or she will suffer." The metallic voice stopped.

Dumb, I stared at the silent phone. They thought Rae was my sister. They knew where the people I loved were, where Rae was, where my mum was. Easy targets. My mind was rolling, my heart felt like it was cracking open. Rae was in trouble. And it was my fault. She could be killed because of me, or because of Coco. Because of a bag of diamonds that weren't mine. I was furious, and terrified.

I called back but the connection was dead.

No answer phone. I called Rae again, but this time the phone didn't even ring. It was flat. I tried her house but that rang out. She was gone. My brain tried to stutter reasonable explanations. There weren't any. This couldn't be happening. But it had already happened. I couldn't stop it.

I could go back to the bar and get hold of one of the crew. But they wouldn't be there now at this time and if I risked everything on that or taking that flat apart just to get information on Coco or find out more about Erik and I failed or turned up nothing, whilst they had Rae? It didn't bear thinking about.

Dislocated from the reality of ten minutes ago, I dressed, packed the rucksack and then unzipped my jeans, relieving the ache in my bladder directly down the tiny discoloured sink.

23

Rae - Tuesday May 11th

Manchester

It was morning. I knew this because of the dull ache behind my eyes in response to the light; light that I had been trying to shield myself from. Either someone had mugged me or I had the hangover from hell. One side of my head hurt really badly and the throbbing was obliterating all thoughts.

I stretched out my arm, finding nothing. Scott's side of the bed was empty. Sheets untangled, pillows untouched. He hadn't slept here. But he was back. That much I knew instinctively. Guilt rippled through my veins.

I sat up slowly and reached for the glass of water, sipped at it and tried to piece things together. It was a hangover. I remembered getting drunk. Hit and run drunk. Messy, sprawling, on-a-mission drunk. A zillion different fragments were suddenly jostling for recognition. Everything blurred and I didn't know exactly what had happened between my last drink and now. Vague images were floating into my head. Voices. An argument, Alex, Scott, Jazz.

Volcanic worry filled the parts of me that weren't choking with nausea. Oh God. Shaking I lurched to the bathroom. Hanging onto the side of the bowl, focussing on the cold enamel trying to calm the swell that was rising again like seasickness, my head throbbed out of time. Again I retched. The floor beneath my knees was hard. Scott? Jazz? And Alex and work and, oh god, I was ill. Eventually when I stood up and fumbled my way to the shower, to wash it all away, to try and clear the pounding in my brain, real memory started to come back. Oh fuck.

After the shower it was time to get straightened out and get to work. I couldn't believe I was meant to be at work. No way did I feel able to face Alex in this state. I couldn't function with this headache and after yesterday I was at a loss. I needed to be on good form, not lying in the wreckage. I struggled into my jeans, co-ordination limited, and grabbed at the nearest top from the chair, something, anything, just one I'd left on the clean laundry pile. A black v-neck, soft cotton and long-sleeved. Where did I leave my phone? I had no idea. But fresh air would help. I wandered down stairs and there was a note from Scott by the kettle.

"Hi. Last night you said you needed to sit down and talk about things properly if we want to try and sort this out. Do you want to meet for an early lunch?"

I burst into tears. I could go into town and see him but I doubted that he really wanted to talk to me. And it might be better to leave him alone. I didn't know what to say to him anyway since I didn't remember exactly what I'd said last night and until I did, it was best this way. 'Right?' I said to Tiara. She jumped up on my lap, and head-butted my chin.

"You hungry?" I asked.

'Miaow.' She looked deep into me with her bright pale green eyes and I was crying all over again. I was being pathetic. Tiara just sat and waited, then realising she wasn't getting fed she lightly curled into a ball and slept on my knee whilst I sobbed and sipped.

I sat drinking water slowly for what felt like hours in that stillness, avoiding the house phone and concentrating on trying to quell the vomiting, both of which thankfully, finally, halted.

"Hi baby, let's go for a drink. I'll call you later," Jazz had emailed.

I didn't even know what to think about that.

I needed to see Alex first before I tried to work anything out about Jazz. I had to see him on neutral territory, somewhere out of the warehouse before we were back in work together. I wouldn't know how I felt about any of this until I did. Because, somewhere buried deep down, I was frightened that Jazz might actually have been right weeks ago when he'd said I was 'very much in love' with Alex. And that was the one complication I could well do without.

I got up and made my way to the kitchen. I pushed two slices of thick bread into the toaster, made a cup of tea and swallowed two paracetamol. Then I dialled his number.

24

Jude - Monday evening May 10th

Antwerp

The plane landed late. The recent vein of airborne luck had dried up and three hours delay meant it was nearer 7p.m. than mid afternoon. They had Rae. My mind kept sticking on that one thought. I had no information on Coco. I'd been forced into leaving Barcelona without getting any nearer to finding her and someone wanted me on a job.

Those photos of Rae were printed in my cortex as I repeated the pattern of baggage collection then locating a taxi. A white Mercedes pulled towards me and I climbed in. The driver checked his rear view and caught my eye. "Holiday Inn please."

The Holiday Inn was just outside of the City Centre towards Northern Antwerp according to the websites. Apparently this was the cool part of town. It didn't take long to drive down the wide streets. Fifteen minutes after leaving Antwerp Airport the cab stopped outside the hotel. I gave the driver twenty Euros swung the navy rucksack back onto my shoulder and strode into the modern glass-fronted building with no intention of handing over my passport for the usual security check.

The receptionist smiled as I approached. She was wearing a transparent white blouse and I could see her white bra. Her hair was loosely tied and she was attractive, I lowered my shades and corrected my eye level, raising my curiosity to her face.

"Hi there, I think I have a reservation," I said.

"Certainly. You think?" she replied, smiling, her lips parted in question.

"Well, to be honest," I said dropping one tone with a smile, "I didn't book it myself, it was my new PA."

The receptionist fluttered her eyelashes and smiled again, she had the finest shadow of dimples. I hadn't seen dimples for a while.

"What's your name please? I will need your passport to confirm."

"T. Black," I replied giving the name of the man that was on the email. There was the sound of keys being tapped on the keyboard on the desk hidden just below my line of vision.

"Ah yes, here we are. Room 505, on the fifth floor, one of our luxury suites. It has already been paid for, the booking and payment went through online. Your PA is not so bad," she laughed gently. "The reservation is for five days. Is that correct?" she was so earnest and sweet, with lovely full lips and soft dark hair.

"Pardon?" I said. Christ I had to concentrate.

"Sorry. Yes, the account was settled at time of booking. The reservation is for five days. Is that incorrect?" she looked concerned.

My mind tumbled. Five days. Five fucking days.

I had to get a grip. "No, no, that's right. Sorry, I am just really …" I paused then and picked up the beat looking directly into her brown eyes, "… tired."

The girl flushed faintly, I watched as her skin fused with a delicate shade of red around the base of her throat but she didn't lower her eyes, she held my gaze and handed over the room key almost in a trance.

"Enjoy your stay Sir see you soon."

I took the plastic key and allowed my fingers to brush hers. I didn't reply, just smiled as I slipped the shades back in place and walked to the elevators. The passport remained in my rucksack.

I entered the silver elevator and pressed number five, the top floor. Within a second I was suctioned up the lift shaft. It was a turbo lift. I felt queasy as the doors snapped open and I stepped into the hall looking for the numbered arrows.

There was a highly polished oak table with a large square glass of flowers on the wall directly in front of me and a heavy wooden and glass door to the right. I pushed through and the first door was number 510. The numbers decreased. My suite was at the end of this corridor.

The key slid comfortably into the black wall lock and the small round light on the corner of the box switched to green. I turned the handle and let myself in. The visions of Rae seeped to the front of my mind. Those images never left, all I could do was push them away. I swallowed hard, right now I was here and she was God knows where.

It wasn't a suite of two rooms, but more a large bedroom with a living area, all decorated in crème and dark red. Everything matched. The walls were crème; one was covered with silver framed sketches and designs, the opposite scattered with silver framed black and white photographs of boats. The cushions and the bed coverings were blood red with a crème pattern. The artwork looked original, and there was no fourth wall – or at least not much of one.

I stared out of the huge glass windows onto a perfect harbour view. There was a balcony, a table and two chairs. This was the back of the hotel; the yacht harbour below had its own terrace, restaurants, pubs, clubs and bars. I vaguely remembered that too from the web guides. The locals called it the "Little Island," where the beautiful people congregated. It seemed like a miniature Monte Carlo, created out of sheer opulent luxury. Coco would love it.

I opened the patio doors and stood out onto the terrace. Leaning forwards onto the white handrail and looking across the harbour I wished I were a thousand miles away. Dread crawled over my skin like beetles. Erik meant business. No dingy back street room, no hiding. This was fast track to the fast lane. I was down with the big boys now.

Going straight and staying clean didn't matter one bit. I was back under. Whatever I was meant to do was within the next five days. I was going to find Coco in six days time and I just prayed wherever she was that she had six days, but the fucking worst part was that for now Rae wasn't going anywhere at all. That's if I succeeded. It didn't bear thinking about otherwise.

I yawned my way to the bathroom and stared at a stranger in the mirror. The Barcelona tan made my eyes look greener, sharper. My hair was scorched white-blonde and longer than I ever wore it. Without the partying I looked lean, less bloated. Stubble had grown over my chin and down my neck. I laughed. I could be a yacht owning racing driver. What better way to be invisible in a place where everyone looked as if they were somebody? Not exactly low profile but then I'd never been much good at that part of things. Another reason why I'd given up because I'd noticed that mostly, people tended to remember me.

The patio doors were wide open sending a peaceful breeze into the bedroom. Exhausted I crashed onto the nearest bed.

25

Rae - Tuesday May 11th

Manchester

"Hello?"

"Hi Alex, it's me. Rae."

"Yes I know. It's called caller I-D. What do you want?"

Aware of how ridiculous I was going to sound I suddenly went very quiet.

"Hello?" he asked again.

"Oh God. Alex I'm sorry, please can we talk? I mean about everything," I said, digging an imaginary hole with my toe in the carpet, as the toast pinged noisily.

"What was that?" Alex asked riptide fast as ever.

"Toast. Why? Do you want some?" I said smiling at the phone.

"Toast? I didn't know we had a toaster at the office."

"I'm not at the office."

"You're at home. Aren't you meant to be working for me today?"

"Well, yes. But I'm not, I couldn't. Look, Alex, the thing is …" I began.

Alex cut across me, interrupting me before I could finish, his voice escalating like swirling flames.

"This is what I was talking about. I knew this shit would happen. He fucks you around, you get upset and you don't turn up for work. How long have you worked for me now? But this is how you treat me! I'm your fucking boss. You have a row with your bit on the side and you don't show up for work! Consider this your notice. I tell you what - you don't even have to work it - I'll make it easy for you. You're fired."

"Fired? What? Alex? You can't do that. Come on! Don't be like this, please don't, please just listen one minute," my voice was breaking.

"What's the matter? Never been fired before?"

"I was ringing to talk things through with you, to … say … to see … a clean slate, can we just forget yesterday? To start again? I am sorry I didn't make it in, but …" I was starting to cry, I couldn't believe it, I was crying, tears were falling down my face and I lost my voice. There was no way I could tell him how confused I was feeling. Just no way would those words come out.

"There are no clean slates with me Rae. I thought you of all people knew that. Pick your wages up next week or better still ask Lola or your mum to drop in if they're passing. We're done. Then tell that new boyfriend of yours I won't be seeing him this weekend either. See ya."

The phone was dead and it was over. Just like that, all gone. I gagged. His words hurt so much I stood hugging myself physically. After yesterday, I thought he was the one person I could trust. How wrong can you get?

I searched everywhere eventually finding an old Nokia phone of Scott's which still had credit on it. I plugged it in to the charger and emailed Jazz the number. It began ringing instantly.

"Hey baby, how are you doing?" Jazz asked.

"Fine. How are you doing?" I answered on autopilot.

"You don't sound fine, what's wrong?"

That kindness was enough and I burst back into tears.

"I've lost my phone and Alex fired me."

"Where are you?" he asked shortly.

"Home," I choked.

"On your own?"

"Yes." I sniffed, appalled at myself. I hardly cried ever and now I was a limp wreck.

"I'll see you in twenty minutes," Jazz ended the call.

Eighteen minutes later the doorbell rang. I opened it and walked back into the house, Jazz following. He waited until we were inside before he spoke. "So, what happened with Alex, exactly?"

"I told you what happened."

"You said he fired you?" Jazz was staring at me incredulously.

"Yes," I said shortly, shoving my hands in my jeans pockets.

"But why would he do that?" Jazz repeated.

I didn't give him eye contact as I sighed, "It doesn't matter does it? It doesn't change anything between you and me where I work, so what difference does it make?"

Jazz shook his head slowly and took a step towards me, "No of course not but Rae baby, it would have been a mistake to tell Alex about you and me."

"I don't understand. Who said I told him about you and me?" I countered. "And anyway what has that got to do with anything?"

Jazz leant towards me, towering like a mountain. His shoulders seemed larger than I'd noticed before. I took a step back but collided with the doorframe, he was making me nervous but that was silly, so I dismissed the thought, Jazz wasn't the least bit threatening. But even so, I could feel the difference in his mood. His mouth was close to mine as he whispered in my ear.

"I am just saying that I think the fewer people who know what we are doing here, the better for you in your situation with your fiancé. So, aside from Alex, who else have you told?" he touched me with his forefinger and thumb as he spoke, lifting my chin so I could look directly into his eyes.

"No one. I didn't tell anyone. Alex guessed," I said.

"That's a good girl. It's not hard to tell the truth is it?" Jazz smiled at me, the usual beam of sunshine sent direct to my heart from his lips.

I shook my head. He took a step back and let his hand drop. He walked into the kitchen and plucked a glass off the draining board, turning the cold tap on to let it run. I stood, watching him make himself at home.

"He fired you because he doesn't want you sleeping with me. He is jealous. So instead of telling you that he has told you some shit about what a big womaniser I am and how I'm only going to hurt you. Now you've forgotten everything we've shared together and you believe him," Jazz continued conversationally in between drinking his water.

"I haven't forgotten anything. Why on earth would he be jealous? He's not jealous, trust me."

"But you believe him anyway don't you?" Jazz ignored my questions as he tipped the rest of the water down the sink. The glass made a hollow sound as he set it down on the side.

"I'm not sure really, Jazz, to be honest," I said quietly unable to stop myself. "Look, I don't know what we're doing here with this."

He walked over to me, cupped his hands around my

face and kissed me. The feel of his lips on mine softly silenced my anxieties. The taste of his tongue, his hands in my hair, his body growing hard as he pressed into me with more urgency stopped my thoughts. He pulled away then and smiled at me. "What are we doing? We're having fun, aren't we?"

"Yes," I nodded, gasping as his fingers hit their target. We were having fun. His hand was in the front of my jeans, exploring my panties, gently stroking their lacy softness and sliding inside. He lowered the zip to gain better access and slowly but surely his fingers were working their magic. I was responding to that touch, wanting more. He moved his body in close, pushing up against me, letting me feel how much he wanted me, as with his fingers he brought me closer with each touch. Another second was all it would take and I would be right there and then, abruptly he stopped.

"I had better get out of here, in case anyone comes home early," Jazz retracted his hand smoothly and shrugged his way into the hall. He was heading to the front door before I even realised it. "You're free tomorrow now you're not working so I'll call you and let you know where we're meeting."

It was more of a statement than a question and Jazz didn't wait for my reply. His words melted into the breeze of the open door, leaving me zipping my jeans and standing alone in the hallway, not knowing who to believe, Jazz or Alex.

Scott came home, late. At least he came home. I was thankful for that. But my stomach still hit the floor faster than gravity when I heard his key in the lock. I couldn't help it. I was anxious around Scott big time now I was sure I couldn't stop seeing Jazz. I felt guilty permanently. But simply breaking up with Scott wasn't anywhere near as easy as I thought it would be. I had no idea what I'd said to him last night when I was drunk but all I knew was until now I had been in total denial about everything. I was only just realising that ending things between Scott and I with no emotional mess was an idiotic fantasy.

Naively I had thought that seeing Jazz had meant that Scott and I were over. As if being with one cancelled out the other. But whenever I saw Scott my heart twisted. They were worlds apart and whatever I felt for Jazz, I didn't think it was love because I knew I still loved Scott. And that felt different and although I wasn't in love with him, the very last thing I wanted to do was hurt him. Only I couldn't see what else to do.

"Hi Scott," I hesitated half trying to get up yet also unwilling to disturb Minx who was sitting next to me on the couch, her tailed curled protectively round to her nose, a coal black cushion. Tiara came running in skipping happily at Scott's feet as he entered the room. She'd obviously been outside. There was a dull silence as he stood and looked at me, his arms hanging limply by his side, one hand still holding onto his battered briefcase, shoulders dipped. "I left you a note earlier," he said.

"I know, I'm sorry," I said, feeling helpless.

"You didn't come in," he replied.

"I thought about it," I replied. "Look I wanted to see you, I really did. But I had the worst hangover and it has taken all day to feel better."

He stared at me, his grey eyes the colour of granite, and I felt a slow flush spread across my cheeks as I saw the pain I'd caused.

"Do you feel better now?" he asked then as he

dropped his briefcase. He looked like a stranger in our home, standing in our hallway. Jazz had seemed more at ease. I dismissed the comparison as fast as it arrived, dispelled the image of the two of them in my brain. This was Scott and this was his home, our home. Fuck, I needed to work out what to do with my life and fast.

"I sort of feel better. A bit," I said.

"Have you eaten today?" he asked.

The love in that simple question caught me off guard. I stood up then and went to him instinctively, reaching my arms out to hug him and hold him close, but he didn't let me. "I'll cook us something," I said, as the tears came.

He nodded and turned, heading to the stairs.

26

Jude - Tuesday May 11th

Antwerp

I heard knocking as I woke. My neck was stiff and uncomfortable. The knocking grew louder, more insistent. Feeling drugged, I opened the door to a young black-suited hotel porter.

"Bonjour monsieur. This was to be delivered to you upon arrival. Please accept our apologies for the delay," the man gave unnerving eye contact. He held out a case and stood sharply to attention, as if he were on Royal Guard.

"Thank you," I replied, taking the black leather case. He nodded courteously then turned and walked back down the corridor.

I dropped the case on the bed and opened the bathroom door to a white marble bath, white floor, burgundy mosaic walls and black woodwork. I stripped before stepping into the walk-in double shower in one corner of the room opposite the bath. There were two showerheads and a switch to select between the large flat round disc or the torpedo shape. I turned the temperature dial and water tumbled down, drenching me, drowning the sleep-fog out of me.

I cleaned my teeth and pulled on a pair of Levis and a vest that needed washing. A rumble in my stomach reminded me that I was starving but the briefcase seemed to be gaining more of a presence. It was a small men's attaché case, expensive black leather. I clicked the locks either side of the three number dials. No combination to crack, surprisingly the case opened instantly. Inside was a slim line silver PC. I slid a hand into the grey leather inner pocket of the case up against the lid of the briefcase and found a disc. I opened the notebook. It sprang into life as I picked it up and went over to the desk, pulled the chair back and sat down to Microsoft Windows.

It asked for a password. Fucking ridiculous. How the hell was I to know what password to use? I rubbed my hand over my eyes, got up again and rummaged through the bedside table. There was a small red file containing all the relevant hotel numbers, I dialled reception.

"Good morning how can I help?"

"Good morning. What time is breakfast served today? Is it possible to have room service?"

"Breakfast is available between 7 and 10am daily in the Great Room. We can provide room service. Is that for yourself or do you have a guest staying with you sir?"

"No, just me. Thanks."

"Room 505 isn't it sir?"

"Yes."

"Thank you. I will connect you. Can you hold a moment please?"

"Sure."

By the time the waiter was at my bedroom door, I had achieved zero except for the self-control needed to stop me launching the fucking thing into the harbour. I stood aside as a trolley was wheeled into the room. Delicious smells tore at my appetite. Breakfast looked substantial, a platter of eggs and cheeses, a breadbasket, fruit, pastries, coffee and fresh orange juice.

The waiter left discreetly. I pushed the trolley to the balcony, pulled a chair out, and poured coffee. I hadn't eaten properly in days. I grabbed the laptop, trying not to feel guilty about Rae as I ate, wondering if she was getting regular food.

When the screen asked for a password instead of trying to bypass it and hack the system, I entered the name of the man on the piece of paper. "Terry Black."

Nothing happened.

I tried again, this time using just his first name, "Terry" nothing. Next I tried the name of the hotel. "Holiday Inn."

Nothing.

Antwerp." Nothing.

Both of my names. Nothing.

Then on impulse I tried "Mr Jude" which is what the psycho had called me on the phone.

It worked. The screen cleared. Cautiously I put the disc into the drive. It whirred, clicked and then display opened.

Contents: DVD.

Word document.

Database.

I hit the first one on the list, opened the DVD folder, double clicked and waited. The image shifted and changed as the programme sprang into life. Stills of a grey oddly shaped building, maybe the same place, maybe different buildings, flowed past, it was hard to tell. All the views were taken from the outside. The scene changed to indoors, a video made by someone walking down corridors until an office door came into view. It was shot on a small camera, maybe a phone or flip-cam, nothing of quality. I checked the file, no information or clue in the programme as to origins.

The place must be of importance but what the fuck was the message? There must be something obvious that I was missing. I restarted the thing.

After the corridor walk, the view changed. It was dark. The perspective zoomed towards something. A body in an awkward position filled the screen. A body bent double, blindfolded, gagged and limbs restricted forcefully. Rae! She was unconscious. The camera paused on her motionless figure. Breakfast churned violently.

The third time I watched until the view was back outside, in daylight. This time I knew where we were. I recognised the sign written clearly on the side of the building from the web.

Antwerp, World famous Diamond Centre.

The DVD file ended. I opened the word document folder, air catching in my throat. I didn't know what Erik wanted but it didn't matter. I couldn't fight a mechanical voice with no other leads and even if I could, I already knew that I would do whatever he wanted.

I had four days - they had Rae.

Numb, I opened the first of the documents that had appeared on screen. It was a data list. There were first names, or surnames, in some cases I couldn't even determine which but there was only one name for each phone number. They looked like dealerships or company names. It was some sort of business directory.

I opened the next file. I was looking at what appeared to be a scanned picture – a blueprint. Building plans. I zoomed in on areas with the mouse. This wasn't making sense. All I could see was Rae. Poor fucking Rae.

I closed the print down. There was one more document. I could barely concentrate as I opened it and found instructions to call the number centred in black text. There was no name, just a number. I reached for my glass of orange juice and downed it, viciously denying the urge to open the mini bar in the fridge, grab the vodka bottles and tip them into the naked juice. Instead I picked up my mobile and called as directed.

"Hello Mr Jude, we have been waiting for you. I trust that everything is to your liking and you are finding the Holiday Inn comfortable?" The voice was cyber-metallic and unnatural.

"What do you want?" I asked fists clenched, sweating.

"I don't believe you are a stupid man Mr Jude. I am sure that you have read the information we left with you. Let me fill any areas of uncertainty for you. You are in Antwerp, the Diamond Centre of the World. You are now in the Diamond City. Your hotel is in fact nearby the centre for the majority of the diamond traffic worldwide. Am I making myself any clearer?"

I exhaled noisily, the sound making my teeth on edge. "What do you want from me? You want me to help you pull something off – is that it? Why do you need me? You could have anyone."

The virtual-voice on the other end of the phone laughed. "I have you Mr Jude and for various reasons that pleases me. Since I am feeling pleased to have you on board you should be flattered. Let us say that it suits me but that isn't all," the voice laughed again. "Listen closely Mr Jude. You will pull together a team and your job is to get yourself plus a very select group of others into the vault at the core of the Diamond Centre."

"The vault?" I inhaled so sharply I nearly missed his next words.

"You need an alarm expert who works at the centre, Louis Visnovitcz, a Polish Jew. He is essential. Locate him, find his price and enlist him. One of my employees will be with you directly and that person will oversee your choices. If you do the job successfully your sister shall be returned unharmed. There are specific boxes in the vault that I am interested in. I will text you these numbers. Afterwards you personally will deliver the van to the destination by six am Saturday 15th May. That ends our agreement. You then walk away. There is a fund being made available to you for supplies. No police, no outside contact to your family. No personal information to be given to any member of the team or your sister will be dead before the call is even over. Do as I ask and she will be returned un-harmed after your successful completion of the job. Is that absolutely clear?"

"Yes," I answered. A one-word detonator.

"Good, I am glad that we understand one another. I will be in touch. Start soon Mr Jude, time is not on your side." The call ended and a text came through. I flicked it open – a number sequence, the boxes he wanted from the vault. I stood in silence, stunned.

After all that he had said I'd replied: "Yes."

My head was throbbing with rage, what kind of idiot puppet was I? He wanted me to get a team into the World Diamond Centre and blow the fucking vault. The sentence on that would be life. More than one time over if a jury got hold of me. If not, it was still a double life sentence - my life and Rae's. And probably Coco's or maybe they'd already taken that payment. I had no idea how she'd got involved in this. But if I ever found out by some sick miracle Coco was in on it voluntarily, I was going to hunt her down and kill her myself.

Fuck-tired, I sat with head in my hands for the longest time. I considered texting Jazz, and taking the risk, to ask him to get the word out on Rae, maybe he could even find her. He knew so many people, and I trusted Jazz completely. Jazz wouldn't be watched, or if he were then he'd know about it. A second later I dismissed the idea. Couldn't take the chance. Jazz would get involved personally and so would Alex, if I told him. Neither of them would ever hand over to the police then sit back and wait. And the minute either of them were involved their families were at risk too.

Right now Erik had the power. I didn't know where Rae was. She could be anywhere in England, here in Antwerp, in Barcelona or outer frigging Mongolia for fuck sake. If Jazz or Alex waded in when Erik had said tell no one and somehow he found out … The consequences didn't bear thinking about.

I tried to sort out the chaos in my mind, but couldn't get past the scale of it. A vault. *That* vault? If this was such a big fucking job, why would he want me?

It didn't make any sense. The guy had taken Rae. Coco planted the ice on me. I was the link. It had to be personal. But whatever the reason, there was no time for the why me scenarios, and I shoved them out of my mind. If I let Rae down she was as good as dead. And even if I went straight to the fucking police, by the time they would find her, *if* they even found her, I would be dead. This guy meant business. The only way out was to go along with this and to get it right. Somehow.

I grabbed a bottle of water and poured it in, my throat was so dry. I looked at my watch. It was after one. I had already lost this morning and yesterday. Less than four days. The walls were closing in on me.

I had to get moving, fast. Mechanically I repeated the job checklist, need to know my way round the city, go buy essentials, and start on the people-research. Contacts were the most essential ingredient. I needed a watertight crew and someone who knew how to blow a vault. I corrected myself, not someone who knew how to blow a vault, someone who could blow *that* vault. And be ready to go in three and a half days time.

Jesus. I needed a fucking miracle.

27

Rae - Wednesday May 12th

Manchester

I looked at Scott's old phone again, I still hadn't found mine. But there were no new text messages and no voicemails. Not one single new anything. I flicked through the inbox to make sure and then deleted everything to give some space. Just in case something was queuing and not getting through. I waited. Nothing. I slammed the fucking thing down on the table and opened my email on the laptop. The white screen glared at me, no new messages. I checked the spam folder and that was empty. I stood away from the computer and taking a deep breath walked to the back door and lit a cigarette.

    I hated having to wait to hear from anyone and Jazz had said he would get in touch. I thought he meant by phone but I just didn't know for sure. Unpredictability was the essence of his charm or at the very core of his being, I wasn't sure which. But either way, my impatience was killing me. It was only 11.30 a.m. and I had seen him yesterday. It wasn't like it had been two weeks or even two days. He had said he would be in touch and I was utterly incapable of waiting with good grace. Clearly I *could* wait but I wasn't doing it well.

I wanted him to finish what he had started in my panties yesterday in the hallway. Then I laughed as the thought re-played through my mind along with images of him and me together. The truth was that I *always* wanted him to finish what he had started in my panties. I needed him to cool that fire. The less I had of him, the worse it got. I couldn't think about anything else. As for him seeing other girls, Alex had no reason to lie but nothing changed the fact I wasn't prepared to give Jazz up on anyone else's say so. I couldn't. Yet no matter how hard I tried, I just couldn't stop thinking about him.

Tiara and Minx were playing hide and seek in the grass that needed cutting, pouncing and chasing each other. They were happy, enjoying the weather. I finished the cigarette pushing thoughts of Jazz away, trying to clear my mind. The birds were nibbling grain from the feeding tray, a safe distance from the cats and Scott and I were on an official break after last night. It was dinner at strangulation point. The conversation had been stilted and pointed. My chest heaved at the memory as the weight of it all hit me again.

"So, what you're saying is you're not happy?" Scott gripped his cutlery as he spoke.

I nodded. "Did you want me to move out?" I asked eventually, across the untouched bowl of salad.

"We've just got engaged! Why would you want to move out?" his eyes never left mine, searching, asking.

I shrugged, instinctively lowering my eyes like shutters in case he somehow saw the reflection of the images in my head. Hot thoughts of Jazz burned me from the inside out and I flushed as the heat hit my skin. I hadn't told him. No matter how drunk I'd been the night before, I'd not told him about Jazz. And I couldn't do it now. I wanted to but I couldn't. I loved Scott and I was a coward. There were just no clean, mess free, easy solutions to dish up with the pasta and sauce.

I looked at him and took a deep breath. "I love you… You know I love you but love isn't enough and I need a break … to think things through. We can't get married if I'm not sure. It's not fair to either of us."

"I don't understand where this has come from? What else is there apart from love?" he said.

"I've just told you, I need a break to think about us, properly. That's all there is to understand," I repeated.

He took a drink of water. I watched his Adam's apple bob up and down. He set the glass back on the table. "That's it? You're saying you love me but you're not making any sense Rae. You said you wanted to talk."

I pushed the white shells around in the red sauce, smearing bloody stains against the white bowl. "I haven't got anything else to say."

"Fine. If you want a break then take a fucking break," he didn't bother to continue the pretence of eating. He stood up, shoving the chair back so hard it almost toppled and stalked across the room, pouring himself a whisky that filled half a glass. "Whatever is going on in your head Rae work it out fast. When you've done that, maybe you can let me know what fucking planet you've been on lately," he said knocking the whisky back in one go.

A universe of words filled my mouth but none of them came out. Scott turned away, switching the TV on, loud. The conversation was over and there *was* nothing else to say. I wasn't going to tell the truth, I couldn't. It was like someone had zipped my lips together and I felt sick for deceiving him but this was survival.

I couldn't handle Scott thinking we were breaking up over anyone else. No matter how much I hated what I'd just done, I knew that my feelings for Jazz were separate to my feelings about breaking up with Scott. One thing had nothing to do with another. It was the only way I had come up with of getting through this.

The miserable aftertaste started to fade slightly as I hung the laundry out on the line and I wondered again what Jazz was doing today. I switched the laptop back on to check my inboxes for the zillionth time. No new messages.

I sighed. Whilst I was online I may as well get on with some job hunting, I needed to find work. It was one long dull morning and I was vaguely trawling through the Manchester online job search website when the phone buzzed with an incoming text.

"Do you know the service station at Junction 10 on the M62 North?"

That was a weird question. It was Jazz or at least from his number. I picked up and pressed call. No one answered. I had no idea why Jazz would be asking me about service stations. Maybe his car had broken down and he needed help. I redialled and waited whilst it rang several times and went to message.

I sent a text instead. "Is everything okay?"

Thankfully this time I didn't have long to wait for a reply.

"Yes, sorry I can't talk right now. Do you know the service station I mean?"

"Yes. I've driven past it. Why?"

Text buzz, reply: "When you come off the motorway at J10 there is a hotel at the far end of the car park. See you there at 6 p.m. this evening. Room 145. Bye for now. Big X."

We had a date! I wasn't even bothered why it was in such an unusual location. Whatever the reason was I was sure I would find out later that evening. I set off upstairs to choose what to wear, worrying about what excuse I was going to give Scott for that evening's absence. Then, with a jolt I remembered, we were on a break. I didn't need to give him an excuse at all. I could do whatever I wanted. Equally so could he. That thought made me feel queasy. I didn't like the idea of Scott being with someone else. Confusion flared like smoke, clouding everything.

28

Jude - Tuesday May 11th

Antwerp

Erik had set up a bank account exactly as he said he would. I accessed the money at a cash point in town and bought what I needed before going back to the hotel. There was hope he would set Rae free when the job was done but I knew better than to believe in anything. Hope was cruel enough, but belief required faith and that was something I just didn't have the luxury of. My phone buzzed as I left the stuff on the bed and opened the message. It was another photograph of Rae.

The image hit me between the eyes. I couldn't think straight. She was blindfolded and gagged, her body covered in ropes, her limbs twisted and tied together.

What the fuck were they doing to her whilst I was spending money at her expense? A loud knocking at the door interrupted the panic, clutching the phone I looked through the spy-hole. It was the concierge. I tried to stay calm.

"Ah, good afternoon sir, this arrived for you at the desk and the courier insisted that you were to receive it instantly," the man handed over an envelope, and left.

The door closed as my mind remained stuck on that photograph of Rae. I could barely concentrate as I opened the padded envelope. I tipped the contents out, a black iPhone. I switched it on. It was charged and surged into life. A text rang through.

"*I hope you are making progress. You don't have long and you will need my help. Call me. TB.*"

Who the fuck was T.B? Terry Black?

Just then my old phone rang. It was Jazz.

"Hi man, how are you?" I said feeling the strain.

"Hey you. Don't hi man me! Where the fuck have you been? I thought you'd fallen off the face of the earth."

"What's up?" I asked.

"Nah. Nothin. Whatchya upto? Did you get everything sorted? Your mum's worried about you, she's telling anyone with ears that you've not been in touch. Where the fuck are you?"

"Busy. Things have been hectic," I replied rubbing my chin, I didn't dare give anything away. I couldn't run the risk of Erik taking anything else out on Rae.

"All right man, whatever, just checking in," Jazz said. "You are okay though?"

"I'm … okay. Thanks."

"Good! I was beginning to think disappearing acts were a family thing."

"What are you talking about?"

"Well … I saw Alex over the weekend and he mentioned that your cousin Rae wasn't in work."

"What's it to you where she is?" I replied, pacing across the room.

"Hey take it easy, I'll come round to yours later. We'll talk. It's not about what it is or isn't to me, I thought you should know, the girl's vanished."

"Christ Jazz. She's engaged for fuck sake! You said you weren't doing anything about that," I replied as fury exploded. He'd lied to me. "I didn't think you would go near her! That's my family!"

I needed to hide the fact I knew Rae was missing for as long as possible. Fuck knows I had more to worry about than who she'd slept with, but he'd lied to me.

"I didn't say that. Listen man, I have to go. Speak later," Jazz persisted.

"No. I'll be in touch," I ended the call.

That conversation hadn't gone anywhere near where it should have done. Trusting Jazz was an immediate reaction, instinctive, not something I ever thought about. But I needed time to think, and time was the one thing I didn't have. Rae had been kidnapped and I was involved in the biggest job of my life flying completely solo, without anyone to watch my back. I was just as trapped.

Minutes later the new phone bleeped again. I flicked open the text. *"We need to meet. See you at the Lime Bar in 15 minutes. T."*

There was no let up. Rae was my cousin and this was my job. The last thing I needed was someone watching me, eyes reporting back to Erik every minute, when I didn't even know who was fucking who. I downed my orange juice and checked my watch. I had twelve minutes to find the bar and Terry.

Luckily the Lime Bar was easy to spot. It was the least glossy of the harbour bars, tucked away in the far corner of the square and had an altogether different, rougher, style to the rest. At first glance Lime Bar was brown and wooden. Stainless steel chairs and tables were set out on the decking. A green neon lime disgraced the wall behind the bar. My eyes adjusted to the shadowy gloom and I saw double seated booths along the back wall. The music was loud, industrial and I recognised Nine Inch Nails coming out the speakers, the noise reminding me of Rae, as if I needed reminding. She was everywhere.

"Bud," I said to the barman. His eyes glazed, barely focussed as he passed me the cold bottle. I drank, sitting on a stool with a good vantage point, slightly away from the open doors.

Five minutes later a couple walked in, ordered drinks and went and sat in a booth. Five minutes after that a man sat down, opposite me. He too got a Bud, and drank, tipping the glass bottle to his lips and licking his lips suggestively. I took the phone out and was about to hit the key to find out where the fuck Terry was when the girl from the couple walked over, interrupting.

"He likes you," she spoke in an accent I couldn't place, nodding at the guy opposite me.

I laughed, "Thanks. But I'm cool."

Behind the shades I looked her up and down; she was wearing a small black bikini top and tiny denim cut offs, revealing long legs. Her skin was the colour of pale honey. She wore no make up and had crisply-defined muscles, a washboard stomach with abs that were barely hidden each time she took a breath. Twitching violin strings stretched from her neck down to jutting collarbones. Her hands were webbing, tendons and sinew that fluctuated beneath her skin.

Her hair was cropped, feathery, black and wet, as if she had just stepped out of the shower. She was undeniably sexy but I preferred feminine women with long hair. This girl exuded invulnerability. She was tall, angular; cheekbones sharpened by a blade. Her slanting pale green eyes pierced me to the core. I was attracted and repelled all at once.

"We should go somewhere private," she insisted.

"Not today baby," I replied. "I'm waiting for someone."

The girl nodded. "I'm Terri."

I pushed my shades back and stared, "You're Terry?"

"Yes, T E R R I, short for Teresa. You were expecting a man weren't you?" Terri laughed. "Let's get out of here."

"What about your date?" I asked.

"Date?" her eyebrows creased her forehead for a second as she shook her head slightly. "He's not … Don't worry about him. Let's find somewhere quiet."

"We can go back to my room and talk there," I replied.

"Okay," Terri slid her shades on as I left a few coins on the bar as a tip. She didn't appear to have a handbag, or anything else except her shades that she was now wearing.

Then I mentally re-adjusted as I realised *she* was waiting for *me*. I had never been anywhere with any woman who didn't have a bag or take ten minutes to gather herself and her belongings, to pick up wraps, and lose her phone. It was disconcerting.

Terri walked fast and in silence. We reached the hotel swiftly. Once in the room I opened the fridge, "What would you like to drink?" I asked revealing a mini bar stacked full from beer to champagne.

"Water. Thanks," Terri replied, wandering across the thickly padded carpet until she reached the wall of photographs. "These are good," she looked closely at the black and white's with the silver frames. "I love sailing."

I shrugged as I poured a large glass of mineral water for her and grabbed another beer for me.

"Where are you staying?" I asked handing her the water.

"Around," Terri replied.

"Oh I get it, you know where I am but I don't know where you are?" I took a swig of the beer. It slid down my throat, cold.

Terri sat down on the bed. "I don't think you'd know if I told you."

"Whatever. Let's get down to business. What do you want?"

Terri shrugged in silence and drank some water, before setting the glass on the desk. She removed a phone from her back pocket, and her fingers flickered across the screen.

"Here," Terri said.

It was the Diamond Centre again. The map showed the main streets that formed the Diamond Quarter.

"And?" I asked.

Terri enlarged the right hand corner and the view changed. I was looking at similar plans to those on the notebook.

She traced her finger along the tiny walkways with a tight smile. "I know this place well and I have a lot riding on this. You're going to have to learn to work with me. Fast."

"Don't you mean *you* are going to have to learn to work with *me*?"

Terri closed the screen. She was sitting on the bed and got up slowly. She walked over to the desk and perched, leaning backwards against the wooden chair and table. I watched her take another sip of water. She was almost eye level.

"I don't have time for games." I said turning toward the balcony. I needed air.

I was at the double doors when I felt bone firmly under my chin and something sharp pricking my skin, pointing into my throat. She was behind me, forearm jammed tight against my neck. Where the fuck did she get a knife?

A second later I realised, it was the letter opener from the desk.

"Now," said Terri, "Those games of yours. Are we going to play nice?"

29

Jude – Tuesday May 11th

Antwerp

In deadly stillness, Terri lowered the blade, dragging the metal lightly along my skin as she did so. I turned to face her. With two inches between my face and hers, the challenge was almost audible. As Terri stood like marble I touched my throat where the sharp point had been pressed. I'd never hit a woman. But I came close in that instant. Instead, I stood as still as she was and under that yolk of restraint I aged another ten years.

The tension in that small space was brittle thin. A shard of glass had a softer edge. Breaking the invisible barriers between us I pushed past her and poured a large whisky. Sweat trickled under my arms and across my back. I downed the whisky, kicked off my shoes and then pulled the shirt up and over my head, flinging it across the room. Scoring a second whisky, larger than the first, I grabbed the laptop and sat down at the desk.

Terri stayed on the balcony. Eight minutes passed before she walked over and perched on the edge of the desk. I could feel her presence, like a cat in a corner.

She peered at the screen. "You don't spell it like that," she said gesturing at the name I had just punched in. "It's got a hidden K, here" she said pointing again.

Without looking at her I corrected the typo and then went over the building plans. I needed to get to know the place back to front, focus on the street plans and devise the exit route. I worked in silence as the afternoon melted into evening.

Terri stretched, "Have you been through everything?"

"What do you think?"

"You don't want to know what I think."

"So what are you still doing here?"

She didn't answer and threw the door to the balcony open. A gust of cool evening air hit me.

"Fuck off, will you?" I spat.

She stood, hand on hip. "Have you even looked at the local police servers?"

"How am I meant to hack into those?"

"Move out of my way and I'll show you."

I folded my arms and moved back a small distance.

"Fuck's sake Jude." She leant over, keyed in some complex string commands and waited. I could see the pulse ticking in her neck. She smelt like citrus.

"Look," she said softly, as the website revealed route maps.

"And?"

"Jesus Jude. This is critical."

"You think I don't know that?"

"Do you?"

I raised my eyes to hers, saying nothing.

"Fine." Terri said, moving backwards.

Her small breast brushed my arm and a current of electricity scorched my skin. If she felt it, she didn't show it. But her eyes caught mine, and I felt the heat in that glance as keenly as if she were naked, hot, against me. Seconds passed in silence, until I yawned loudly.

"I've had enough of you for one day," Terri snapped. "Phone this guy and get him on board. Fast."

She scribbled a phone number on a piece of notepaper, her hand a balled up fist in my chest as she punched the paper into me.

I snatched the number, barely resisting temptation to crunch her fist in mine. Silence. She looked at me, her eyes taunting.

"Close the door on your way out," I said.

Her face was next to mine when she spoke, her breath on my skin. "Don't fuck this up. There is not enough time to even shit wrong here."

I kicked the chair back and stood up. Animal like we were facing one another again. She turned and left, the door slamming behind her.

I checked my watch, anger simmering as she left. A moment later, equally as quickly, it passed, leaving hunger soaring. I picked up the phone.

"Good evening. I'd like room service, please," I said, pouring another whisky.

"Certainly, hold please." There was a pause as I was reconnected. "How can we help?"

I ordered food and waited on the balcony, in the cold. As the clouds gathered above, I stood trying to reason with the chaos and tension in my mind. Everything was a priority. I needed to know the area completely and I *had* to pull the right gang together in a tiny amount of time. Vault jobs almost always ended in disaster and this one was as big as they came. It was foolhardy. No one sane would want to take this on at short notice. The alarm guy Erik had named was necessary. I'd looked him up, knew his details but I still had to buy him somehow. Then sort the rest out. I was in so far over my head that paranoia oozed through my concentration like an oil slick. I couldn't shake the suspicion that Erik was fucking with me.

I lit a cigarette and drew half of it in one breath. Maybe I *was* being played.

The thought whirred around and around. I couldn't believe anyone would take a chance on leaving the planning so late for such a huge job. The dead guy at the Quays must have been big if he was the centre pin of all this. So why wasn't there a back up in place? That back up couldn't be me. It didn't make sense.

My head pounded. Rae was fucked and so was I, because however I looked at it, the bottom line was still the same. Erik had Rae, Coco was fuck knows where and I had no choice. Terri was a law unto herself and the thought of being around her for any amount of time didn't fill me with an emotion near joy.

The waiter arrived with chicken salad and fries. Whilst I ate I went through the information I'd accumulated. It didn't feel like much. I took the last whisky from the mini bar and didn't even bother with the glass. One move at a time, I told myself.

I looked into sourcing the raw material for breaking the vault. Thanks to Google, I found an array of local places to buy the basics, except I was no mathematician. I was only even aware of this shit because of a good friend back in Amsterdam. I knew that we needed the specification of the concrete used in the vault door in order to work out how much explosive would open it. But I didn't have the information, and I couldn't begin to handle that responsibility. I rubbed my eyes, sore and tired, and tried to think it through, again.

The easiest way of making a bomb was using *TATP* or *HMTD*, the exact same cheap bang used by the average terrorist. Buy ingredients over the counter; solid fuel camping tablets, enough peroxide to go and some acid, didn't need to be brains of Britain. But the simplest bombs to make were as volatile as hell. It wasn't just living through making the compound. The other problem was getting it down into the vault. Heat or friction, in fact, anything like normal movement would set it off and we'd all go up.

I stretched. It was almost impossible to believe that Erik would leave the detail until this late. Yet he'd made it clear. So, even if I had been set up, it still didn't matter, there was no choice. I had to follow through. Rae needed me. And I needed an expert. I lit another cigarette.

It was almost dawn. Drinking the last of the whisky and watching the shifting skies through the balcony window, I felt time closing in on me faster than I could breathe. My brain refused to switch off and stop thinking about Rae. I didn't know where the fuck Coco was or if *she* was even still alive but when I caught up with her … I couldn't finish the thought. I was seriously off balance and uncomfortable trusting my own instincts. Second-guessing myself constantly was getting to me. I had a lot on my mind, way too much for sleep.

The room was still dark, dawn hadn't broken, and after three hours of restlessness I threw myself into the shower. I was sitting on the bed when I saw the brown envelope on the carpet. It had been shoved under the door.

Shock ran through me. More photos of Rae, A4 size, big black and white images, harsh and vivid. There was nowhere to hide from the visual assault. Head shot side view. Rope coiled over her head, snaked around her neck, a noose tight on her skin. Rae with ropes wrapped around her neck.

I stared at another photo. A full body shot. These were much worse than those sent to my phone. It was the size. I couldn't get past it. Dramatic reality shook me. Her eyes were wide and staring as she choked on the gag, her bare legs pulled back and attached behind to her wrists, her shoulders met in the middle. A thick black leather strap buckled around her neck, leather strands down her torso, cross wise, above and below her breasts, pulled from her neck down through her centre, tight between her naked legs. Fuck knows how many hours a day they kept her like that. I couldn't bear to look and couldn't look away. Where the fuck was she? Frustration burnt like venom, seeing her in this state and yet not being able to get to her, to help her, was agony. I had never felt so useless in all my life.

Downstairs I made my way to the dining room but the sight of the other guests holidaying and sleep-stirred with their breakfasts laid out perfectly, made me nauseas. The smell of food in the stifling hotel air hit my stomach. I ran for the exit.

I walked across the harbour, forcing the photographs out of my mind, as I turned left into town, heading towards Central Station, and on to the Diamond Quarter. The Quarter had originated years ago with the trade route from India where the first diamonds and gemstones were cut before they filtered through to Europe in the 1300's. Antwerp's sparkling history dated back to 1530. This was where 80% of the world's diamonds were cut and sold.

Almost five centuries ago Orthodox Jews had created the Diamond district.

The impact of the place hit me and I stood motionless, in the center of the world's gem trade, mesmerised. Several buildings made the Diamond Quarter literally a "quarter". The main one was The Diamond Centre and that was the largest in Antwerp's gem district. The buildings had been here for hundreds of years, and within these walls age-old commerce was the age-old tradition. The lives that had passed through here... Wars, feuds, generations and still the trade went on, constant. Yet these buildings had withstood it all. I could almost taste the fragrant smell of money and diamonds emanating from the brickwork. Fucking hell. *This* was a job.

I began walking past security cameras, those revolving mechanical swans high on the building walls. I passed tourist clusters and businessmen. The Diamond Centre was protected by twenty-four hour police patrols on pedestrian streets and by dozens of those silver surveillance cameras. It was impossible to see every one of them and I didn't expect they would all run from a single security zone.

I kept walking. I made a complete circle of the place on foot. I knew it would get busier as the day progressed. This was business time, the first half of the working day, where appointments were made and meetings were held. People were mostly in their offices, but the inner streets contained a vibrant energy. I could sense the undercurrent and feel the excitement crackle through the cold exterior. I heard it in the footsteps of those hurrying into glass lobbies. The job was massive, an overwhelming challenge. No team together yet and the deadline was in two days time. Im-fucking-possible. Yet the thrill of the slimmest, tiniest, insane glimmer of a 'maybe' made me hotter than any promise of sex.

The police presence was subtle. Patrols ran to a tight time schedule and as yet I hadn't passed more than a couple of security guards, strutting like peacocks across the square. I continued around the outskirts until I reached the metal barricades that prevented unauthorized vehicles entering the district. The Diamond Centre itself required special access passes for entry and had twenty-four hour guards.

I turned back towards the hotel, my thoughts full of security and caught site of a young woman bending down to pick up a little girl. I watched as she swung the child up high into the air, her long blonde hair flowing outwards with the movement. As the child settled in, legs tucked around her waist, the woman saw me looking and smiled. I checked my watch as I wandered over, smiling in return.

30

Rae - Wednesday May 12th

Manchester

The motorway was clear. Despite the rush hour, traffic flowed and I was at the junction within forty minutes of leaving home. The grey tarmac of the car park blended into grey skies. Grassy verges skimmed the roadside, crows squawked noisily and lorries drew to a grinding halt at the fuel station. This wasn't the Lowry Hotel by a long chalk.

I drove across the car park as Jazz had said and followed the road round. Sure enough there was a hotel at the back. I stopped the car and switched the ignition off. I checked my hair in the mirror, grabbed my bag and feeling more than slightly over dressed in a body skimming black dress and a pair of new heels, I set off to see where room 145 was and to find Jazz.

A small fountain attempted some sort of scenic levity. Gargoyles rested next to granite fish and spouted water incongruously. A few bushes lined the pathway but any lasting semblance of landscape gardening was laughable. The entrance to the hotel was more like an Inn. I opened the main door and glanced across the reception desk. No security and no one attending. Anyone could walk in or out.

The hallway was orange and the windows were dirty

with motorway grime, double-glazed and Swiss cottage style, with latticework PVC that should have been white. At least it wasn't noisy. There were stairs to my left and a corridor straight ahead of me. I looked for a sign to indicate which direction the numbers were and saw nothing. I reasoned that 145 would be on the first floor, so I hit the stairs, new shoes sticking slightly to the carpet. For the fiftieth time I wished I was wearing my usual jeans and docs. I felt so out of place, like an escort, a woman dressed to please and contracted to an allotted time for sex. My mind was playing tricks on me. Jazz had better be in a good mood as mine had evaporated.

Number 145 was on the first floor. The brass numbers were tarnished. I stood outside for a moment and caught my breath before knocking lightly. The peephole in the centre of the door seemed to glow darker for a second and then it swung open.

"Hi, how are you doing?" Jazz said smiling. He raised an eyebrow and made an "mmmm" sound as he nodded approvingly at the dress and heels. That look made me glad I'd made the effort.

"What are we doing here?" I asked as I walked towards him, suddenly feeling full of sunshine and smiles simply at the sight of him. Anywhere was fine as long as I was with him.

He answered with his mouth against mine, his lips warm and soft. As we kissed hello I felt his hand move to the zip of my dress, drawing it down like a caress as his fingertips stroked my back. His lips traced a line down my neck, teasing and nipping. Then I felt his tongue licking where his teeth had been, sending shivers through me all the way down my legs to my toes. He kissed along my collarbone, blowing gently, teasing the hollow at the base of my throat and along my shoulder.

Jazz whispered, "I have my camera with me again today. You don't mind do you? You'll let me take photos won't you baby?"

I nodded, "What do you want them for?"

He smiled, kissing me, breathing heat against my neck, "For when I'm without you. Do you mind if I record it too? I'd love to keep it."

I was hot and aching and Jazz was talking softly as his fingertips stroked all the way down my spine, neck to buttocks and back again.

"You want to film us?" I asked, not sure I'd heard correctly.

"Of you baby, not us. I want to record taking the photographs of you and how beautiful you look, of the expressions on your face, of your gorgeous sexy body, so I can watch how exciting it was," he said making me gasp, softly whispering right into my ear. "Well what do you say? Will you let me?" he paused, his thumbs now gently circling my nipples.

I wanted him to continue, my nipples were tight against my bra and I could see how aroused he was. I ran my fingers lightly over the swollen bulge in his trousers. Clearly the thought of filming the photographs turned him on even more.

"Sure, if you want to," I smiled at him and he smiled back. His eyes were dark and full of sex. He walked to the bed, opened a bag and took out another camera. I watched as he removed a fold up tripod and attached the camera in the corner of the room, opposite the bed.

He picked up the square Canon digital and fixed a large wide lens to the body. His eyes met mine as the camera whirred into life. And like before, a sensual thrill ran through me, as every snap of the lens sent a shiver of ice-heat over my skin.

One tiny click in the dead silence captured that moment between us and sealed me to him. It was like being fucked by the camera lens, private and intimate. Our secret.

"I really love those shoes baby. Did you buy them for me?"

I blushed, and nodded.

"They look so sexy with your tattoos. Here, sit on the chair? There that's right, in front of the camera, now take the shoes off, now the stockings, just leave your underwear on, oh wow, Rae, that is so fucking hot, yes …"

I leant forwards seductively, allowing him a perfect view of my cleavage in the dark red and black Agent Provocateur push-up bra-set I'd bought especially for him, breasts framed and held. I was gently skimming the lace, back and forth, fingertips curving over each rounded shape and then lingering between, pausing to rest briefly on the soft skin where I needed his touch. My nipples were hard. I cupped them just once, almost offering myself to him before running my fingers lightly down my torso and along my thighs, down the front of my legs, all the way down to my feet where my toenails were painted the colour of dark cherries. I held his glance. I knew what I was doing to him. He was watching, hypnotised by my hand sliding into my black and red panties, my fingers gently teasing and playing where he wanted to be. I could see it on his face and I loved that look. The camera in his hand was momentarily forgotten. As I stood, I caught site of the thick white ropes lying on the bed and knew what was to come. The expectation just made me hotter.

31

Jude - Wednesday May 12th

Antwerp

"See you there in twenty minutes."

I was speaking from a bathroom and the reception on the phone echoed like a tin rattle. I hoped he had heard me. Re-entering the bedroom carefully as I did not want to disturb the sleeping girl, I lifted my jacket from the chair at the end of the bed and left, quietly. I'd been waiting for the call from Louis the alarm expert for several hours. As the lift arrived I knew there was no chance to go back to my hotel and shower. Being late wasn't an option.

The early evening sun sank between cotton clouds, and the city's skyline looked down on me, impassively. I felt the fleece of my jacket, snug against my neck, the fresh air acting like espresso. I ran my hand across my chin. I needed a shave days ago, felt rough and looked it too. Jazz would have said that wouldn't harm. I missed Jazz like a brother. Manchester was a universe away.

I opened the glass door to the café and made my way to the counter. There was a small queue. As I waited, I thought of Cerise the au pair who I'd left in the cheap hotel room. Erik's database held meticulous details of Louis's routine. Every day the old man was visited by his grandchild and her au pair, and true enough I'd seen them both this morning at the Diamond Quarter. The girl didn't deserve to be dragged into this, but neither did Rae and it wasn't like I was keeping her tied up against her will. Cerise was pretty, which made it easier, and she had enjoyed herself. But the instant I recognised her she'd become my back-up insurance policy. If the meeting with Louis didn't go well I was going to have to see her again, soon. Only I didn't want to dwell on that.

"Hello, can I help you?" A French voice broke my thoughts.

"Two please," I said pointing at patisserie beneath the counter.

"Would you like coffee?" A young girl, her brown hair tucked into a white cap, smiled.

"A large filter thanks."

I found a table in the soothing warmth and several minutes later the girl brought the coffee and wrap over. Taking a gulp of the bitter hot coffee I checked my wrist again. It was almost time and I was willing to bet that this guy would be punctual.

Seconds later a man walked in, nervously plucking at his watch as he glanced around the room. He was wearing a beige golf jacket, balding, mid to late 50's, looking exactly like his snap shot on Erik's file. I nodded casually towards the stranger and half raised my hand.

"Hello. It's not warm today is it? Have you ordered? Oh yes, I can see that you have coffee but the English have tea." Louis spoke as fast as he moved, his tone anxious. He stood next to the table, fidgeting.

I took a level breath. He was going to panic. And panic was a liability in any job. I moved my chair slightly back and pulled out the other chair for Louis to sit down. As he sat I caught the eye of the pretty girl behind the counter and gestured that she should bring another coffee and pastry over.

"You don't mind if I eat?"

"No, please," Louis replied as the girl brought the order.

Whilst I finished, Louis ignored the coffee and cake, and stared at the floor. I mopped my lips on the serviette.

"Well?" I asked.

He removed his glasses, cleaned them on his handkerchief and leant forwards, his small eyes twitching, "I have the documents."

"Do you have them with you?"

"Yes but we must discuss this," Louis spoke quietly, urgently. "I can't do what you want."

I took a deep breath. "There's nothing to discuss. You will be well rewarded. But I want you and the documents," I said, my fingers casually strumming the edge of the table.

Louis raised his head, eyes meeting mine. "I will cut you a good deal, half of what you suggest, but please, you have to leave me out of it."

"No, and I am sorry Louis, but you absolutely need to be there," I said.

There was a quiet pause. Tiny beads of sweat were beginning to break out on his forehead. He shook his head as he spoke, voice dropping even further. "I can't. I have worked all my life and I can't jeopardise my retirement with something like this. I'm prepared to sell you the paperwork."

I sighed, my heart heavy in my chest as I picked up the phone. Images of Rae flew into my head faster than I could push them away. I knew how he was going to feel, but I had no choice. "Insurance policy," I said, as I showed Louis the photos.

I sat and watched the colour drain from Louis's face as he stared at the photographs of his little granddaughter. Photographs that I'd taken a few hours earlier. The child was smiling at her au pair Cerise.

"You will be there," I said.

Louis didn't respond. He stared at the phone, shaking his head.

"Take the money and do the job or they'll use another way to motivate you."

The older man shuddered, his voice shrill. "Stay away from her."

"Once you agree," I said nodding at him.

"You'll be better off with someone else, can't you see that?" Louis lowered his eyes, twisting a serviette round and round white fingers.

"It has to be you," I replied.

"You give me your word she will be left alone? No one will go near her?"

I saw the love for his granddaughter crack open all over his face. I had him. I nodded, not trusting myself to speak.

"Then I'll do whatever you want," he said sighing as he reached into his inner pocket. He held out a USB hard drive. It was such a small innocuous piece of technology, black plastic and a slice of metal. I took it, and pushed it into my jeans pocket, snug. Then as I slid my shades back into place and stood up, I removed an envelope from my own jacket and left it on the table.

As he sat immobile, I spoke softly into his ear. "Relax Louis, she'll be fine and you're gonna be very rich." I patted him on the shoulder as I turned to leave. "I'll be in touch later today."

As I walked out the café the air was cool, evening had fallen. Nausea spiralled into relief. Louis knew the alarm structure and key codes better than anyone else alive. He had to be there. But he wasn't the sturdiest member of any team I had been a part of. God knows what I would have done if I had had to physically threaten the au pair, never mind the granddaughter. I'd been worried I would have to get Terri's contacts to take them both as hostage until he'd agreed. I didn't like where my mind had been headed and my gut clenched uncomfortably as I lit a cigarette.

There was no time for scruples. Rae's life was on the line every minute of every day. Walking faster as the nicotine hit, I shoved the worries aside. Securing Louis was a start, nothing to get excited about. I still needed to get the rest of the team in place and ready.

Once back at the hotel, I started work on the laptop, memorising plans for the layout of the diamond centre. The new phone rang; number withheld.

"It's Terri."

"What?"

"Have you contacted Wolf yet? The guy whose number I left with you?"

"Back off."

"You stubborn asshole. There's no time to argue, get in touch with the Wolf and get him on board. We need him."

"What we need is …" I stopped, realising she had cut me dead. A text came through as I was furiously calling her back.

"Be at the Bovine by 10.30pm. T."

What the fuck was the Bovine? I checked the web. Apparently the Bovine was a biker bar in downtown Antwerp and Terri wanted me to meet her friend there tonight for a drink. I felt choked as anger flared.

Standing outside on the balcony with another cigarette, I realised dinnertime was long gone and my appetite had waned days ago.

The sky was purple, staccato lit by toffee-orange street lamps. I had less than thirty minutes to get to the bar where Terri had arranged for me to meet Wolf. The air throbbed with music from the downtown bars, and the splashed beer on the pavement reeked as I walked. It was sensory overload with nothing pleasant. The reeking fumes of rubbish from overflowing green plastic dumpsters and restaurant bins made me gag as rats scurried through the rotting spillage on the concrete.

I found the bikers' pub by the roar of heavy metal before I even saw the sign. The Bovine was centuries old, and appeared to actually be part of the old city wall. A black solid iron gate guarded an entrance across a flagged beer terrace packed full of drinkers. As I walked around the building I saw a side entrance. I ducked under the short ceiling and made my way to the bar, through thrashing jukebox sounds. A few years ago I would have thought this was place was exciting, now I just didn't want to be here.

There was no sign of the lightly built man that had accompanied Terri to Lime and I felt punctured by stares as I waited.

The barman had a thin scar running cheekbone to ear, and rings on every finger. He narrowed his eyes. "Drink?"

"Bud," I said, reaching for the change.

He passed the bottle over in silence and I drank slowly, it was 10.24pm.

As I glanced around the room, I was sweating. The group sitting near the pinball machine had that back exit covered. There was barely enough room on the stools for each man's bulk, their shoulders almost meeting as they sat with four full pints on the small, round, wooden table. No one was drinking. The singular guy casually leaning against the doorpost to the gents could cut off anyone fleeing from that downstairs window.

Shifting slightly, I looked over my right shoulder at the front entrance. Six longhaired, metal pierced Hog riders, wearing enough black leather for a herd of cows, stood in a row hardly talking. Bovine suited the clientele as well as the place. The pub was much smaller than I'd thought it would be and almost all of the guests were on the patio, drinking outside.

I was paranoid. These people were socialising, out with their friends. And yet, I couldn't dismiss the fear curling through my gut. I estimated there were about three genuine customers, eleven tough guys in total, and me. I was going to drink another mouthful of this beer and get out. Every nerve in my body was screaming that Terri had set me up.

I pulled the phone out to text her as a lean, wiry man with collar length black hair entered the room, using the back gate. He slid past the pinball machine and past the four sitting at the small table. Not one of them gave him a second look. I almost recognised him but couldn't be certain. He was ordinary, indistinct. Slight as a shadow he made his way to the sidewall where he lit a rolled up cigarette. The woman at the table next to him was in her early twenties with dull raven hair, red lipstick, and black gloves. She was drinking and talking to a life-worn rocker. He seemed unsteady as he stood. The man I thought was Wolf hugged him, as if to greet an old friend. When the three from the pinball crew joined them, the slim dark haired man walked away.

In slow motion horror I watched as the three stepped back, and the body fell towards the table. The girl began screaming, the sound piercing the jukebox.

I was at the door before I looked back.

One glance showed her drenched in shattered glass and beer, the bare skin of her legs smeared in blood whilst a dead man lay in her lap. A fight broke out between the gang at the pinball and the bulk from the door. Muscle men smashing tables and bar stools, using broken wood as weapons. There was no time to think. I ran through the guests on the terrace, back towards the hotel.

32

Rae - Thursday May 13th

Manchester

Twenty-four hours after being at the hotel with Jazz and the glow hadn't dissolved. It was like being drunk, or drugged, and sobering up was a reluctant process.

I gazed the computer as an email came in, I checked the screen. Disappointment filled me. It wasn't from Jazz. It was from Sara, my best girl friend who'd moved to Paris.

"Hi, I'm here! Can you make 9pm tonight? Can't wait to see you."

"Hi, sorry I can't – but have a lovely couple of days."

"Are you okay?" asked Sara.

"Fine. You?"

"Should I pop round to yours? We said we'd meet up, remember? When you were over with Scott!"

"I know and I'd love to but I can't, sorry, I'm really busy with work and uni."

"Oh okay. Speak soon then?"

"Sure. Have a nice time."

There was no point in seeing her. I didn't want to share anything going on in my life and wasn't in the mood to listen to hers, and besides, Jazz might call and I wanted to be around. I lit another cigarette, gazing at the garden, and not seeing anything other than the memories of yesterday.

Jazz did things to me that I hadn't even realised I'd been longing to experience. I wasn't innocent, I knew what sex was about, but this – or rather he - was like nothing else. I sighed as the sensations flooded through me, taking me elsewhere. I had been tied up, blindfolded and gagged, it was purely physical but at the same time it wasn't. I couldn't explain it. A part of my mind thought that maybe I should be scared, but I wasn't. The more he did to me, the freer I felt.

Somewhere, deep inside, I thought I was losing it. Because the minute I stepped into a room with him, any room, anywhere, nothing else existed and nothing else mattered. The problem was that I didn't seem to be able to concentrate on much else, apart from needing to know when the next time would be. Every single minute when I wasn't with him, or knowing when I would be with him, dragged.

33

Jude 1am Thursday 13th May

Antwerp

48 hours to heist

I stood in the shower. Water thundered down my head into my eyes, trying to wash away the images. But they were stuck in my mind on auto-play repeat. The reality wouldn't fade. The blood on the girl's legs. The look on her face … Her screams. And his body as it fell into her lap.

I had to get a grip. Rae was everything, and all that mattered was securing her freedom. I needed to find a way to do this.

I went through it again. There was an alarm guy to get us in who would be no good on the job, and Terri. Erik had said four, or five, others plus me to get the loot out. I had two confirmed so far. From what I'd just seen of Wolf, he was a slick, capable hit man. I shook my head, numb at the thought of working with a cold-blooded assassin. My gut wrenched. Terri *had* set me up, as if I needed a reminder that could be me dead at any time. But the most crucial person on the job was the explosives expert. Without one we weren't getting into the vault.

Sitting in my towel at the desk, I flicked through the menu on my old phone looking at contacts from Amsterdam who moved around. I used to know people who would jump at the money in this if I wanted to go head to head with Terri. I needed a few hands that I trusted, and at the same time I didn't *want* to bring people from the past into this. I didn't want to be in anyone's debt afterwards. I had stayed away for good reason. But Rae's risk factor increased if I didn't and I couldn't pull this off alone. Yet, I doubted anyone would be free at such short notice. Erik had set me up to fail, but I was not giving him the satisfaction without a fight.

The one name that kept coming back to me was Danny. The guy was a known quantity in this business. We'd been good friends, and Danny was more than a nice guy. Danny was a genius who could blow anything wide open. But Danny was very choosy about which jobs he worked. If he still worked.

I chewed my pen, and pressed his number. It rang out. No answer and no voicemail. I redialled, left it for two rings. Then called back, using the old code.

"Yeah?" an American voice answered.

"Hello mate."

"Who is this?"

"Someone who was in Amsterdam and knows how to party Dutch."

"It's after midnight and you're talking about Dutch all nighters! Jude, how the hell are you doing?"

"I'm sorry it's been a while. I'm forgetting my manners. How're things?"

"All good. What's up bro?"

"Are you in Europe at the moment?"

"Actually yeah, just back in the old city. You here?"

"No. I wish I was. I've got a situation."

"What's up?"

"Too much for a phone call and I don't have a lot of time."

"What time do you have?"

"Forty-eight hours."

I heard him exhale.

"Shit! What you thinking?"

"Your speciality. Tight."

"Where are you?"

"Antwerp. Fancy a mini-break?"

Danny laughed, "You're insane! That's what I like about you Jude. You haven't changed one bit. Haven't heard from you in how long? Then, 'Hey, let's kick some ass in forty-eight hours!' Sure man, I'm in, it's been a while since I had a challenge."

I grinned. "I didn't say it was a challenge."

He laughed again and then his voice dropped, "You've been out for so long that you wouldn't be calling otherwise."

"Fair point. The first flight is in seven hours, come straight to my hotel when you land. I'll text you the address."

"Excellent."

"Danny?"

"Yeah bud?"

"It'll be good to see you."

"You too."

I was looking forward to seeing Danny, and that feeling of relief lingered after I put the phone down. Terri, the explosives expert, the alarm guy, and me.

Another two team members and we would be ready, one more if I gave ground on Wolf.

It was after 2 a.m. when I opened the laptop and booked Danny's flight, yawning I sent the reservation. I would just check the confirmation had gone through and then try to get some sleep.

I opened my hotmail account and my stomach shot through the floor. I saw a stack of mail from MR ABC. More photographs of Rae. Colour shots, close ups of her restrained wrists, or the back of her shoulders, arms and head. Seeing her tied and suspended made me sick. My cousin crucifix-like, arms outstretched, eyes dark, hollow and empty. Rae, ropes bighting into her wrists, hanging and limp. Others of her blindfolded, and gagged.

When I eventually fell asleep nightmares tortured me. I woke like I'd been pulled out of an anaesthetic two hours later around 5am and on instinct checked my mobile. The battery had died. I reached out and plugged it into the charger and switched on. It flew into life with incoming texts. Girls 'do me now' kind of stuff, from names I didn't recognise. Texts from Jazz asking 'what the fuck was going on,' 'where the fuck' was I and 'why the fuck' wasn't I returning his calls. A worried text from my mother, could I get in touch and why was my phone off? I sat up, pointed the camera at me, made sure there was no background other than the wall behind me and clicked. Added text:

"Hi, I'm staying in a nice hotel having fun in the sun, on a break, out partying, be in touch in a few weeks when life chills out. Hope you're okay. X."

She'd get it when she woke up. I wouldn't be in contact for a while if the job went well as I'd need to lay low. If it didn't she'd hear soon enough anyway. On voicemail there was single, short terse sounding message from Alex. "Jude, where you at?"

"Taking a break with a sexy blonde!" I replied by text.

But I had no answers for Jazz. I filled the kettle, made a coffee with hotel instant that tasted the same the world over and sat down at the laptop to go through the centre plans again. There was nothing else. This was my life. I had no idea where in hell Coco had gone. I didn't know where in God's name my cousin was being held and the only gateway to either of them was finding a way through this maze. It didn't matter if I felt like I was drowning and that it was impossible. The only thing which counted was getting Rae back.

If I followed instructions I might have a heartbeat of a chance. In the half lit hotel room I drank the coffee and studied the plans.

34

Jude - Thursday 13th May

Antwerp

Sunlight bled through the window. It was just before 8am and I was jumpy. Without rest my mind was beginning to dissolve the boundaries between panic and reality, and when I tried to focus, there wasn't much solace to be found in reality. The short lived relief that Danny was on board had been obliterated by the new photos of Rae. Instead of being glad that he would be here in a couple of hours, it added to the sense that the timing on this was way out of control and I wasn't going fast enough to keep up. I was standing on the balcony, smoking another cigarette, when the phone started ringing.

"Be downstairs in ten minutes." Terri said, loudly.

"What do you mean?"

"Jesus Jude, is everything a battle with you?"

"It's not even eight and you're in my face," I dumped the cigarette.

"Get your ass out of bed," she retorted.

"How do you know I'm in bed? I could have been up for hours."

"We have a heap of shit to do today so if you're not up, get up and if you are up get ready and meet me downstairs in the hotel lobby," Terri ended the call.

I was hitting redial before the thought had even

finished.

"What the fuck now?" Terri rasped.

"Get in line bitch, I'm running this thing." I replied, heading to the shower.

"When will you get it into your head that you can't do this without me you fucking idiot and that feeling you have? It's mutual. Don't make me wait."

I don't know who clicked off first that time. I was out the shower and in the lobby six minutes later, drinking more coffee and waiting by the red leather armchairs. Breakfast was happening around me. I had no appetite and felt like over the last few days I'd had at most half an hour nap in a gravel pit.

Terri was to the second punctual and turbo charged. Wearing a black tracksuit, knees marching like pistons she came over, sat next to me and pulled down her shades.

"We don't have much time and I don't want to argue every step of the way so let's just get on with it."

"What do you think I'm doing?" I said.

"Did you go to the Bovine last night?" Terri asked, her eyes sharp.

"Yeah, what the fuck was that about?" I shook my head as the memory tumbled back.

Her whole body changed, the air oozed out of her leaving her thin like paper. Her shoulders drooped as she took a deep breath. "Wolf had a debt to repay, it was something Erik needed taking care of."

I noticed the vulnerability and reacted to it instinctively, "What did the poor bastard do?" I asked hearing my voice get softer, as a cold shiver ran through me somewhere beyond my bones. For that second I wasn't sure if I meant Wolf was the poor bastard or the guy he had left dead.

She heard the tone, maybe mistook empathy for pity, I don't know but I saw her guard rise back up. She ignored the question.

"Let's go," she stood, clearly expecting me to follow her.

Images of Rae mingled with the dead man from last night and cascaded like Niagara Falls through my brain.

"I'm waiting for someone this morning, I can't just leave," I put my hand on to her arm to slow her down.

She lowered her voice, "We need to get on. Text whoever you are waiting for and get them to meet us as soon as possible." She tore off the corner of the newspaper, wrote something down and pushed the scrap of paper towards me.

"What's this?"

"That's where we're going. We need somewhere safe to talk." Terri didn't wait for a reply and stalked out the lobby.

I followed Terri outside the hotel to a sleek black Porsche parked in the area reserved for taxis. Wolf was waiting behind the wheel. When Terri approached he got out and slid into the backseat next to Louis.

"What the fuck is he doing here?" I gestured at Wolf.

"He's with me," Terri snarled. "Stop fucking around Jude and get in the car."

I took a deep breath, swallowing the feelings of hatred toward Terri, and sat down in the front. My legs were twice the width of hers, taking up most of the foot well. I was too big for this car and I could feel Louis's knees in my back.

"Where are we going?" I asked.

"To a management consulting retreat. I've hired it for the day. There'll just be us onsite and a couple of staff who provide food and then leave. It's won a lot of awards here," Terri replied as she manoeuvred the Porsche through the early morning traffic.

"You are fucking kidding me? We have less than forty hours! You're certifiably insane. How do you think can we go 'team building' all together in public as a single group? What the fuck are you on? You know damn well I have someone coming here this morning. I have to meet that contact, he's critical."

"Don't you ever listen?" Terri's eyes were flint-hard, "I just told you it is private. The place costs a fortune to hire. We need somewhere secure to sit down together and discuss this, and fast."

Before I could reply I felt Wolf move behind me. He spoke quietly and precisely into my ear, "Just call your contact and tell him to meet us there. If he's not from here tell him to call a cab. We have a lot to do today, so the sooner we all get there the better."

He was leaning through the small gap between Terri and I, his arm and body scythe-like. There was a silent threat from his proximity. A moment later he turned the radio on and settled back in his seat. The tension didn't alter as music pitched through six speakers, leaving the inside of the car claustrophobic.

This wasn't the time or place for a fight. I slid the window down and text Danny. His reply was almost immediate, said he would be there shortly and he had just landed at the airport. I noticed he didn't ask any questions and neither did Louis sitting heavily in the back.

Thirty minutes later stones crunched beneath the tyres as Terri drove down a large swooping drive. A beautiful white cottage, as pretty as any tourist postcard, sat framed by rolling green meadows. Rose bushes bloomed near the entrance. A bright gurgling river flowed by the white building, water gushing over rocks as tall trees lined the other bank. The sense of space was breathtaking.

Terri walked toward the front door as I bent the seat back for Louis. He nodded at me, avoiding eye contact as he unfolded his legs. He hadn't spoken two words.

My thoughts filled with Rae. I flicked my phone to check any new messages but there was nothing and the phone was blank. I switched it on and off then hit it a couple of times against the palm of my hand.

Wolf was watching. "There's no mobile reception here, it's a retreat," he said the gravel barely making a sound as his light footsteps followed Terri.

I stared after him. This was surreal.

35

Jude - Thursday May 13th

Antwerp

The boardroom was full of light, with large windows and French double doors looking out on the gardens. Terri, engrossed in her notebook, fingers flickering across the keyboard, didn't raise her head as I walked in. The computer was plugged in to a grimy yellow cable lead. There wasn't even wifi here.

Wolf had taken a seat at the table next to her, whilst Louis sat quietly nursing a cup of coffee. I realised I was pacing the fourth time I saw the same view. I sighed, and tried to slow down as I walked back along the length of the room without looking at my watch.

"Jude you're driving me nuts, sit the fuck down," Terri's voice was sharp.

"We've done nothing since we've been here and the morning is passing," I snapped.

"We can't start until everyone is here," Wolf replied.

"Where's your contact?" Terri replied.

"Since he's just flown over maybe he doesn't know where this place is." I hissed.

Seconds later the door swung open and Danny walked in.

"Hey man," I said, slapping a hand on his back.

"About time," he said, flashing a smile, red hair falling

into his eyes. He went straight to the coffee machine, "Anyone want a drink?"

Terri replied. "Thanks, two black coffees here. Louis do you want anything?"

Louis shook his head.

"Let's start," Terri said.

Wolf's arm rested on the back of her chair, as Danny settled in next to me.

"My plan today is to take us through the main points first and then tackle each section in detail. We'll start with security. Louis, you created the alarm key codes?"

"Yes," he said hoarsely.

"How do they work?" she asked.

"They are operated by a keypad in a concealed panel near the doors on the ground floor. A string code relates to the ground floor entrances and is changed regularly. The numbers are chosen by computer, the centre's security personnel use a scrambler to select them." He replied.

"The security guards have access to the updated codes weekly so if the code was set Monday it would still be the same until midnight on the following Sunday night?" Terri asked.

Louis nodded, "Correct. Each guard slides his card into the reader at the main entrance when he starts that week's shift and the card updates automatically."

Wolf spoke, "I have the codes for this week."

"How?" I asked.

"I've been working as a guard there for six months," he said, barely glancing at me. "I have a pass, as does Terri."

"Louis, if you set up the codes can you bypass an emergency shut down?" Danny asked.

I looked at him, "What do you mean?"

Wolf answered, "Well it's unlikely the card won't update but we can't use those to get everyone in. Each person has to swipe and the security is set so tight after hours there isn't enough time for more than one person at once. There are also cameras."

"That's not what I mean," Danny said looking at Wolf.

"What do you mean?" I asked.

"If something goes wrong could Louis prevent the alarm shutting down all the exits?"

"There wouldn't be much time once I broke into the alarm circuit but yes I can stop the doors at the front of the centre locking from the main entrance-exit keypad." Louis said nodding at Danny.

"The cameras are 180-360 degree spinners, they record activity and change the view at staggered intervals, every angle's covered. That place is Alcratraz."

Terri stood up and clicked something toward her laptop. A moment later the floor plans for the World Diamond Centre were projected clearly onto the blank wall.

"There is one single central security office. Each side of the building, all entrances and exits are system controlled. The fire escapes are alarmed, the doors, everything but they've circuit broken it. So, to disable all the alarms for the whole building you would have to take them down one by one within a certain time limit," Terri paused.

No one interrupted.

"The only doors that are separate are at the main entrance as they have the override facility, for fire risk. The fire escapes are alarmed but aren't locked, obviously, and the best way out in event of fire is via the main entrance. The CCTV cameras are in the central office. It's all hooked up to the police and there's every security measure you can think of and some that you can't."

"P.I.R?" Danny asked.

Louis nodded, "Yes."

"Where do they have the infra red detectors Louis? In the vault or in the passageways?" I asked.

"I wasn't involved in planning where the sensors were placed," Louis replied.

"We won't know until we're in but we'll see them, I couldn't really go round marking down where each sensor is as preparation," Terri said.

"I know where most of them are, from walk-around duty," Wolf added.

"How are we going to get round them?" I asked.

"There is something we can use," Danny said. "The problem is there are no beams, it's not like you can see where they cover, but when a body moves the heat signature changes. The detectors pick that up and set the alarm off."

"Great," I said, shaking my head.

"I can sort it," Danny said. "How are we going to get into the boxes when we're in the vault?"

Terri laughed, "Well Jude? How would you like to get into the boxes?"

Danny interrupted, "Someone had better have keys. Cutting our way in will take far too long. Who knows which numbers we need when we get in there?"

"I'll give you that information on the night before we go in," I replied.

Louis, sweating and mopping his brow, caught my eye as he replaced his glasses, "I have access to some of the keys. I can get some from the dealerships. Terri can get hold of others, isn't that right?" Louis nodded.

"So, Terri, when were you planning on getting the keys? Or did you want to waste time with more games that you already know the answer to?" I said.

"Tomorrow," she replied, shortly. I watched as she and Wolf shared a smile without any humour.

Wolf saw me follow their exchange and his eyes narrowed as he turned, "Ready for the real fun Jude?"

"Fun?" I asked.

"Assuming we get in, past all the security to the boxes, get them open and emptied in the time we have, we then need to get out." Wolf said.

Terri pointed to the plans, "Here's the guard's sentry box."

"Jude checked security with you not longer than ten minutes ago and you said there was one central security office," Danny replied.

"That's for the building," Terri said.

I looked at the plans again, "The vault is guarded in two places?"

"Yes and no. Daytime yes. But there is no real entrance at night into the vault from the building that would need guarding," Wolf said. "There is a normal security patrol within the building as anyone would expect and these guards here do their walk around the vault from the sentry box," he touched the map and ran his finger along a route.

"The guard sentry is situated here," Louis pointed to the corner of the map.

"That sentry box is past the steel barrier entrance into the underground car-park. The double gates and the iron hatch that comes up from the ground are at the top of the slope, and protect the entry at street level," Wolf said.

I rubbed my hand over my head. "The bottom line is that we need access to that vault and Danny here is more than able to get us in."

Danny nodded, "I'll handle that the old fashioned way."

"But as we've all just said the vault isn't the only problem here Jude," Terri said, speaking far too slowly, her tone of voice patronising, sneering.

I stalked round the table to her chair and stared down at her, "I am aware of that, so let's start at the beginning since I've clearly lost you somewhere."

The left corner of her eye ticked with her attempt to control her temper. I enjoyed the reaction. "Try and keep up. Louis can get Danny and I in to the building. Both Wolf and you have passes to get in. Right?"

I didn't wait for a reply, "There is one central office so that means the guards have one starting place for their patrol. The cameras are run from that same place. Wolf has the guard's rota and he has a uniform – you're similar in size so you can borrow one. Disable the cameras both on ground level and in the vault. I don't expect either of you to take down all the levels in the place but it won't matter as we'll have the security under control where we need it. We can get past the infra red detectors once we know which ones they use. So, let's divide it up. Security - that's your problem. Alarms, that's Louis' problem. Leaving Danny to concentrate on how to blow the vault and me to deal with the exit route, which I've already sorted," I turned away from her. "Danny, as soon as you decide what kit we are going to need, we'll get it."

"That all depends on the thickness of the concrete," Danny answered with a grin.

There was a bang as Terri slammed her hand down on

the table. "Stop being simplistic! The cameras are focussed on every aspect. They record the doors, the front gate, the underground car park, the security entrance to the vault …"

"Jesus. What is your fucking problem?" I clenched my fists, barely keeping them by my side.

"You're my fucking problem!" she shouted.

"And you're wasting my fucking time!" I shouted at her, my mind consumed with Rae and how little time she may have left.

"This is not some back street shed! For fuck's sake!" Terri hit the table so hard that the coffees spilt leaving dark black puddles. She lowered her voice. "This is the World Diamond Centre. We have to get in *and* we have to get out and you're the only one wasting time here."

I opened the double doors and stormed outside into the spring day. I stood, gazing at the sky, my thoughts full of Rae. I loved her so much. The plan should have been sorted by now. I needed Rae's freedom secure, it was not possible to leave anything to chance. There *were* no second chances with this. We succeeded and Rae lived. It was that simple. I took one last deep breath, pushing away the images of Rae in ropes, and walked back indoors.

Terri stopped talking and looked at me. "Yes?"

"None of us have enough time. Today is the only day Danny and I *have* to sort the raw materials out and as we're in the middle of the countryside it feels like this job isn't going to happen. I can't afford that. So believe me when I say I will do whatever it takes," I was twice her size as I leant over her, arm down either side of her on the table.

She was beneath me, glaring through stone eyes. Wolf was on his feet and I felt rather than saw Danny, faster than light grab him in an arm wrap, and hold him back.

"The only way I can think of is to disable security, go in at ground level and then blow the vault wide open. We get out the same way we got in when we're done. Isn't that right Dan?"

I could almost hear Danny's head move through the dead air, as he nodded before he spoke. "Just give me the specifics on the door thickness for the vault and we'll get out of here."

I stepped away and pulled the chair out next to her, metal legs scraping violently against the carpet with the force of the friction and sat down.

Danny slowly let Wolf go. He was by my side a second later.

"You lay a finger on her, even once, and that will be the last thing you ever do." He said eye level with me.

"All that matters is this job gets done. Whatever happens afterwards is anyone's game." I stared him out.

"Get some air," Terri said. "I need to explain something to him."

Wolf didn't reply as he left the room.

"Jude." Terri forced a smile. "We won't be able to just get in or out of the vault, that's the whole point. If it were so easy it would have been done before. That vault door is solid concrete re-enforced with stainless steel. It can't simply be blown open. It's in a confined space, look at how it's built," Terri pointed at the blue print projection.

"The entrance to the vault is at the back of a concrete square, opposite a wall. It's been specifically designed that way so that any blast down there will kill. In other words try and blow your way in and we all die. There is no room for an explosion. You can't hide around the corner as each side of that square has been built to a specification that a blast will travel or asphyxiate, and that is assuming you can even get down to the vault. What did you think? That you got in via the front door? That you just walked into the building and then took the stairs down to lower ground level and hey presto you found it? No. As we have been trying to make you understand, there is just one exit and one entrance. One is via the building and one is via the car park."

I looked at her face. "You know of a different way to get in? Don't you?"

She nodded, and smiled like a glacier in sunshine.

36

Jude – Thursday 13th May

Antwerp

29 hours to heist

I'd barely got back in the hotel when the phone began ringing. I saw the time on the screen as I picked up. It was 8 pm. Terri's voice a laser in my ear, "We're meeting for dinner. Wear something appropriate."

"Dinner?"

"You do eat, right?"

"We go live in how many hours? And you're arranging dinner dates?"

"Get a cab, we're at the 'Establishment,'" she said before the phone went silent.

The large oak doors of the gentlemen's club swung open. Crystal chandeliers hung at regular intervals across the elaborately scrolled ceiling. I stared, numbed by the opulence, as a man wearing full black tie commanded my attention.

"Good evening monsieur, do you have a reservation?"

"Name of Black."

The Maitre D ran a long white finger down the list of names hidden from view, turned theatrically and began to walk. He led to a set of regal doors, pushed both open wide and suddenly I faced the dining room. The hairs on the back of my neck rose. I felt sweat prickle beneath my shirt. The place was full, diners in every space, except for one table. I followed the twenty paces to the vast oval with only two occupants, Terri and her assassin.

The Wolf's wiry presence didn't fit with any ease into this room. With short jerky movements he reached for his drink. Terri, chameleon like, blended into her surroundings. Wearing a crème dress and lilac wrap she looked like a wax orchid. When she saw me she retracted her lips by way of greeting as the maitre D withdrew a chair. As soon as he left I pushed my chair back so fast it nearly toppled.

"What the fuck are we doing here?" I stopped myself physically pointing at the absurdity of the place.

"Eating dinner together," she said glaring from serpentine eyelids.

"This is a fucking joke!"

"Get over yourself! Lower your voice. This place is the ultimate in discretion. No one is interested in who we are or what we are saying or doing. Sit down."

I stared at her, feeling my mouth open and close like a goldfish. "Don't you get it? Why choose somewhere like this when we should be lying low?" I replied, sitting in the chair nearest to her.

She leant toward me, eyes flint, "*You* don't get it. Do you know why no one gives a damn? Because everyone has their own agendas! You have no idea who is here. Believe me, I know this city, *this* is the safest place for us," she hissed, turning her back on me. She began speaking fluent French to Wolf.

I reached for a cigarette, and realised the place was no smoking. Shoving the cigarettes back in my jacket knowing that I was going to stay made me very uncomfortable. But allowing Terri the satisfaction of having won an argument was the least of my worries. All the tables were fully set with thick silver cutlery, crystal glasses and fresh flower posies. The large windows had long, sash heavy, velvet curtains. The walls were covered with old-fashioned mahogany panelling. Groups of diners were sat eating and laughing together, quietly. It was very much business as usual, an old style gentleman's club. I had no idea who these people were. And I didn't want to know.

The waiter re-appeared, his eyes travelled the length of his nose before he addressed me, "An aperitif perhaps Sir?"

"Whisky, on the rocks," the words came out like bullets.

He left and the drink materialised a moment later. I took a slug, then another and a third. The whisky was all but gone. Terri was still deep in conversation. This was madness. Rae's life was on the line whilst we were out playing gentlemen. But more than that, I felt like Terri was making a deliberate announcement to Antwerp's criminal elite directly from within the beast's underbelly.

I stopped still at the thought. That was exactly what she was doing. There was no hiding intended. This was all about the display only I didn't have a clue who the players were and I was blind to the rules. But Terri wasn't - she'd deliberately ensured that we'd be seen with her - so whoever's line of vision she was targeting would then make it their business to know who we all were. Not that it mattered. I was out of here as soon as the heist was over, one way or another. Dead or alive.

I drained the last drops of whisky. The ice hadn't even begun to melt.

The waiter arrived with a man in a smart navy three-piece suit, wearing a striped shirt and a cravat. He looked like a wedding guest who'd lost his way. As he took the seat next to me he glanced around the room and smiled. He sat for a second, and then as soon as the waiter left he sprang up like a jack-in-the-box and enthusiastically kissed Terri's cheeks.

I watched Wolf react to the newcomer's arrival, his face colouring as he slapped him on his shoulder. Wolf knew him, and ignored him. The wedding guest didn't seem bothered, and settled himself back in his seat, noisily.

"All right mate. What're you drinking?" he asked me.

Londoner, I thought as I remained silent, and another subliminal waiter arrived. Louis appeared and offered tepid nods of greeting as he took a seat next to Wolf.

Wolf in a grey suit a size too big, his neck sitting like a turkey's gullet in the large white cotton of the shirt, leant forwards in silence, using his menu as a face shield. The wedding guest was watching me. I could feel his curiosity boring into me as I put the wine list down, "And you are?" I asked, leaning back in my chair.

"The driver," the dark haired man replied. "But you can call me Spike," he continued with a wink. "Pleased to meet you mate." He said offering me his hand.

I reached over and shook the dry hand as I looked into his eyes. The smile didn't reach the centre of his lips.

I tugged the collar of my shirt away from my throat, loosening the top button. I had had nothing to do with choosing any of these people. And yet it *was* clearly meant to be a team meeting. So where was Danny?

I swirled my third whisky around the heavy tumbler. By the time the mains arrived I'd phoned Danny six times, his phone was off and I had no idea what was going on. Reading my mind Terri followed my gaze to the empty seat at the table.

"Where the hell is he?" she asked.

"Thought you knew everything," I replied, forcing myself to relax my grip on the glass in my hand.

"He's your fucking contact," she snapped.

"This is your fucking party! Did you even tell him?" I put the glass on the table in front of me, stopping myself from smashing it. There'd be an explanation. I knew there would.

"Of course I told him!" Terri glared.

The photographs of Rae were surging into my mind, vivid images with no escape. Tomorrow at midnight we would be going live and I wanted to get out of here. Spike's voice grated my ears, a semi-drunken, blurred rumble.

"It's all good to go my end, the rest is up to you guys. Afterwards, come over for a bit, I'll take you out," Spike was chatting to Terri.

Terri was sober, and her face wore the same look as a cat toying with a half dead mouse. Suddenly she smiled at Spike, a real smile. Wolf noticed, and abandoned all pretence of not listening to their conversation, his expression unreadable.

I glanced at Louis as he manipulated his main course across his plate. Mine was tuna steak. "The food is good," I said, not hungry.

"Yes, it often is here," Louis replied.

"So you know this place?"

"I've been here several times," Louis shrugged and stripped white pieces of breast from his baby chicken with the silver utensils, folding each piece high onto the prongs of his fork followed by a selected portion of vegetables. Every mouthful a carefully constructed country's flag, striped and unified.

It sent chills down my spine to watch, I couldn't eat like that. Food deserved somehow to be eaten randomly. I took another hit of the whisky as I looked into his eyes and lowered my voice. "You are sorted for tomorrow night, right?"

Louis stopped eating, and nodded, "Please if there is any way we can…"

Seconds later there was the sound of metal hitting china as Wolf dropped the solid knife and fork to his plate noisily. "Pardon?" he said, leaning in towards Terri and Spike, involving himself directly with their conversation.

"Yeah, well as I said, it's all about being in the know." Spike patted the side of his bulbous nose.

"That's not what you said. Do you think I am stupid?" Wolf leant forwards another inch, the tendons in his neck stretching ominously. "Repeat yourself, now."

"Okay then, I said that *everyone* knows that job fucked up because the pigs were in on it."

"Who was it who told them?" Wolf spat, fingers curled around his knife.

"Gentlemen, remember where we are please," I said, placing a hand on Spike's forearm, my gaze never leaving the Wolf's eyes, as the room surrounding us seemed to fall silent.

"He is talking about things he knows nothing about, the stupid fool, how can you entertain such an idiot," Wolf rattled off to Terri in French ignoring me. My French withstood the first part but Wolf spoke so fast with such venom that it was impossible to follow the rest.

"We are professionals, act like it," Terri hissed in English as she covered his hand with her own. Wolf's eyes were tinged with red, Terri removed her hand and the knife lay redundant on the white tablecloth. Louis inched his chair away from the table, his seat directly between the two men. Slowly Terri managed to calm Wolf and Spike fell silent. Louis kept his eyes focussed on his feet.

"Enough bullshit. Is everyone prepared for tomorrow night?" I said. "No fuck ups. And I want everyone and I mean everyone drinking water from now on."

Spike glared at me. "You're not my fucking boss," he said picking up his whisky glass.

"That's exactly what I am," I replied, palms sweating.

But Terri was faster. She whispered something in his ear. Spike tilted his head at her in reply and put the glass down.

Seconds later the waiters brought five petite fine bone china plates and set one in front of each of us. Finally one centre display arrived, laden with an array of fruits and sorbet. I checked my phone again. There were no new messages, nothing at all from Danny. As Terri helped herself to raspberry coloured sorbet and blood red grapes I stuck the phone back in my pocket and chose what was in front of me, rich jewel coloured cherries with translucent sorbet. I slid the silver ice-cold teaspoon into my mouth and the unexpected sharp taste of fresh lemon surprised me. I wondered if Rae had eaten lately and my appetite vanished.

37

Rae - Thursday May 13th

Manchester

I woke up slowly, unclear what day it was. I saw the grey numbers on the white digital clock. It was 11.32 a.m. Sleep was a thick fog, and each morning I found it harder to struggle free.

I hadn't heard Scott leave for work. Not that we'd seen much of each other recently. I looked at the white walls and the pine chest of drawers, and felt dislocated from normality. The absence of familiar photographs of Scott and me on holiday, laughing, on one of our earliest dates, tugged. This was home, yet it was not home, a world within a world.

Since I'd moved into the spare room we weren't doing anything productive about working out our issues. All we were doing was living a lie. I reached across the pale lilac sheets, searching for the phone to call Scott and see if he was free to talk sometime today. His work number was ready to go, and I was about to press the dial, when I changed my mind. My one overwhelming issue in this relationship was Jazz's presence as a third party and the need I had for him.

I lay staring at the ceiling, if I was happy I wouldn't have slept with Jazz. Not that that was Scott's fault. Or maybe it was. He had stopped making an effort a long while ago. But I'd stayed. So I didn't know whose fault that was, I only knew where we'd ended up, and that was somewhere I hadn't expected.

On my way to the bathroom, the house phone rang. With no intention of picking up, I let it to go to answer as I cleaned my teeth. My mother's voice filled the speaker, her tone shrill and critical.

"Morning Rae, although it's nearly lunch-time. I heard Alex fired you. Have you tried to get another job? I know your college work is keeping you busy but it won't pay the bills. I have your wages here. He rang and asked me to pick them up. Must have been some row if he didn't even want to see you. Give me a call."

I reached for the towel and wiped my mouth. Dismissing the feelings of resentment at her lack of sympathy or support was never easy. I was used to it, yet it still burnt. I wondered how Jude was. But the thought of Jude made me angry. I was livid with him for telling Alex and there was no way I was going to contact him first. He owed me an apology or he could go to hell. Jude would find out the score when he surfaced, and I was pretty sure I didn't need his opinion on my life, either. Besides Auntie Lola had said he was off on his own for a while. Jude would come home when he was good and ready, or when the money ran out. He always did.

As I got dressed I realised I had a waiting text message. The phone memory was full. I lit a cigarette, despite our usual rule of not smoking inside the house and cleared out the inbox, one by one. Fifteen minutes later the phone beeped and the new message appeared.

It was from Jazz. "Hey baby, how are you doing? Text back! X."

Tiredness evaporated at the simple joy of hearing from

him. Obediently I sent my reply: "I'm good. What are you up to?"

The phone started ringing, flashing his number.

"How are you doing?"

I laughed, happy at the sound of his voice. "You should read your text messages! I just told you, I'm good. You?"

"I'm okay, could be better."

"What's up?"

"Nah, nothing important."

"Did you want to see me? Can I help?"

"Seeing you always helps. Actually, yeah, if you're not busy, do you have any free time today?"

"Sure! I'm free and as I'm on an official break with Scott I'm even officially free. When were you thinking?"

"Thirty minutes. I'll pick you up."

I had fed the cats and got changed again by the time his car pulled up. I grabbed my bag and went to meet him, the morning's earlier mood all but forgotten.

"Hi," I said smiling.

He nodded, brooding, his eyes deep set and dark.

"Where are we going?" I clicked the seatbelt in place as he zoomed off.

"Mine," he said his lips forming a tight line.

I hadn't been to his before. I didn't even know where he lived, in the short time we had been seeing one another it was hotel rooms or he'd come to visit me. I was intrigued.

"Where is that?" I asked touching the side of his face with my hand. He nudged against the caress but didn't reply.

"You're quiet," I said a little later.

"Driving," he replied, his eyes fixed firmly on the road.

"You said you wanted me to help you with something?" I ventured, twisting toward him, legs curled and tucked beneath me.

He glanced over at me, and there was a smile in his voice, "No, I said seeing you always helps." He took his hand off the steering wheel and slid his hand inside my skirt, his touch making me wet.

In response I ran my fingers in a line all the way down his thigh to his knee, and back up again as he drove. My mouth went dry as I touched his groin for the second time and felt the heat through his trousers against my palm before he pushed me away, leaving me wanting.

"Later baby."

The day was beautiful and I was hot. Sexually I felt on fire, like I always did when I was with him, alight with the promise of what he could do to me and how he made me feel. I folded my arms, sighed, and stared out of the window as we waited at traffic lights.

I didn't know who I had become lately, and it didn't matter. All that counted was the present moment when I was with him. He intoxicated me. I couldn't get enough, too much wouldn't have been enough. My panties were damp, my nipples chafed against my dress within minutes of seeing him. Expectation and desire ran through my veins, sense and rationality long gone. I felt carefree.

The car pulled away from the lights and we continued, turning off into a side street. Trees lined the avenue where Jazz drew to a stop on a road full of large old houses, with gables and pointed rooftops. I hadn't seen a recognisable sign since we left Stockport, as we had driven through picturesque stone villages on the way to the Peaks.

"Where are we?" I asked.

In reply he grabbed me and lifted me over his shoulder in a fireman's lift, "Here is where we are!" He said spanking my bottom.

"Put me down!" I squealed.

"I'm taking you in! I don't want my nosy neighbours enjoying you! I want you all to myself! You're mine during the time we spend together!"

"Put me down!" I laughed.

"Okay!" Jazz dropped me back on my feet. Whilst I blushed he picked up a black shoulder bag out of the car, and then slammed the boot shut, heading for the front door. I stood smoothing my dress down. Jazz stopped and turned, holding out his hand for me to catch up. I ran toward him brimming with happiness.

The building was broken into flats. The walls were painted white and there was a vibrant cheese plant thriving in the sunlit hallway. The space was open and airy.

Jazz rummaged in his huge black bag for keys and as we headed up the stairs he was talking, "This place is nothing special, I don't live anywhere fancy. It's not Alex's pad, so don't have any big expectations," he said as we reached the top floor.

The door was solid and wooden with a spy hole in the centre and no doorbell. He slid the key in the lock and I followed him inside. There was mail on the floor. Clearly Jazz hadn't been home in a little while. He read my mind, "I haven't been around much lately," he said as he bent down and picked it up, only to leave it scattered on the counter like a paper fan.

And the next moment he was kissing me. His tongue in my mouth, his hands in my hair moving my head towards him at the angle he wanted. I could feel his urgency and that pace flowed through me. I tore at his clothes, opening his shirt, reaching for his belt buckle. All I wanted was this, to be with him. He lifted me up easily and carried me into the bedroom, my legs wrapped round his waist, laughing as we bumped into the wall, kissing as we stumbled, together until he threw me down onto the bed. It was a four-poster yet I barely noticed as he landed next to me, his hands covering me. He slowed down, gently biting my skin, the heat of his breath making me shiver as he stroked from my stomach up to my breasts, and down again, playing, teasing. I was still wearing my summer dress as he pulled the straps down, taking each nipple into his mouth using his teeth, nipping, sending shockwaves.

Cupping his head in my hands, I pulled his face to mine, kissing his beautiful mouth, wanting more, I was hot, wet and desperate for him to fuck me. My skirt tangled around my hips, panties pushed to one side, I needed him inside me. And just when I thought he would give me what I craved, he stopped.

"What's wrong?" I whispered.

"Sssh," Jazz got up, pulling me to my feet so I was standing too, but on the bed.

He lifted the straps back up on my dress, instantly concealing my nakedness. He pulled a blindfold from his trouser pocket and securely fastened it around my eyes. Blackness. I didn't know what he would do or when. I liked it that way.

"You look so beautiful, the way the light catches you …" He murmured.

I was standing as he left me on the edge of the mattress. Seconds passed and then I felt the binding softly encase first my left wrist and then my right. I smiled quietly. I could hear his movements and sense where he was by the direction of the air in the room; the same gentle flow carried the smell of his aftershave. He lifted my wrists as he bound them separately first and then together.

Now my arms were in front of me, resting against the front of my legs, the warmth gathering between my shoulder blades filled me with anticipation. I felt the thickness of the rope as he slipped it over my head. It lay against my skin and cooled me with the kind of weight that didn't hit the scales, heavy on the base of my neck with the sober stillness of the knot hanging down my back. He didn't speak. He slipped the noose up high, beneath my chin, snug and comfortable then lifted my wrists and re-attached me so I was hanging. I guessed I was between the two bedposts and the headpiece was attached to the bar across the top. My bodyweight rested on my feet but I was precariously balanced, and the tension between my wrists and the rope going up from my neck, was making me ache.

I heard the camera click. Then he touched me, stroking my shoulder and upwards along my arm over my bound wrists to my hand, to my fingertips. And back on the underside, whispering briefly into my palm and all the way down, pausing to kiss the inside of my elbow then dipping over my collarbone.

The thrill as I felt him move down my torso and between my breasts, lightly over my nipples hard and aching, was bursting through every pore. Skimming each side of my navel and up, over to the other arm where he started again. He was using the rope, the cotton thick end with the softly frayed cord. He trailed and swirled across my body.

My legs were quivering as he teased all the way down my spine and paid special attention to each of my buttocks, just underneath the rise of the curve where buttock met leg. The longing I felt surging through my body was killing me. I needed to be naked against him, not trapped in this dress. I reached forwards to kiss him, blindly guessing where his mouth would be, meeting nothing but air. I could have cried out, but instead, with great effort whispered. "Please?"

He stopped and placed his finger on my lips. I was coiled tight, desperate for more and thought I had ruined the moment; that he would pull the blindfold off and that would be *it*.

I knew him well enough by now. If I misbehaved, I lost everything. Jazz would stop. And not resume. I held my breath and stood absolutely still. A minute passed. And then another, in aching silence, I stood as still as marble.

Then I felt him beneath the skirt of my dress. First his fingers sliding along me and then his tongue. Jazz was gently nibbling at my panties, licking further, tasting and driving me wild, making me gasp and each time he took me nearer to the edge I found it harder to keep my balance. With each and every flickering lick of his tongue, with deliberate soft slow movements of his mouth he pushed me. I could feel myself begin to give way. I couldn't help it I could feel the intensity building up. I was gasping with the effort of control, because as soon as I lost it, I would slip.

He was driving me to it. The noose around my neck was snug. My arms were hurting, straining against those restraints, my body needing me to stop fighting him, to give in but I couldn't, I'd hang and he knew it. He had to. And just as he kissed me with his whole mouth, just as I felt him that deeply, it happened so hard and fast that I was sucked in and right in the midst of that violent orgasm my feet slid, my neck pulled tight and all went black.

38

Jude - Thursday 13th May

Antwerp

27 hours to heist

The waiters hovered, reaching for desert plates, sliding between us like slugs every five minutes. After the last dessert plate was collected, and unable to wait another second, I paused by Terri's chair.

"I'll be in touch."

"Jude!" Her hiss hit me like a dart in the back as I left.

The Maitre D stood, a redundant skittle in a tenpin-bowling alley, as I stormed past him. I didn't need escorting to the exit and I was hitting redial on Danny's number before the doors had swung shut.

The walk back to the hotel took twenty-five minutes, Google provided an adequate map, but the constant rejection from Danny did nothing to calm my temper. The hotel was busy, guests spilling into the lobby from the bars, music throbbing as canapés circulated on silver trays. Someone was celebrating their special birthday. My phone buzzed with a text, throat tight, I opened it:

Danny: "I'm out. Heard a rumour via fucking Amsterdam! The walls of the Establishment are paper-thin. You should think twice."

My world snapped in two. I dialled but the phone rang out. I text him:

"Call me."

I sent another: "Name your price. I thought we were friends."

No reply.

I felt sick. There was no point in holding back, but my finger paused on the button all the same knowing I could live to regret it, and still I sent the third: "Whatever you want in return. I'm begging."

Less than twenty seven hours to deadline and no vault guy. Rae was dead without Danny. Images filled my head, thoughts of what they would do to her. I made it to the bathroom before I lost dinner.

Afterwards I sat down on the bed. Danny hadn't replied to text or calls and I couldn't sit around waiting. How did anyone in Amsterdam know what the fuck was going down here in real time? My mind skipped back to Spike talking about a job that the police had been informed of and the row he'd had with Wolf. Co-incidence? There were no co-incidences; co-incidences didn't exist. I knew that. Someone here was talking. There wasn't another explanation. I took a deep breath. I was in this over my head, completely blind. I was the only one who didn't know who the hell I was dealing with and what the hell was going on.

But they did. They all knew each other.

I flicked through my phone looking for Ross, a Northerner who had moved down to London. He was an old contact, a party animal, from when I was living with Coco. I'd supplied his club way back and we'd caught up in Manchester a few months ago.

"Hi Ross, how are you doing?"

"Jude? You fucker. You think I've forgotten you bagged my girl last time I saw you?"

I laughed, hollow and fake. "Ross, what can I say, I was an asshole."

"Yeah you were."

"Sorry man I'll make it up to you. Listen, I'm in a spot, need to speak to Zed. Have you got his number? He changes it so fucking often I don't have it."

"The cleaner?"

"Yeah and it's urgent."

"Okay man, but you owe me. I'll text it."

"Deal. Thanks, Ross." I said as the text came through, genuinely grateful as I killed the call, dialling the new number as fast as I could.

"Zed?" I asked.

"Who's that?"

"Jude."

"Jude you motherfucker, I thought you were dead."

"Soon with the way things are going."

"What's up?"

"I need information, the kind that doesn't get back to anyone."

"Where are you?"

"Belgium. Someone's talking, any word on who?"

"Come on. You know I don't hear names," Zed said.

"I will owe you man, anything at all. I'm in over my head here."

"So get the fuck out and disappear someplace, fast," Zed laughed.

"Seriously?"

"I've known you since you were the pain in the ass kid on my patch stealing my punters and dealing crap. Okay Jude for old time's sake. Do yourself a favour and vanish.

Anything going down in Antwerp is way above your kind of shit. What happened?"

I started to crack as I rubbed my hand across my brow.

"Coco … She got me into something I can't get out of."

"Then get rid of that woman she never did you any good. Be careful kid. Take my advice, walk the fuck away and go back to your straight life. Best thing you ever did was get out. Look me up when you're someplace sunny."

Zed didn't wait for a reply, leaving me staring at a dead phone for the second time in an hour. I hadn't told him I was in Antwerp. I'd said Belgium. Maybe it was obvious, but either way, he knew. Which meant whoever was behind this, knew Zed. It had to be a contact of Coco's gone sour. For the millionth time I wished she had never asked me over to Amsterdam, or had told me the truth instead of landing us all in this fucked up bullshit.

I checked my phone again, and saw my reflection staring back at me from a blank screen. Still no word from Danny. Since I'd been here, the one person with all the answers, and who got off on playing me, playing everyone, was Terri.

I lit another cigarette, staring out at the water, over the balcony. I was running out of time.

39

Jude – Thursday May 13th

Antwerp

25 hours to heist

The honey coloured whisky in the glass tumbler didn't last long. I drank, paced the bedroom, poured another and then repeated. It was numbing my senses but not nearly fast enough. The conversation with Zed swam in my mind, making everything unstable. My thoughts kept circling around one person, Terri. This was all a game to her. *We* were a game. I thought back to dinner, how she'd deflated Wolf, then soothed Spike with that whisper into his ear. I'd no doubt she knew exactly what to say to Louis too. She was pulling everyone's strings. Only, if I was fucked so was Rae.

Draining the glass, I opened every email on the laptop and forced myself to look through the photographs, one by one. There had to be something, anything.

But there was no clue in the images or on the return email address, nothing I recognised. I ran the email address through a free ISP mapping programme, but there was nothing useful. I got a country location as to the UK but that was it. The sender could have been anywhere using a proxy. Those photos raked my insides, like barbed wire through jelly. I loathed them. I would never have to see them again and I'd recall every detail. I couldn't phone the police, I couldn't get anyone to try and find her, if they failed to keep quiet or if the team had someone on the inside, Rae would be killed. I could never live with that.

Yet, with the way Wolf had so easily taken out the man at the Bovine I wouldn't have to live with it, I'd be dead within an hour. If word had got through to Amsterdam it wouldn't take a genius to block a leak from me. There was no guarantee Zed hadn't slipped a word to someone about our call either. He owed me nothing and I knew it.

Fact remained that there was no other way of getting Rae back. No way out of the job. There was no way out of any of it other than straight through the centre.

I picked my phone up and text: "My hotel bar, 20 minutes. Urgent."

Time for one more drink, I looked at the bottle. Empty. No small bottles left in the fridge. I opened the wardrobe and pulled out a perfectly laundered black shirt, yanked it over my head, attached silver skull cufflinks, and picked up my mobiles. I made my way to the lift and down to first floor lounge, The Harbour Terrace Bar. The door to the lift opened, exposing a room of noise and people, the impact was crushing.

There was cabaret on this evening. A woman in a black sequinned dress, floor length, sang smoky, sultry notes, to a man playing New Orleans blues. White lilies in thick glass vases sat on square tables as waiters threaded through clusters of small groups. I hadn't realised that the bar would be this busy. The red leather chairs were all occupied. Hotel guests had materialised, immaculate, and in multitudes, downstairs.

I walked towards the bar man standing behind the long glass bar.

"Hello good evening, there's waiter service at the tables so if you would like to find a table …"

"Double whisky, single malt and I'll stay right here thanks," I said sitting on a stool, bad mood spilling out of my open necked shirt. Anger spread in thick layers across the surface of my skin like emulsion. He served the whisky in silence and shrank to the other end of the bar.

The Harbour Terrace was a drinking space on the harbour side of the hotel with a large balcony reaching out above the water. My phone buzzed loudly, I read the text, "Where are you?"

"First floor bar." I stared at the screen expecting a reply, but there was none so I slid it back into my pocket, the movement causing me to sway on the stool.

I wanted a refill, my glass was nearly empty, but the barman was chatting to an attractive woman at the other end of the bar near the entrance, his attention firmly, deliberately elsewhere. They seemed to be sharing a joke until he turned his back to serve another guest and the woman walked purposefully towards where I was sitting. Terri! I hardly recognised her. She was wearing a dress covered in black and pink flowers, with a tiny short skirt that accentuated her long legs. The pretty dress seemed at odds with the rest of her. She looked at me.

"You're drunk," she said, eyes cold.

"Want one?" I asked not waiting for an answer as I drained the glass, ignoring her.

"Where's the fire?" she asked.

"The fire?" I repeated.

"What do you want? Company to get asshole drunk after you walked out on dinner?"

"You fucking bitch. You really are something special. A class act."

Her eyes narrowed, "Jude, I don't know what's upset you but don't speak to me like that, I don't deserve it and it doesn't look good."

"It's all about appearances with you isn't it? How things look," I swung round on the stool to face her properly. "Well look at it this way, if you want me dead stick a bullet in my brain. Too easy, you want me cornered, nowhere to run. That's what gets you off. Right?"

Terri stared, "Jude, I don't know what you're talking about but if you want an argument pick your surroundings better."

I looked around at the bar, crowded full of 'expensive people' watching cabaret in their nice clothes with their neat uncomplicated lives. The sight of them made me want to numb it all even more.

"I'm not nearly drunk enough, I want another fucking drink."

"Fine then lets go to Lime," Terri said.

"That shit-hole? Okay, Lime. You don't fit in here anyway, you trashy whore," I said softly as I got to my feet, checked that phones and wallet were in place and realised that once again Terri was waiting for me. It was unnatural.

"Fucking Christ. What is it with you?"

"I don't trust you," I answered as I leant towards her, struck by the unexpected smell of her perfume, rich and sweet. She pulled away glaring at me, walking out of the bar and down the hotel lobby towards the huge glass double door exit. I was behind her in an instant. She was not leading me all the way to Lime like something on a leash.

"What is wrong with you?" she spat. "We have a job to do in just over twenty-four hours time and you're drunk! Sleep it off and get yourself together. Fast!"

I jabbed my finger at her, "I'm going nowhere until you've heard me out." I stalked off down the harbour towpath towards Lime. This time I heard her footsteps behind me.

Terri caught up with me, "Will you listen to yourself?"

I grabbed her skinny elbow, tugging her towards me. "You listen! But why would you? It's not your life on the line is it?"

Terri wrenched her arm back, "All our lives are on the line. That's the deal, it always is. C'mon let's get some fresh air and calm down."

"I don't want fresh air, I want another drink," I answered, leaving her where she stood.

A minute later she caught up with me again. We walked in silence, and then Terri stopped. "Jude, just tell me what is going on? Please? This isn't getting us anywhere."

Terri was standing still, her back to the inky water, leaning, resting on the marina railings behind her. We were by the harbour on a quiet secluded part of the pathway at the back of the hotel.

I turned to her. "Why was Danny a no-show at the club dinner?" My fists were thrust so tight into my pockets that my hands felt dead.

"I didn't hear from him so I guessed he'd had a change of heart, wanted out."

"Right. You're in the mood for guessing games, okay, let's try again, why do you think he couldn't make it?"

"I'm not in the mood for any fucking games! Danny

changed his mind whatever! I thought you were a pro. I thought you could handle yourself don't tell me this is your first time. I should have known, you're nothing but a spoilt little rich kid. Look at you, you've never been on a job and I bet you've never even worked a full day in your fucking life. I don't know why the fuck Erik insisted on you. You're..." she stopped.

"*You* know *nothing* about *me*," I said, anger, pain and whisky oozing from my pores.

Terri was staring up at me, her face millimetres away, her usual veneer of smugness missing. And in that instant sobriety hit me like a brick in the gut.

"I've worked it out, Erik's your boyfriend. That bastard sets people up, exactly like you do. Like that poor fuck at the Quays."

"What poor fuck at the Quays? What are you talking about? I haven't got a fucking boyfriend. So Danny let you down, get over it instead of getting drunk like a fucking kid. Find a replacement fast. Stop taking everything so personally."

I started laughing, "It's all fucking personal. The one person I bring in, you send off. You have no idea what's at stake for me."

"I haven't sent anyone anywhere. What are you talking about? We have a job to do in just over twenty-four hours. Do you have any idea what will happen if we don't get it done? If Erik finds out things aren't watertight?"

"That's what I'm trying to tell you! But you arrange a point scoring game to impress fuck knows who in a place full of ears. You're the fucking amateur. Because of you we lose a man essential to getting us in there. You're full of shit."

"Me full of shit? I've got a fucking physics degree! I've

been stuck in the Quarter for more than three years. We set up a gemstone dealership specifically for this! This is my *life*. Every person but you was handpicked - you know fuck all and yet you come in here at the last minute … "

"Like I wanted this? I might know fuck all but the rest of the fucking world knows everything. Danny said the heat was up and the word came out of Amsterdam. That's why he pulled out."

"That's ridiculous. How the fuck can anyone in Amsterdam know anything? If you stop acting like a brat long enough maybe …"

"Maybe what?" I hissed, fury won as I gripped her hard by the shoulders, trying to shake some sense into her, hands encompassing the tops of her arms, pinning them to her sides. I had her up tight against the cold metal railings, my hips pressed into her pelvis.

Terri tried bringing her knee up into my groin but I read her like a book and jammed my forearm under her chin against her throat, clumsily echoing her threat with the letter opener three days ago.

"I'm done. Try anything and your neck will be snapped before you hit the water."

My body weight held her against the railings.

"You stupid idiot we're on the same side," Terri snarled back.

Her body softened against mine as she shifted on her heels abruptly and fast. The movement parted her thighs and the change in balance forced me against her full contact, my leg sliding between hers. She rocked her hips and thighs either side of mine. Her eyes challenged me and she didn't break that eye contact. Her lips were near mine as she whispered. "Do it."

I didn't move.

She spoke again, softly, heat punctuating her words. "Fuck me."

Almost crushing her as that wave of desire tore through me, I kissed her. With my tongue I tasted her lips. Her legs wrapped around my waist and in that instant I had her lifted onto the railings, skirt up, underwear off. I was unzipped and inside her, fucking her like it was the only way of anyone surviving this.

40

Rae – Thursday May 13th

Manchester

I was choking, gasping for air. Tears stung my eyes. My heart was pounding through my head, I felt sick, faint, couldn't catch my breath. Dizziness overwhelmed me. I tried to be calm and to concentrate on breathing. But I was having an awful dream. Terrifying. I woke up fully, swimming in anxiety and reaching for the glass of water by my bed, but as my eyes opened I knew the glass wasn't there. This room was totally empty. Memories sprung back. I wasn't at home. And that hadn't been a dream.

I tried to catch my breath, to think through the anxiety, to stop the panic tightening my throat as I looked around, but it wasn't working, and fear rising like a tsunami I touched my neck. It stung and the skin was burnt. I was on my own. Where in God's name was Jazz?

My stomach lurched at the thought of him. I had to clear my head. I needed a drink of cold water desperately. My legs were unsteady as I stood up. I felt flimsy like paper. I'd been lying on a dusty carpet in an empty room, no ropes, and no four-poster bed, just me alone. And I was naked.

There was a tiny corner window between a sloping ceiling and a wall. I peered through the glass and looked down on a big garden. The flat sounded silent. I took a deep breath and tried the bedroom door handle. With relief it clicked open. I don't know why I expected to be locked in, that was ridiculous but I couldn't shake the thought and all too suddenly it hit me that I didn't know Jazz nearly well enough.

A dark realisation filled me, spreading like eerie mist from my feet and up through my entire body. I didn't know where I was. I had no idea what the address was here, he hadn't said. And no one at all apart from Jazz knew where I was either.

41

Jude - Friday May 14th

Antwerp

16 hours to heist

My phone was buzzing. The screen showed a new text from an unknown number. "Check your email." My stomach clenched and I was out of bed, sleep vanished leaving my heart pounding and my mouth like sand paper as I struggled with the rush of bile that text had brought.

As the server collected email, I remembered Terri, the feel of her and the smell of her perfume lingering on the sheets, surrounding me. Last night flooded through my mind, fucking her hard by the water I'd so nearly lost control. Maybe I had lost control. Yet she'd come back here with me. Right in the middle of this claustrophobic insanity, being with her was the only thing that had made sense.

There was no time to think about any of that now. The heist was tonight and there was no one to get us into the vault. Fear snatched at me again as I washed my hands and face, the bathroom mirror reflecting the roughness I felt.

I opened the inbox. There was the name Mr ABC in black bold letters. The email was blank, with three files attached. I clicked the attachments and could hardly take in more photographs of Rae, taken from chest up, blindfolded and gaunt, wrists tied. I dialled the number on the text. Voicemail. No one ever picked up.

"I'm here. I'm doing what you want. Leave her the fuck alone!"

Seconds later another new email came in from Mr ABC. A single photograph of Rae, with a noose around her neck, what was he saying? That she wouldn't be alive long enough for me to finish the job?

The numbers on the inbox escalated, more emails coming in. I opened the first one to a photograph of my mother, laughing, smiling, and on her mobile. Shock froze every thought. I opened a second photograph of her getting into her car.

The third photograph, Alex's little sister, Zara, outside school with her friends, a fourth, Zara coming out of school, a fifth of her being collected by my mum and another of them both at our front door.

Next email: "Fix the team problems fast or your sister dies. Break the deal or call anyone and both the child and your mother will both be in ropes within the hour."

I was numb. My mum didn't deserve this. Neither did Zara or Rae. I hadn't even done the fucking job and I'd blown it. I reached for my phone to call Alex. He had to protect Zara and my mum, get them out the country, anywhere away someplace. I stared at his number on the screen. But I couldn't dial.

Erik would find out. How could I explain to Alex that Zara was in danger because of me? When he realised that I'd kept all this from him until now, Alex would be furious. But what had this got to do with Alex? The only threat to Zara's safety was Alex's connection to me. If

Alex knew anything at all about anything, he would've told me.

Yeah right. Like I had told him about Rae?

No matter what I tried to focus on, all I could see was my mother, bound up like Rae, their faces interchanging. Every time I shut my eyes, it was as if Rae was already dead. I saw her swinging from that rope night and day. Zara was lined up next. I felt sick to my stomach. I couldn't let anything happen to them.

Forcing the images as far away as I could, I stood at the window. Panic seeping through. There was no escape. This was reality.

I opened the door to the balcony. The skies were blue, cloudless and airless. People milling around on the walkway below near the marina, an engine crashing into life shot through my adrenal levels like bombs. Their lives were normal. My head hurt with the effort of staying calm. People were everywhere, crawling like ants through rotting picnic remains.

The tourist explosion was due to the Diamond Women's Games 2016, which started today. It had to be why we were here doing this fucking job now. Timing was everything and for one week a year Antwerp went Tennis crazy. All security and attention would be focussed elsewhere and with so many people in the Diamond City this was the easiest opportunity to slide unnoticed into the chaos.

I pulled the doors shut, forcing myself back into the room. I needed a drink. I stood at the mini bar, staring at the freshly stocked shelf of glass bottles, wanting to rip the tops off the lot of them. And instead I headed back to the bathroom.

After the shower I checked my email again, it was like a nervous tick, something that I didn't want to do but was compulsive. Nothing new in the inbox, I found meagre comfort from that at least. I looked at those photographs of Rae and then flicked over the images of my mum and Zara, the tension vibrating inside me. Zara was a child. I couldn't lose this. I couldn't take a chance that every part of this was going to fuck up. There was far too much at stake.

I made coffee and picked up my phone as I checked my watch, knowing I should be hungry. I'd lost my appetite days ago.

"Danny, it's me. I am fucking desperate. I need your help. Whatever you want in return I'm there. Please. Call me." I was begging and I knew it, and it didn't matter. I needed Danny, not one other member of that team would have my back. I lit another cigarette, ignoring the roaring pain in my gut.

It wasn't like I hadn't tried to replace him. I considered going to Terri so she could get another one of her contacts in, but I didn't want to do that. I still couldn't be certain she wasn't feeding information back to Erik. I'd been drunk last night. I didn't know for definite if Terri had been straight with me or not.

I couldn't trust myself any longer, let alone anyone else. I knew for certain now that it hadn't been down to me to get the team together. I'd been played. I would have liked to see what happened if I had pulled a team, two sets of people for one job. At a guess Wolf would have taken them out. Maybe it was a way of sourcing the competition and getting rid, whatever. I didn't know but I couldn't take the chance on failing completely to get anyone from my side into this team. I didn't want to die on the job or be the fall guy. I couldn't go in completely alone. I couldn't take the risk he wouldn't make my family suffer.

The thought crossed my mind that it was all about Danny. Danny was choosy and securing his place in any team was a coop. I didn't believe the mastermind behind this would have left anything to chance but I couldn't take that risk either.

Without Danny we were one short right at deadline. And we couldn't be. The heist was going ahead tonight with a full crew in place whatever it took. This was about family and their safety was the only thing that counted. I logged onto a website for cheap flights, found what I needed and made a reservation. I sipped at the coffee, the dark heat keeping me focussed as I made the call.

"Hi Jazz, it's me," I chewed my finger and in the split-second silence, heard his intake of breath.

"Jude you fucking bitch. Where the hell are you?"

"Antwerp."

"Antwerp? What the fuck are you doing over there? I've been calling all week. Your phone's off, you don't reply to my texts. I thought some motherfucker had taken you out!"

"Long story man. Look, I've booked you a flight, get yourself to the airport," I hit the send key as I was talking to him. Jazz would understand. He was family too.

"What the fuck? … Are you serious?"

"I'm serious."

"What's going on?"

"I'll tell you the details when you get over here, bring your tool kit."

"The tool kit? Okay I get it. So, that's what kind of shit you've been up to."

"Jazz ..." I sighed. "It's not that simple."

"It's always that simple. When's it on?"

"Soon as you fly in and we start the party."

"What in hell are you playing at man?"

"I told you. I'll explain when you get here."

"Jesus Jude you've lost it. I could be in the middle of fuck knows what and you just want me to drop everything and bail you out?"

"I don't need you to bail me out! I want your fucking help. Not the same thing and I don't have time to argue."

"Jeeez man, you called me!"

"Fine. Are you in the middle of fuck knows what?" I shoved my free hand in my pocket trying to control my temper.

"No. Nothing I can't get out of."

I took a deep breath, "Jazz, why are you being like this? You know me and I'm telling you straight I've not lost it. I'm not fucking around." There was a pause. I tapped the phone against my ear impatiently.

"But you won't tell me what's going on?"

"You know how it is. Are you going to come or not?"

"Okay. Where am I meeting you?"

"Call me when you get here."

"Fine. I'll be in touch. See you later."

It was nearly one o clock. Eleven hours to go. I got off the phone and checked my messages. A text had come through.

"You have no team and you are running out of time. There will be consequences. I've had a lot of fun with Rae. I wonder if your mother and your pretty little cousin will enjoy being fucked just as much."

My knees buckled. The air rushed out my lungs, red smoke surged into my head and I was dialling the number. He never picked up. I felt myself snap as the words came spitting out.

"You fucking coward, that's your style isn't it, watching in the shadows, spying. If you've got something to say, say it to my face straight or stay out of it. The more you screw with me the less the job will get done. You want that job doing don't you? So you listen to me you sick fuck. I will hunt you down and rip you apart. I don't care how long it takes. If I'm dead, someone else will do it for me. You've got me. I'm doing what you want. Leave my fucking family alone."

I was sick of the fear and the nausea and the pain. I was walking down to the harbour before I realised where my feet were headed. As I stood by the water, light reflected from the sky on the surface. People were everywhere. There was no peace, not from my thoughts and not from this situation. Not until it was over.

42

Rae - Thursday May 13th

Manchester

I walked out of the room into the hallway, the carpet soft beneath my bare feet. The door to the room opposite was half open, I pushed it wider, saw the four-poster bed and felt physically sick. I took a deep breath, but there was no sign of the ropes or my clothes. And no Jazz either. It was as if he didn't exist and we hadn't done what we had done. I touched my throat, the blistered skin attested otherwise.

Overwhelmed by the silence of the flat, I wandered into the kitchen. Empty space greeted me as I looked around for a glass. It was immaculately tidy. There was nothing out of place. I opened the nearest cupboard to a stack of white dishes and assorted mugs. I took a mug and filled it with cold water. As I drank I tried to concentrate, I needed to get out of here. I was cold, naked, and had no idea where my shoes were. I hadn't seen any of my things anywhere. I wanted my clothes, my bag, my phone and my purse.

I finished the water and realised that Jazz had moved the mail. There was no address left out for me to see. I walked into the adjoining lounge and looked around, my bag wasn't there either. I was certain I had left it in the kitchen before he had picked me up and we had gone to the bedroom. The flat was almost empty. There were hardly any personal possessions, just simple furnishings. There was a television in the lounge, an i-Pod dock, speakers, table and chairs and a sofa. No pictures, no books, nothing to say this was anyone's permanent home, least of all Jazz's.

I heard the door. A large lump formed in my throat then fell into my stomach, embarrassment soaring through me.

"You're awake. So, how are you doing?" Jazz said smiling.

"Hi," I said blushing, standing in his kitchen in broad daylight, stark naked.

"You were asleep so I went out to get some things. You okay?" Jazz asked.

"I'm fine. Thank you," I replied my voice belonging to someone else.

"Good! I've got dinner. Salmon pasta, crème sauce and wine, okay?" Jazz said, lifting two full shopping bags down onto the counter.

I wanted to go home but Jazz had been food shopping. I realised that he didn't think I was going anywhere. I took a step backwards, toward the bedroom.

"Everything all right?" Jazz asked, glancing at me in the silence.

"Yes, I just didn't ... think ... I was staying for dinner."

"Well you said you were on a break with Scott so you don't have anything to rush home for," Jazz smiled. "Spend the night. That's what you want, right? More time with me?"

"Yes." I said swallowing hard, stopping myself from touching the burn on my neck. "Of course I'd like that.

But I really should go home first and feed the cats. I'll drive back later. Where are my things?" I said hoarsely, barely able to give him eye contact.

"Nah, it's silly to leave and come all the way back. Don't worry, am sure your ex will feed the cats. You go take a bath and get cleaned up. I'll start cooking," Jazz clicked the front door and slid his key in, locking the mortise as he spoke.

"I haven't got anything to change into." I said quietly, trying to breathe deeply enough to stop the tears falling. He wasn't going to let me simply walk out of here.

"Rae, stop being silly or I'll think you don't want to be with me and after everything you've said I know that isn't true. You can wear something of mine to keep you warm. Go relax on the sofa, watch TV, whilst I run you a bath. Your clothes are in the laundry. I'll put the machine on later," Jazz brushed away my objections as easily as cobwebs as he forged his way past and left the room.

The normality in his voice did nothing to calm me and I felt like I had just stepped into *The Stepford Wives* or even worse, *Rosemary's Baby*. As I heard the sound of the bath water running into the tub, I had to forcibly stop myself thinking he was going to push me in headfirst and drown me.

43

Rae - Thursday May 13th

Manchester

"It's ready," Jazz held the bathroom door open, and waited.

The gentle fragrance of sweet, soft, vanilla wafted toward me. The tub looked innocent, almost welcoming, but the raw skin from the rope burns on my wrists and base of my throat stung viciously as I lowered myself into the hot water. Tears rolled down my cheeks. The bubbles were pretty glistening fairy tale castles; with a finger I traced the top of the beautiful frothy white fortress. I wished I could climb inside one of them to find my prince charming, and then laughed at myself. I hadn't wanted to be Cinderella since I was eight.

I winced as the water caught the delicate skin on the back of my neck. Jazz's bathroom was a light honey champagne colour, with chrome and white fittings. It was feminine, incongruous. I expected charcoal or black, something cool, stylish, like Alex's, with a row of subtle spotlights and sharp edged angular mirrors. Not this. The bath was long, my toes didn't reach the end and it was enamel or ceramic. I didn't know what it was made of but it wasn't plastic, as my bones hurt where I lay. It was hard, unyielding. Like Jazz.

Soaking went someway to soothing the ache on the

surface of my body, but the pain inside went deeper. A week ago the prospect of a night with Jazz, the two of us alone at his apartment and I would have been beside myself. I wouldn't have been able to think about anything else. Yet now here I was and all I wanted to do was go home. But home wasn't home any more.

I had broken apart the soft knit security and love that Scott and I had shared. It had never been perfect, there was no romance and he just didn't want me the way I wished he did. I wondered if he'd been unfaithful too. But I knew, whatever he had done, that he would never have made me feel like this. The thought of ever actually being afraid of Scott was alien to me. I hadn't been afraid of any man until now.

I was sat in a bubble bath, sobbing. I had ruined my engagement, lost my job, and thought I'd fallen for my ex-boss, but instead of trying to sort all that shit out, I was sat in a bubble bath! In the apartment of a man who thought absolutely nothing of tying me up, hanging me and then deliberately pushing me sexually until I was unconscious.

The biggest joke was that this was supposed to be fun. Being with Jazz was supposed to be the best fun I'd ever had. It's what I told myself all the time. I bit my lip. I had feelings for him, I knew I did.

But it was like being inside a vortex, there was no sense of ground with Jazz. It was all speed and heat and need. And spending time with someone who was happy to leave me to come round alone, naked, lying on a floor in an empty room just wasn't me. I should never have allowed anyone this kind of control over me. I had no idea what I was doing with my life and it scared me. Right now, all I wanted to do was get out, and score something, anything, to take my mind off this. But even that wasn't 'me' anymore.

The one thought that kept swimming around and around in my head was that Jazz did not seem bothered in the least about what we had just done or the impact it may have had on me. He had zero consideration for my emotional state at all. And that hurt.

The door to the bathroom opened making me jump.

Jazz handed me a thick fluffy white cotton towel. "It's time to get out, dinner is almost ready."

"Fine, I'm done," I hesitated as I pulled the plug, instinctively wary about him seeing me naked again. But with no choice I stood, taking the towel from him. He left, leaving the door open.

A cold draft clung to my legs fixing the bubbles to my skin as I walked into the kitchen, in the towel, feeling yet ever more fragile.

"Where's my bag?" I asked.

"It's around someplace," Jazz replied, his back to me as he served squares of stuffed pasta, drizzled olive oil over each and tossed salad from a packet into a bowl. Then he reached for the saucepan and spooned a pastel pink sauce containing chunks of salmon on the top of the pasta cushions.

I swallowed back the vomit as it rose in my throat. The food looked inedible. I stared at the table, two small bowls of green salad, silver cutlery and a bottle of mineral water. He handed me a white pasta bowl and a large glass of cold Chablis. This civilised normality was absurd.

"Go sit down," he said.

"In my wet towel?" I asked clutching the heavy food bowl and the large glass as I stood staring at him.

"Whatever you want but you could always put on the

robe I left out for you on the bed," he sighed, shaking his head.

I set the food down on the table and practically ran to the bedroom. I was desperate to have clothes on. I had left home wearing my sundress, a pair of panties and my shoes that morning. My dress wasn't on the bed and nor was my underwear. Maybe he had put them in the laundry as he had said but I couldn't understand why, the dress would have been fine for me to just get home in. But I wasn't going home. Jazz had indeed left me a robe, a white robe. It was clean and warm. I started to look for my bag but couldn't see it anywhere.

"Rae, come on, dinner is getting cold," Jazz's voice sounded from the other room.

I went into the lounge and smiled as best as I could, my features felt like they were made of rubber and my mind was numb. I didn't know what to think or feel anymore about anything. Breathing regularly was as much as I could manage. As I sat down Jazz reached towards me and kissed me on the forehead, his lips leaving an imprint.

"Do you feel better after your bath? You said you liked salmon. Pasta with salmon is good for you, nutritious, right?" Jazz said as he drank from his water glass and then picked his fork up and dissected one of the large pasta pillows.

"I feel ... yes." I said vaguely and picked up my fork and stabbed a chunk of salmon. I didn't trust myself with the crème sauce. "It's great, thank you." I looked up at him after a few moments. "The fish falls apart, very ... It's nice, perfect, thank you." I said again as I ate some more and then started on the pasta. I had no appetite but I was going to need energy if I was going to make it through the evening sane. The tension between us was brittle. Jazz wasn't stupid but I didn't believe he knew me that well. As I forced myself to eat, I forced myself to smile, the panic rising inside me threatening to escape like gas from a bottle. I didn't trust him. A part of me thought I was being irrational and knew I wasn't thinking clearly but I dearly, truly, just wanted to leave and walk out.

Yet, naked wearing only this robe? With no shoes, without my house keys or my mobile phone, without any money? It wasn't going to be that easy.

I wondered if Scott was doing okay and then started thinking about Alex and his family, wondering about Zara and her party. Instantly I felt tears welling up.

"You're very quiet," Jazz commented as we cleared the dishes up.

"I'm tired. Sorry," I said.

"I see. If you say so," Jazz shrugged. "Let's sit down and finish the wine. Then I'll take some new photos of you whilst you are here."

I spun round, "You want to take pics tonight?"

"Why not! You love it as much as I do." Jazz laughed, handing me a re-fill when I had hardly touched the first glass.

I went to the bathroom, shut the door and sat down on the toilet, my head resting in my hands. This was stupid. I should be able to go out there and ask for my clothes back and say that I was going home. It should be simple enough for me to tell him I wasn't doing this anymore, that I didn't want to take photos and I didn't want to stay. But I couldn't get past the fact I didn't know what would happen if I did say those things. It was either risk that or go along with whatever new photos he wanted to take and if I was worried now, I knew as soon as he got those ropes out I was going to be completely powerless.

And that really didn't seem like any kind of fun any more. I flushed the toilet and looked in the single mirror above the sink. My neck still had the telltale thick red welts from where the rope had bitten my skin and burnt earlier. It was then that I realised. There was no way Jazz would let me out of here looking like that. Too many questions would need answering.

44

Jude - Friday May 14th

Antwerp

12 hours to heist

"Spike?"

"Who's asking?" A broad cockney voice rumbled.

"Haven't got time for jokes today, it's me Jude," I laughed, a shallow sound.

"Always time for a joke Jude mate. What can I do you for?"

"I need to check the wheels."

"They're sorted, no worries."

"It's not sorted until I say we're sorted. Where are you now?"

"Out an' about."

"Get yourself to Lime. I'll see you in the car park in ten minutes."

Call waiting:

"Jude."

"Danny?"

"Yeah, it's me."

I exhaled so loud I was afraid Danny had changed his mind. "Are you still there?"

"Yep."

"Jesus man you have no idea how glad I am to hear from you."

"Jude, there's heat all over this shit. Meeting at a club like that is suicide."

"It wasn't down to me. I wouldn't pull that kind of stunt. You're calling, so … you're in?" I scratched the back of my hand.

"I must be mad, but yeah, if you're saying you need me, well, I'm here for you man. We were friends. Anytime you want to talk about it …"

"I owe you. Thanks Danny. I won't forget it."

"I know you won't. We've got to get through it yet!"

"See you at seven tonight, Holiday Inn room 505."

I flicked through the phone on my way to the car park at the back of Lime bar, walking through the groups of people. I owed Danny, Ross and Zed so far. If I survived this they would come calling. Nothing was free. But as Danny said, we had to get through it yet. The job was far from over and there was no point in worrying about debts until after Rae was free and I'd found Coco.

"Louis, it's me, Jude."

"Yes?"

"You need to be at the Holiday Inn by seven tonight, room 505."

"Very well," he sighed.

After the phone went silent, I sighed too. I was standing at Lime Bar car park with no sign of Spike as I slid my shades into place.

Suddenly and without warning my mind was full of Terri. Lime was always the place she insisted on. She drove me insane, infuriated me and I didn't have time to dwell on it. I still thought she might be playing me against

Wolf. There was something between those two, I saw it on their faces and in their manner with one another; they seemed 'together'. Yet she'd said he wasn't her boyfriend, when I'd met them that first time in Lime.

I dialled her number, and left a message. "It's me. Make sure you and the Wolf are at my hotel room by seven tonight."

There was nothing else to say. I almost laughed out loud at myself. I was done with women. I couldn't believe I had given Terri thought-time. It was a woman who had got me into this mess. When this was over I was going to find Coco and get the answers I deserved.

I moved past a woman and a little boy waiting by the pavement, seconds later a taxi arrived, holding the child's hand she folded the buggy and lowered it into the boot. A group of youths in sports gear laughing together were pulling rucksacks off each other's backs. I felt a million miles away from the scenes in front of me. I checked my watch, losing patience, looking through my phone for Spike's number as a silver grey Mercedes stopped at the kerb.

The glass slid down: "Get in," Spike said.

Spike had better taste in cars than I'd have given him credit for. "Nice ride," I said as I opened the door. "Expensive."

He nodded. "This is a waste of fucking time. I said I'd get it sorted," Spike's hands were knuckle-white on the wheel.

"C'mon man, you know I need to check everything. Where's the van?"

Spike accelerated, "In a lock up not far from here."

It didn't take long. The road from the marina swept us out of tourist Antwerp into the urban jigsaw fast. Spike drove towards a sprawling apartment development, similar to something built in Manchester in the late sixties. He pulled up outside a garage and killed the engine.

He squared his shoulders, removed a set of keys from his jacket and unlocked the steel handle in the middle of the garage door. I followed as he pressed the light switch on the wall and pulled the metal shutter down behind us.

There in front of me was a navy Transit van with the back door windows blacked out.

"See I told you it was all sorted," Spike replied.

"Spike, we just need a small van, something easy to drive and something fast! This thing isn't going to go above thirty," I said.

Spike stood his ground firmly, his hands shoved deep into his pocket and his jaw thrust forwards. "You've no idea how much stuff is in them vaults Jude. We'll need this trust me."

"I don't want any shit. Easy in and easy out. This thing isn't going to move."

Spike was unlocking the back door and he swung it open revealing two skinny bench seats and above each on the inside wall, a line of guns. There were six in total, low slung on hooks and casually resting, three on each side. Spike stepped up into the van and sat down on one of the benches.

"Enough room in here for the gear and the team," he said patting the space next to him.

I swallowed hard. "We won't need to be armed like this. The place'll be empty."

"We'll need protection, can't go in with nothing Jude and we're using this van. Tailor made for the job. Can fit the entire contents of the vault in," Spike laughed but I couldn't see the funny side and I wasn't going to argue.

"My hotel seven tonight to go over the plans. Let's get out of here," I tapped my watch. He shut the van as I lifted the door and stepped out into the warm day.

"Got any smaller kit?" I asked.

"You want different shooters?" Spike looked over at me as the Mercedes engine purred and we flowed into the tennis games tourist traffic.

"Yep," I said, checking my phone. There was nothing new.

"What do you think we're going in with Jude? Toys?"

"There isn't any need for that kind of weight. Bring the smaller pieces round to the hotel later."

We drew up to the harbour, and I opened the door.

"Yeah whatever," Spike drove off, his words crumbling into the dust.

45

Rae – Thursday May 13th

Manchester

I splashed cold water around my eyes to cool the skin where I had been crying. I wasn't one of those women who cried gracefully, dripping movie star diamond tears, and looking like they hadn't actually been upset. My thoughts were everywhere.

Jazz was sitting watching the TV in the lounge as I crept into the bedroom, the one with the four-poster where we had been earlier. There were no keys on the nightstand. I pulled open the little oak drawer by the bed, nothing. Gently I opened the wardrobe door. There were no clothes on the shelves. Empty.

"Anything wrong babe?" Jazz spoke from behind me.

"You made me jump," I squeaked crossing my arms. "I'm cold. I wanted to borrow a jumper."

His eyes narrowed as he stared, "You're wearing a robe, the heating is on and you're cold?"

"I don't warm up easily," I replied holding his stare as openly as possible.

"I don't know about that," he laughed, taking the one step separating us until he was right in front of me, so close, we were almost touching.

Then his hand was in my hair, tangled tight with deliberate grip. He pulled my head back briskly so I was looking up at him. Without warning he kissed me full on, forcefully. His mouth was on mine, his tongue sliding over my lips, snaking inside alongside mine, his right hand holding my wrists above me.

With his other hand he dropped his trousers. He was hot and hard against my skin, pushing my robe off and I was naked as his hand slid between my thighs. He lifted me upwards, his arm around my waist, my legs around his and with that heat he slid into me easily. We were together, fast, and slick, and suddenly I was struggling against him, fighting him until he stopped.

"What is wrong with you tonight?"

I wiped my mouth as I looked into his melting brown eyes, at his slanting cheekbones and the jet-black hair that etched his face in ink. I remembered everything I had ever thought about him the first time I had seen him and all the things that had happened since. My vision had been blurred by the fact I wanted him so much and I couldn't admit it, nor could I believe a man like that had ever looked twice at me. And I burst into loud noisy sobs.

Jazz recoiled as if I had scalded him. "What? I kiss you and you're crying?"

"I want to go home," I howled, no longer caring what he did to me. "I want to get out of here and go home, see my cats, and go to sleep in my own bed."

"Fucking hell! You're acting like a crazy child. I thought we would spend a bit of time together and have some fun. I was giving you what you wanted. You remind me of my ex fucking wife."

"Why? Did you tie her up, hang her from a rope til she passed out and then dump her on a floor and leave her? No wonder she fucking divorced you," I spat at him as the tears evaporated instantly into fury. "Now, where are my fucking clothes? Give me my fucking clothes and call me a cab you asshole," I said shaking with anger.

Jazz stared at me, shock plastered all over his face.

Without a word he walked out and returned seconds later with my bag and my crumpled dress. Then he flung open the wardrobe door nearest to him and pulled out my shoes, throwing them across the room at me.

"Go, and you are not coming back. Leave here tonight and we're done," he said.

"Good you fucking maniac! What on earth makes you think I want to see you ever again?" I shrieked as I tore the dress off him and practically rammed it over my head, shoving my feet into my shoes as I lunged for my bag.

He held it just out of reach and paused thoughtfully, stepping back and resting his shoulders against the pale coloured wall. I glared at him, waiting for him to give me the bag, determined to get out of there as soon as he did. I tried to grab the bag again. This time he handed it to me. I opened it, checked my keys were there, saw my purse and phone and turned to the door.

"You know I have photographs of you don't you?" he said before I could make it out of the room.

I stopped still. "So?"

"Well, I am just saying I have a lot of photographs of you, some of which are very ... compromising. Perhaps you would like to buy them from me."

"I don't have any money and you know it. I don't have a job and I'm a student the rest of the time," I said staring him out.

"There are other ways. Maybe we could arrange some kind of payment in exchange," he said, arms folded, leaning back against the wall as he spoke.

"What the fuck? Seriously? I wouldn't have thought

you of all people would have been so desperate for sex that you would have to blackmail me," I said.

"Let's just say that there are things we've shared that not everyone enjoys." Jazz looked at me, his eyes sending shivers through my skin.

"Who said I enjoyed them? Maybe I just went along with it." I replied.

He saw the lie and laughed as he caught me by the elbow and drew me back towards him, his body close to mine and his mouth near my ear. He ran his finger down the side of my face and then traced a teasing line along the front of my throat, down between my breasts to my navel, sending slivers of desire slicing into me like blades.

"My darling Marae," he murmured softly. "Some things can't be faked. We've had a row. It's been an intense day."

"I'm not lying. This isn't me. You don't *know* me."

"I know *you*. You'll want more. You'll *need* more." He said, taking my hand. "But I'm not joking baby, you choose to walk out of here now and you don't come back."

"Why? I just want to go home for a little while."

Jazz shrugged. "So go."

"What do you mean I'll 'need' more?"

"You know exactly what I mean. If it isn't me it will be someone else, you won't be able to stop yourself and not everyone can be trusted."

I stood, lost, as silence filled the seconds gathering weight between us.

"Oh God Jazz," I said, the words expelling something deep inside and breaking the tension. I stood rubbing my hand across my forehead and resting against the doorway. He waited silently.

I took a long breath. "Look, I don't *know* you! I have no idea if I can trust you! And a big part of me thinks I would be completely mad to, after today."

"But why?"

"You're serious? You don't get it?" I asked.

He shook his head. I picked my bag up and walked past him. I kept on walking until I got to his front door and opened it. I didn't stop to think or breathe hardly, I walked downstairs to the main door to the house and opened it, then realised I still didn't have the address. I picked up my mobile and as ridiculous as I felt, I hit his number.

"What now?" Jazz asked.

"I don't know where I am and I can't call a cab without knowing where I am."

"Jesus Christ. Wait there. I will call you one."

"Jazz?" I asked not sure if he was still on the line.

"Yeah?"

"I'm tempted," I said, hating myself.

He laughed, "Baby, I'd be disappointed if you weren't. So, come back inside and we can talk about it."

I took two steps into the hallway, and stood at the bottom of the wide staircase, feeling like I'd aged a century since this morning. Was it only this morning? I could hardly believe how long ago it felt since I arrived. He was right, whatever it was that we shared would haunt me and I knew already that I wanted more of what he gave me. But it felt like I was signing my soul away to the king of hell. Because whatever this heat was, it didn't feel like love. Not any love I'd known.

"Well?" he asked.

"I … can't," I answered, the word tearing out of me more like a sob.

"Are you sure? Before I call the cab and this ends tonight? Come back, let's talk it out and then, okay, if you want we can have a break. What do you think?"

I heard his voice echo, and saw him standing at the top of the stairs looking down at me. God help me because I didn't know what to do, or which way to go.

46

Rae - Thursday evening May 13th

Manchester

"Marae, come on … I would really love you to stay with me tonight," Jazz said again, smiling, as he descended one step at a time until he was within touching distance.

"Tomorrow would be better."

He shook his head silently and another smile touched his lips, but his eyes never left mine. He moved towards the front door and held it open, "I'll call you," he said.

I laughed, "No you won't."

He had the strangest expression on his face. We were over. I knew it.

In a daze I was bending down, picking my bag up.

"Goodbye Jazz," I said hardly able to recognise my own voice as I reached the door, trying not to choke on tears as I avoided his eyes. The air was cold outside. But instead of hearing the door slam behind me, I felt his hand, warm, on my shoulder.

"Here, this is for you - if you wanted to stay, we could try things differently. Maybe you could …" he didn't finish his sentence, his voice sounding as strange to my ears as my own did.

I looked down and saw his hand, he held out his camera to me.

Silence filled the void where the words had run dry. And in that hollow emptiness somehow my mouth found his. I kissed him, tears flooding, leaking down our faces, drowning both of us. He was oxygen. And as fucked up as it was in that moment, in that second, I needed him. I couldn't lose him like this. I couldn't leave and not see him again. That wasn't an option.

Jazz had broken me apart inside but only he could put me back together. Easily he put his hands around my waist and lifted me. My legs encircled him and he walked me back indoors until I was pressed tight against him, resting my weight between him and the wall. It was full body contact. I knew where we were and I didn't care who came in or who went past. I wasn't being an exhibitionist and I wasn't getting off on the fact the door was wide open and we were in a public hallway, it just didn't matter. Nothing mattered. I was safe because I sensed that there wasn't a single situation Jazz couldn't handle.

I didn't want to think about anything else and I cut the thoughts dead.

This was all I cared about. I couldn't help it and I couldn't control it. I was addicted. As we kissed I was tugging at his zip. Urgency fuelled, I couldn't stop, not until I felt him in my hand, then with my legs wound around his waist I moved my hips, guiding him into the hottest part of me. As much as it hurt, what he'd done earlier, somehow, in this fucked up world we'd created, the fact he wanted me as much as I wanted him, stopped that pain.

He slid into me, his eyes locked on mine, his gaze pushing into me with as much force as his body. I held that look and rode him back just as hard. But this time I didn't let myself go, instead I took him to the edge, my hands trailing down his back, over his nipples pinching hard, soft kisses in his ear, biting and licking, tasting his skin, and all the while moving with him. I loved the feel of him inside me, fucking me faster, hotter, and deeper. This time it was him. His surrender pushed me over and despite myself I came hard in the aftermath, clinging to him for those seconds. As I slid down, tears started to fall again but he didn't see.

I wiped my eyes as he arranged his clothes, standing silently, watching as he picked my bag up from the floor where it had fallen and closed the front door.

He held out his hand. "Come on baby let's go upstairs. I don't know if they have CCTV down here but it's enough of a show," Jazz said, his voice like cotton.

47

Jude - Friday May 14th

Antwerp

6 hours to heist

I paced around the bedroom, looking out at the harbour. I hadn't heard a word from Jazz all afternoon. I had assumed he would have been in touch. I needed to know he was on his way and that everything was okay. It was getting later and later and I was jittery, sick at the thought of the job tonight, but Jazz was family. He would be here. I knew it. Because if our roles were reversed I would have dropped anything for him, so it was impossible to believe he would let me down.

Just before seven o' clock there was a knock on the door. I opened it, hoping it was Jazz. But instead a small figure wearing drab clothes stood, waiting. I stepped to the side as Louis scurried in, his movements fast and anxious.

"Have you got the plans with you?" I asked.

Louis tapped his inside pocket and I heard a hollow sound. He pulled out a tube of papers and began to peel away elastic bands and unroll sheets, straightening out the bundle on the desk. He was almost finished when the door went again.

Terri and the Wolf. Terri looking slight and lithe, wearing black jeans and a long sleeve black top, breezed past me, unsmiling.

I stood and let her pass. The Wolf followed, his eyes dark, deep set, darting around the room and resting on the plans. I headed to the table, where the other two were standing.

Terri sat herself on the edge of the desk, close enough for me to feel her presence.

"One last time, Wolf, you and Terri will both be in uniform and go in first, followed by Louis here at the main entrance," I jabbed my finger on the map. "Several of these internal points on the ground floor have alarms you're going to need to disable so we can get to the stairs, but you can access those doors from that keypad?"

Louis nodded silently.

"You two go straight to the camera control room and deal with the visuals."

Wolf nodded as my phone bleeped. It was a text message from Jazz. I flicked it open. "Plane delayed, should be there by 11 p.m. What room?"

"That's tight. Holiday Inn. 505." I text back.

"Excuse us having a meeting Jude whilst you're texting your girlfriend," Terri snapped.

"*He* is not my fucking girlfriend," I replied, the words too loud.

"Who the fuck are you texting?" Her eyes were grey stone but knocking interrupted the argument before it could get anywhere.

I stalked across the room and peered through the spy hole. Relief flared as I opened the door. Danny walked in and clapped a hand on my shoulder with a flash of a smile.

"Hanging in there?" He spoke softly.

I leant toward him, "Thanks man, I'll make this right with you."

Terri glanced at Wolf before she turned to Danny. "Back again? We aren't playing yo-yo here. You're not fucking vanishing again, leaving us high and dry …"

"Enough. Leave it," I said. "He's in."

There was silence. A minute passed, Wolf offered his hand to Danny who shook it.

Danny nodded, "Everything set to go?"

I answered, "Yep. Have you got the stuff?"

"All good," Danny replied.

I heard knocking at the door again. I got up leaving Louis sitting at the desk, Terri peering at the plans on one side and Danny on the other. The Wolf was on the balcony smoking a cigarette and gazing out across the water.

"All right mate," Spike marched in with a black holdall slung over his shoulder. As he dropped the bag down onto the bed a ripple went through the room, I felt it like a living current. Danny and Terri turned away from the desk, Wolf came in and stood as still as concrete. Louis looked up, his attention diverted from the plans.

"Glad to see you had a change of heart," Spike said walking towards the American.

As Spike turned to Terri, Danny remained silent, his eyes flickering over to me, his expression unreadable. Curiosity burned. I wanted to know the score here, but now wasn't the time. Rae needed us. Thoughts of Rae, her body contorted and restrained, fused with images of my mum and memories of Zara.

I took a deep breath, opened the wardrobe, took out two bags and tipped the contents onto the bed. Six rubber masks landed with a wet sound.

"What the fuck?" Spike asked.

Terri picked up the mask nearest to her and stared at it. "Couldn't you have chosen something else?"

"These are cool," Wolf said, fingering the hooded black Batman head. He pulled it on. "Hey I can see really well," his voice sounding distorted.

"You're a real dark knight," Spike laughed.

"Go for it Terri," Wolf's voice buzzed through the rubber.

"Fucking hell," she sighed and then pulled the Joker over her short dark hair.

"If you do run into any guards that should give them a heart attack," Spike said.

I tapped the table and pointed to the plans, "We don't have much time. Louis is going to take the alarms out and as soon as he's done his bit, we go in."

"The guards are going to be there?" Danny asked.

"Here," Terri replied pointing.

"Patrols run at midnight and two a.m. that gives us ninety minutes to get in, empty the vault, and get out just before the two o'clock patrol," I said.

"Yeah but if they're not back until four we could just sit tight and go after two," Spike said.

"No way. If anything fucks up and they find out we're in there, we're sitting ducks. We're not going to be able to take more than we can carry and we'll only have one chance to get to the van," I said, pointing to the exit route. "There is only that one place to park. You can't wait anywhere."

"By four a.m. deliveries are starting," Wolf added.

"Spike you'll be there before two a.m. I've a lot riding on this, don't fuck around."

Spike's jaw was set, "Jude, we've all got a lot riding on this and I think we can afford the extra time to get the gear. I'll bring the van over for the four a.m. …"

I had him by the scruff of his designer lapels before I'd even thought about it. He was shorter than me, my teeth were almost against his skin and I could taste the smell of him.

"You listen to me you fucking idiot, you're the driver. You drive. You don't get paid to think. And you don't tell me how to run this. Got it? *This* goes as I say it goes or *you* get replaced here and fucking now."

"You and whose army?" Spike grunted at me.

"This one right here," I replied.

I felt Danny's hands behind my shoulders, pulling me away. "It's okay we're good," I said stepping back. "Anyone else got any bright ideas they want to share?"

Wolf looked at me then, eye contact. If I had known him better I would have said I had his approval.

48

Jude – Friday May 14th

Antwerp

5 hours to heist

The air in the room was thick, no one spoke. Louis stood holding his mask like an offering at a sacrifice, the rubber quivering visibly.

"Danny, have you got everything we need to get into the vault?" I asked.

Danny nodded, "Covered." His voice sounded even and calm.

"Vault keys? Terri, Louis?" I asked.

Terri flashed hers at me as Louis reached his hand deep into his jacket pocket and pulled out a set of tiny keys hanging together on a small chain. He dropped them into my hand, warm from his body heat.

"Terri, Wolf, you'll need no more than four minutes to get from the camera control room to meet me and Danny. Once we're in you're going for the low numbers on the boxes. Danny will take out the high numbers, and I'm the mid range, here." I handed printed cards with the rows of box numbers they would be responsible for emptying.

"Louis, why aren't you going in?" Spike asked,

stepping closer to the smaller man.

I answered. "Leave it Spike. Louis is not coming into the vault."

"You're not going to be able to get everything out, there's only the four of you, and we need at least five, even six. Louis here needs to take his place in the vault," Spike stated, patting Louis on the shoulder. "You don't mind do you brother?"

"There will be five," I said, with effort.

"Well I can't see anyone else here," Spike gestured, his arm around Louis's shoulders as he looked around the room.

"He'll be here later," I said.

"Who will?" He sneered, squaring up to me, his shoulders pushing forwards.

I shook my head, determined not to lose my temper. "It's under control. Trust me."

"Trust you? After the way you just spoke to me you jumped up little fuck?" Spike threw a punch. I ducked just in time, his fist barely grazing my face before I hit back.

He doubled over, struggling to recover but Danny was faster and bigger and pushed us both apart. "Get a fucking grip both of you. We have a job to do."

Spike grunted, standing up. "You fucking come near me again …"

"You'll do what?" Wolf said, slight and menacing, like a knife between us. He smiled a slick smile. "Jude, do you want a new driver? I owe this motherfucker a lesson."

"Try it you bastard." Spike spat.

Wolf raised his eyes at me, and pointed at Spike grinning, "Well?"

I shook my head, swallowing hard. The last thing we needed right now was a body to dispose of. "No."

"Are you sure?" Wolf repeated.

"Not now," I replied.

Wolf shrugged. "I can wait."

"Tonight is about staying happy as long as the money's good, right?" Danny had both arms wrapped around Spike's shoulders, pulling him back, away from Wolf, away from me.

"The money's good," I said, forcing back the anger.

Danny released Spike. Seconds later, and without a word Spike unzipped the black holdall bag he had brought with him. Terri walked over and peered into the bag.

"I'm not carrying one of these," Terri stated picking up a sub three times the width of her hips.

"For fuck's sake I said we didn't need anything heavy," I threw my hands up in the air.

"Get back in your pram Jude, they're for those who want something sturdy," Spike handed subs to Wolf and Danny who both began testing out their handling. "These are the doll-size," he laughed and handed a standard looking glock to Terri.

"That's better," she said fingering the trigger before sliding it snugly into her jeans.

"Here's yours Jude, and you," Spike said gesturing to Louis.

Louis shook his head, "No, not for me."

"Everyone needs one," Spike said.

"No," I replied. "No violence. There are two guards on duty and we're not going near them, we don't all need to be armed if we're paired up. Only one of the pair needs a shooter."

"Jude you're being naïve," Terri snapped. "He has to be able to protect himself."

"It is quite all right my dear, I can't use one," Louis replied quietly.

"Who's with Louis?" Danny asked.

"Someone of mine will go in with Louis. He'll take care of anything unexpected. Spike you need to get the van here," I said, pointing at the ground level just outside the underground car park. "You know it's a strict time line with nowhere to wait. When we're done Wolf will key in the code at the barrier. It will rise and the gate will sink, as if a security delivery vehicle was coming in but we'll get out. You've got to be there for that exact minute."

"Can't I just drive in and pick you up?" he said.

"You're having a laugh!" I replied. "For you to drive down you'd need a pass and the middle of the night isn't delivery time. It will be tough to get out on foot but we'll still be faster than risking you trying to get the van down, loading up and then getting out. Louis leaves after he has taken the alarms down, the rest is up to us," I said.

Just then my phone beeped. I flicked open a picture message from an unknown number. It was a photograph of my mum, my head throbbed for a second and everything started to swim.

"All right Jude?" Spike asked, leaning towards me. "Getting a bit much for you?"

I snapped the phone away from his eyes and shoved it in my pocket. I turned to them, "The timing is key to getting out. We can't afford to be late."

"I'm not sure if that route we're using as an exit links up to the police directly, it might show any activity," Terri gnawed at her fingernail, the first sign of any uncertainty I'd seen from her. The tension was getting to all of us.

"Well I guess we're going to find out in a few hours time," Danny said.

"I thought your background covered everything," I said.

Wolf turned to me, "She has done more than anyone could have done. The key code at the barrier will give us enough time to get out. Louis, your over ride codes won't work on that part of the system?"

"No, I'm sorry," he said.

We looked at one another. That was the second weak link. The first was getting into the vault itself. But if we succeeded at the vault and then afterwards the barrier didn't rise, the iron gates would stay locked and we would be caged. If the barrier rose, the gates would drop in sequence. The whole thing was a risk. But there wasn't any other option.

"Do not forget we need absolute silence inside the building and the vault. They've got electronic voice recorders built into the security system so no fucking talking whatsoever. Set your watches," I said, checking the time and walking to the bed where the masks and guns still lay. "Nine o clock, take your kit. Does everyone know where they are going to be at midnight?"

"Yeah," Spike nodded, picked up his shoulder bag and walked out.

"You okay man?" Danny asked.

"As good as it's going to get," I said.

"We'll get it done. Never known me not to, right?"

"Never," I replied, and managed a half smile back.

"See you in three hours," Danny said as he left.

Terri, Wolf and Louis looked at me.

"Okay?" I asked.

Wolf didn't speak, just nodded and Terri replied with a slow look and a casual nod of her head, "We're done."

"Terri," I said quietly, reaching my hand towards her.

She stepped back. "I'm out of here," she turned to Wolf.

Wolf curled his arm around her shoulders and walked Terri out as I felt a shiver that had nothing to do with the job.

Louis watched them go with a strange look on his face, "What do you get out of this?" he said suddenly.

"Money," I replied, surprised, fingering the packet of cigarettes in my pocket and pulling them out, offering one to Louis.

His shook his head, eyes narrow and shrewd, "You don't seem like a man doing this for money."

"You don't know anything about me."

"True. However I know people and you're not the same as the others. You don't have money, no, but … That is not it. Do you owe a debt? Or maybe something else?"

"Nah nothing like that," I said, shaking my head and turning away. "We need to get on, Louis, we've a job tonight and that's all there is to it."

"Did someone threaten your family the way you threatened mine?" Louis asked.

Even I heard my sharp intake of breath.

Louis nodded at me, and kept his eye contact as he continued speaking, his voice dropping to a whisper. "You know how it feels and yet you chose to hurt someone else's family?"

I didn't reply. But I didn't drop my eyes either.

Louis was the calmest I'd ever seen him. He spoke softly and slowly. "In another life I would feel sorry for you, if that's what is at the centre of this, but that's not possible. If anything at all happens to my grandchild I will send someone to find you."

There was a silence. Louis broke it. "So, it seems that finally we understand one another Jude." He wiped his glasses carefully on his handkerchief before sliding them back in place.

"Louis, if this goes wrong tonight and your granddaughter gets hurt, you can believe me when I tell you that by the time you've sent people to kill me, I'll already be dead."

Louis didn't reply. He rolled up his map, picked up his small rucksack with his mask and then walked silently through the waiting, open, door without looking back.

49

Rae – Thursday night May 13th

Manchester

"Do you want anything else to eat?" Jazz asked, heading straight into the kitchen.

"No I'm fine thanks," I said. "But I could do with a drink." I dropped my bag down on the floor in the lounge and switched the TV on. The noise was normal, a welcome babble of something nondescript and soothing, I picked up the remote and started flicking through channels.

"Do you want tea? I make nice tea. Or would you like coffee or something stronger?" Jazz reappeared, holding a folded towel over his arm.

I stared at him and started laughing.

"What's funny?"

I was laughing so much I couldn't talk.

"Look Rae, if you don't stop it … I don't know what!" he said, his expression making me collapse further.

"It's you!"

"It's me?"

"Yes you … you look … so British! Like a butler! Like Carson! As if we're at Downton Abbey. Offering tea! It's funny! And today … everything, it's all just so … funny," I struggled to get the words out.

"Downton Abbey? Where is that? Funny isn't how I'd

describe today."

I slowed down, catching my breath. "It's a ... Nevermind. Yeah you're right. It wasn't funny, it was ..." I was still thinking of a way to phrase it all, when I felt a stinging slap across my backside. "Hey!"

"Now that's funny!" he laughed.

"No! That's not!" I squealed and swung round as he swiped at me again with the tea towel. I caught the cloth that time, tugged it, pulling on it hard, bringing him closer, and then relaxed my grip. Suddenly I yanked it so hard that he fell forwards, tumbling into me, both of us falling backwards into the huge cream leather sofa. His mouth was soft as his lips parted, butterfly light. It was a lovers' kiss, languid and sweet. Gently and slowly, with all that I was feeling, I kissed him back.

He peeled the straps down off my dress and lowered his head to my shoulders. With his tongue he lapped at my collarbone and layered kisses against my skin where the rope had chafed earlier. With each movement of his lips he gave me an apology. With each kiss he set my body alight with tender flames. His mouth caressed my nipples to bullet point as slowly he touched me, stroking my legs, the backs of my knees, exploring me with a softness that I'd never felt from him. Then he kissed my toes, my feet and my ankles. Millimetre by millimetre he kissed each leg all the way up until he was between my thighs. He licked and tasted until I was pulling his head towards me and his mouth once again met mine. And then we were both naked, lying next to one another on the huge sofa, skin to skin, pressed together as we melted into one another.

Afterwards he rested his head against my chest. I

wrapped my arms round him holding him close. He pulled me tighter and we lay entwined until our bodies began to grow cold.

Reluctantly, not wanting to break the connection, I shifted. He looked at me his eyes light in colour and a smile dancing across his lips. "You okay? You're quiet."

"I'm good." I said smiling back.

He stretched as he sat up and for the second time he reached for my hand. "Let's go to bed and get some sleep."

I bit my lip, and Jazz caught the look.

"What is it?" he asked.

"Which room are we sleeping in?"

"The bedroom!"

"Yeah, but which? I don't really want to …"

"… Sleep in the four-poster?" Jazz concluded.

I nodded.

"That's fine, the double bed is mine. Come on." Jazz turned to me, eyebrows lifted. "Which side do you want?" He asked.

"The side you don't want!" I laughed.

He tugged the duvet back and then feeling oddly self conscious I sat down and slid in feet first as he wandered off.

"I've a spare toothbrush in here, a new one!" Jazz's muffled voice filtered through the wall from the bathroom.

"That would be great thanks!" I replied already on my feet and heading his way. He opened the bathroom cabinet, his mouth full, lips covered in globules of white paste, his brush stuck in one side of his cheek as he handed me the new brush in its packet. I stared at him via his reflection in the mirror. He was so handsome, even smeared in toothpaste he still managed to make movie stars look ugly. And like I always did when I was with him, or Alex, I caught my breath.

"What?" he said catching my glance back in the mirror.

"You're so fucking gorgeous," I said for the first time actually voicing what had been going round in my head. He was overwhelmingly good looking.

He blushed, "You know I gave you the camera, well if you wanted to photograph me I didn't think it was going to be when I was covered in toothpaste."

"What did you have in mind?" I asked.

"You know what I had in mind," Jazz wiped his face.

Then it was my turn to blush. "So you want me to take photos of you like the kind you took of me?"

"No. I want you to take the kind of photos you want to take. I want you to be yourself," he said as we walked into the bedroom.

"Tonight?"

"I thought you were tired," Jazz smiled.

"I am! I could sleep on a park bench, I'm so tired," I replied sliding my feet back under the sheets again.

"So we'll do it another time. When I get back maybe," he replied as he turned the lights out.

"Get back from where?" I asked feeling sleepy. The bed really was very comfortable.

He didn't answer. Instead he wrapped his arm around me and nestled against me, his body covering mine. His limbs felt heavy as he whispered, "I am glad you came back Marae."

"Me too. Good night Jazz."

"Good night baby."

50

Rae - Friday May 14th

Manchester

Morning streamed through the curtains, the light becoming more intrusive, slowly waking me. I was smiling. I was happy. Quietly, so as not to wake Jazz, I rolled out of bed and softly walked barefoot into the kitchen. I picked two mugs off the draining board, opened several cupboards and found coffee. When the kettle had boiled, I took the drinks into the bedroom, slid back into bed, and gently stroked Jazz's hair as he slept.

Seconds later he was wide awake, checking his watch. "Shit I didn't realise it was so late!"

"It's not late. It's just after nine o' clock and it's Saturday," I said, yawning and padding to the bathroom. I was in the middle of cleaning my teeth when Jazz reappeared.

"No baby, it's Friday. Which means we have to really get going this morning," he said.

I stared. He was already dressed and grabbing his toothbrush, practically standing on me as he reached to the sink to spit.

"What happened? You were sound asleep a second ago."

"I move fast," he grinned at me in the mirror.

"Tell me about it!" I laughed back.

"No I'm serious, I don't mean to be rude but I have a lot of things to do today. Get your stuff, we have to go. I'll drop you back at home."

I wiped my face on the towel in amazement, "What? Right now?"

"Yes. Now!"

"Fine!" I said whilst mustering all the dignity I could manage wearing absolutely nothing.

"Here, get dressed," Jazz threw my clothes at me.

Stunned, I pulled my dress over my head, as the shoes landed on the bed, next to my bag. I put my shoes on, and grabbed my bag. Underwear was a waste of time and I had no idea where it had gone anyway.

"You really are chucking me out after everything we went through yesterday?"

"Oh no," he groaned. "Don't take it that way, look Marae, honey, I'm not doing this to upset you, I have to be someplace, it's been planned a long while and well, that's all. We need to be out of here."

"Can I come?" I asked.

"Not really."

"Oh. Where are you going?"

"Doesn't matter where, but I'm not going with another woman! If that's what you're thinking," he laughed.

"I'm not thinking anything. And I'm ready." I said, trying to ignore the thoughts, and drink my coffee. It hadn't cooled.

Jazz was rummaging around in a drawer. He looked up at me, his eyes catching mine, "Thanks, I am sorry. Okay?"

"I suppose."

"Well you got the extra night anyway!"

"What do you mean by that? It was you who wanted

me to stay!"

"I know and I'm glad you did," he gently butted me with his body as we walked to the door. He locked up and in seconds we were at the car.

"I still don't know your address!" I said as I got and fastened my seatbelt.

"You don't need it. I'll pick you up next time we meet." Jazz said.

I smiled at him. "Yeah okay. That's cool. Fuck!"

"What?"

"I'm going to need somewhere to live," I said as the thought really hit me.

"You and him are really finished then?" he asked.

"Yes. Can't go back, no matter how much sometimes we wish we could," I said.

"Do you regret this?" Jazz asked suddenly.

"No."

"Are you sure? Because I'm not promising anything here, you know, no marriage and babies that shit isn't for me and if that's what you want, then you're better off with Scott."

"No, I'm sure," I said quietly, blushing.

There was a pause and Jazz stopped at traffic lights. Then he spoke again. "I'm actually surprised to tell you the truth Marae."

"What do you mean?"

"When I met you I thought it was Alex."

"Thought what was Alex?"

He nodded, "Women always fall in love with him. I see it all the time."

I was so floored I had no idea what to say.

"See I thought so," Jazz laughed. "You're exactly the same as the rest."

I reached out and touched his arm as he was driving. He turned to look at me for a second, his eyes off the road.

"Alex is Alex," I said. "But you're you."

And I hoped that was enough.

51

Jude - Friday May 14th

Antwerp

60 minutes to heist

My phone was ringing, vibrating through the loose skin of my jeans. I picked it up, stubbing the cigarette out on the balcony.

"Where are you?" I asked.

"Walking through your hotel, on my way to your room," Jazz replied.

The T.V was on low as I re-entered the bedroom, shutting the balcony doors behind me. Checking my watch confirmed what I already knew, we needed to leave in less than sixty minutes. Not much time to catch Jazz up to speed.

I drank half a bottle of cold mineral water and looked through a copy of the plans on my phone. If everything went well I'd leave from the Diamond Centre. If not I didn't want to think about it. But I wasn't coming back to this room. The small rucksack lay on the bed, tightly packed. I was ready.

There was a knock at the door. I felt like a month had passed since he'd telephoned ten minutes ago. It was hard to believe it had been little more than eight days since my visit to Amsterdam to look for Coco. The decade of the past week weighed heavily as I walked across that carpet, turned the solid hotel doorknob and saw Jazz, standing resting against the doorframe, looking exactly like Jazz always did.

Light filled me as I saw him. I hugged him and felt worry thawing as he slapped me on the back. "Hey man, why are we here? What the fuck is happening?"

I sat down on the bed, "Was your flight all right, eventually?"

"We're in the middle of fuck knows what and you're asking about the flight?" Jazz rested against the desk, semi-sitting, legs forward, arms folded, looking around the room. "I don't understand any of this. Do you have any idea what is going on at home? Where is Rae?"

"Don't talk to me about Rae. I asked you if you were seeing her! You said you weren't and you were!"

"The girl's vanished and your family don't even know," Jazz stared at me. "Surely you should be worrying about that?"

"Don't tell me what to worry about!"

"Jude your priorities are shot. This isn't about which cunt I'm screwing!

"For fuck's sake! She's not a cunt! She's my cousin! You fucking lied to me, you said you weren't doing anything about it when I asked you."

"You gave me her number, remember? Rae is a consenting adult, no different to anyone else that you or I screw. In fact, what you said at the time was that she needed 'a good shag.' You saw *my* cousins, both of them. It's fine for you to fuck my cousins but I can't go near yours?"

Looking at his face for one insane second I wanted to

punch him so hard that I'd knock him out. Instead, with great effort I quelled the anger and ignoring him, shoved open the balcony doors. I stood outside in the cool air staring at the water in the marina below, reflecting navy from the empty skies, lights fading in and out. The dark depths held twisting ropes and twining limbs. Shadowy distorted faces, Zara, my mother and Rae were interchanging in my head.

The thought of Jazz playing Rae like he played women, like *I* played women, was sickening. I hated what he was saying but I knew he was right. All that mattered was where she was now and getting her back unharmed.

Jazz stepped outside, and stood next to me above the water, opening his cigarettes. His voice low as he lit up and inhaled.

"What the fuck is going on Jude? Your mother is so high on meds that she thinks you're on Safari. What has Rae's disappearance got to do with the diamonds?"

"What?" I said.

"Here?" he asked, offering me a cigarette.

I took one, "Why would Rae's disappearance be anything to do with the ice?"

"The timing is odd," Jazz said handing me the lighter.

"What do you mean?"

"If you had got in touch sooner instead of going along with whatever scheme you've landed yourself in, we may have found her. If the diamonds have nothing to do with Rae, why did you volunteer for a job five minutes after you found a pocket full of ice in your rucksack?" Jazz asked as he ground out his cigarette, already finished.

I stared at him in cold silence. His logic numbed me. I dumped the cigarette and followed him back inside, in silence.

"Rae's somewhere man, and you're up to your neck. Talk to me."

"Enough talking! I don't know where Rae is. Don't *you* think if I did I would have got her out of wherever she was by now? We have to focus," I looked at my watch, and held my wrist out to Jazz. "We have a fucking job to do. In *forty-five minutes* Jazz we have to be somewhere." I patted him on the shoulder, my gut twisting as I tried to smile. "Man, we only have one chance. Listen, I know what I'm doing, everything is sorted."

"So if you know what you're doing, why do you need me here? You're so full of shit you're starting to believe your own crap, Jude."

I slammed my fist on the desk, "Fuck you Jazz!"

"Look Jude, either you need me here or you can go it alone. Which is it?"

"You're fucking kidding me! Of course I need you. You're my best friend. Some maniac has taken my cousin, our lives are on the fucking line and you're fucking me about," I felt confusion cloud the panic, my throat was dry, palms sweating. Jazz was doing my head in and I wished to God I hadn't phoned him. I was better off on my own.

In almost forty minutes the others were going to be there. But instead of the two of us sorting through plans and being on the same vibe, it was as if Jazz was obstructing me. I didn't get it. I was under so much pressure I didn't know how to trust anyone anymore, not even Jazz. I thought of Terri briefly, and wondered if things would have been any better if I had trusted her. I picked up my rucksack.

"Jazz, I'm going, with or without you. I called because I thought you'd understand. If you can't that is okay, but there is one favour you can do. Lie to my mum for me. Never tell her I fucked up robbing a vault in the middle of the diamond city and her niece was kidnapped under her nose or she won't be on valium she'll be on fucking heroin for the rest of her life."

"Christ! You're doing the vault? Tonight? Why didn't you fucking say so? Come on, what do we need to do?" Jazz looked at me.

I shook my head at him, everything felt distorted. "Here, this is the layout," I swiped open the plans on the phone and hit zoom, tracing the pathways in and out of the centre with the keys as Jazz stood with me, staring at the map intently. "Two take out the alarms, two take the CCTV, two wait til that's done and then we're all in, leaving the driver in the van. The inside team meets here, central, easy access once the cams are down, you can't get lost as it's a direct route, see, from where your starting point is. We take what we can carry and the van will be waiting at street level. Ninety minutes, six of us, but only five are going in. One by one drop off when we get out, no contact split. I'll deliver the van when it's over. We're connected. All you have to do when you get in is trace that route I've just highlighted."

Our phones bleeped. Mine to say the message had been sent successfully and then almost simultaneously Jazz's rang for the incoming hit. He showed me he had received it. I nodded, "Good. We're sorted," I said.

"Fuck man," Jazz said, "You seem organised."

I shrugged. "These are for you," I said, unzipping the rucksack and pulling out a gun and a rubber Joker mask.

"Nice," Jazz said, fingering the weapon then he picked up the mask. "Who are you? Fucking Batman?" he said eyebrows rising.

I shook my head, "No, I'm the same as you. Louis, who you're partnering, is Batman and the guy who's with me is too. Have you got your kit?"

"Jude that's sick, Batman and Joker," Jazz laughed. "Who is Louis? I thought *I* was with you. Yeah, I have the tool kit," Jazz said, unzipping the inside of his jacket lining and showing me.

"Louis is our alarm guy. Go in with him as back up and keep him calm. He will need you to work with him to disconnect the system shit-fast if the over-ride fucks up. The bottom line is we won't even get in if Louis can't undo the alarms."

"So everything is riding on him?"

"And on you," I nodded.

Jazz frowned, "If he's unreliable why is he doing it in the first place?"

"He's one of a kind. He helped set the systems up," I replied.

"But he's not going in the vault?" Jazz repeated.

"No, we have an arrangement, he's just there to do the electrics," I said, checking round the room one last time to see that I hadn't left anything personal anywhere. It was clear. I'd thrown away all traces of myself. The laptop was in a locker at the train-station along with a copy of as much detail on Erik and the job that I had. I'd left a note about the locker in an envelope at hotel reception with a request for it to be posted to the chief of Belgian Police first thing tomorrow. Regardless of what happened to me tonight, I was covering my mum, Rae and Zara as far as I could.

"Time to go bro," I said, slinging the rucksack on my back and holding the door open for the last time.

"Man. This is one hell of a rush," Jazz said as we

walked out.

52

Rae - Friday May 14th

Manchester

Scott was out when I got home. Home. The word was ironic. I didn't have a home any longer. Jazz had kissed me softly and driven away, the tyres leaving black scorch marks on the road. He hadn't said where he was going, or when he would be 'in touch' and this only fuelled my insecurities. Moments after he left I realised I didn't like how I felt about him, which only confused me more.

I couldn't think clearly when I was with him. I was glad I had stayed last night or I thought I was. But, now, in familiar surroundings, I was a long way from being comfortable about the four-poster bed experience. And as I flooded with anger, I knew that staying meant I'd given him control all over again. Jazz made me feel off balance and adrenalin fuelled. He put me on edge. After the predictability and staleness of my relationship with Scott, I was beginning to think that part in itself, was addictive.

The cats meandered around my legs, so happy to see me that I felt guilty. Upstairs, the smell of Scott's aftershave and the scent of the drying laundry choked me with memories as I jumped in the shower. Afterwards, I started packing, folding jeans and t-shirts, underwear, a few changes of clothes. I was only taking the basics for now, but Scott and I were done. It hurt, but as I'd said to

Jazz, from some things there was simply no way back.

When the suitcase was packed, I picked up the phone.

"Hi, Auntie, it's me, Rae."

"Hello darling, are you all right?"

"Not really. Can I come and stay for a few days? Scott and I are ... we're splitting up."

"Oh Rae I'm sorry, of course you can you know that. He told you he's been seeing someone else?"

"He's been seeing someone else? He never told me!"

"Oh no darling! I'm sorry!"

"I can't believe he's cheating on me ..."

"Has he said who?"

I burst into loud noisy sobs. "No. He didn't even tell me."

"Well then maybe it's not as bad as all that? You know what these things are like."

"It's not been working out but it's not ... only him, I can't marry him. We can't go on like this."

"Just come over."

"I thought it for ages anyway. And now you've said that, and we were breaking up because of ... because of me ... what I'd done because he'd been treating me like crap."

"Just put the phone down and come round."

"Have you heard from Jude?"

"No, but he won't have a problem. He loves you like a sister."

"Okay. See you soon."

I grabbed my bag. I had no idea what was happening in my life, my relationship with Scott was a total fake and he hadn't even told me. I thought we were engaged.

And if Jazz and I *were* seeing one another then I wasn't

skulking around, hiding. I didn't even know if I wanted a relationship with Jazz. Everything was so screwed up. But one thing was for sure I wasn't telling Jude anything over a telephone. He'd find out when he got back if I was still living at his house. I was not leaving him a voicemail. He was going to go ape-shit when he found out about me seeing Jazz, if Alex's reaction was anything to go by. For one brief second I considered going to Sara's. I could phone and go stay with her, really sort my life out. But I didn't want to leave Manchester in this mood, as I knew I wouldn't come back.

53

Jude – 1 a.m.

Antwerp

The World Diamond Centre

Streetlamps lit the chilly night air as we walked toward the old city. The streets were deserted and the building loomed fast. I glanced at Jazz, my chest tight at the memory of our ugly conversation in the hotel room, but he was here, he'd come through, and that took Rae closer to freedom than anything else.

We needed to split up. I stopped, pointed at myself and gave a flicker of a hand movement to the right. Jazz nodded, he was to go straight ahead and meet Louis. I glanced at my watch. Twelve minutes before one. Twelve minutes to get in.

Jazz grinned, his teeth white and reflective, "Don't fuck up."

I shook my head and pulled the rubber mask on. It was thick against my face and I felt the fear dissolve momentarily in that anonymity. Walking against the wall in the dark shadow of the drainage trench where the leaves fell. I stayed close to the bricks, where CCTV couldn't reach.

It had been weeks since Coco planted the ice on me,

and it felt like a year ago. Five long days of drowning in fear for Rae's life had passed and it was finally show time. The checklist in my brain was running circuits. Without thinking I knew Louis had several minutes to disable the alarms at the main doors and key in the over-ride code. That was essential. His presence would give us the chance of a safe exit if anything went wrong before we even got into the vault and needed to abort. Whilst Louis was taking out the front exit alarms, Terri and Wolf would be using their passes at the swipe-card security entrance at the side of the building to get up to the central control room. They would reset the recording in the cameras over to the disk footage taken last week, of when all was quiet.

A single figure crossed the street before becoming part of the darkness at the side of the building. I sent a fast prayer that it was Danny, with his rucksack and right on time.

Seconds later we both arrived at the back entrance, and stood together at the door, staring at unbreakable re-enforced security glass. A camera was pointing at the exit from within. A camera that was still red and active, as we waited against the bricks in dead-silence. Nine minutes to be in the vault on schedule. The red light was still active. We couldn't open the door.

Louis should have disabled that alarm at the front exit by now. When he was done all security lights would change to green. That was our signal. We'd have thirty seconds as alarms and cameras went down all over the centre. Terri and Wolf would replace the CCTV footage after Danny and I had used this back entrance. Jazz would be in via the front and Louis could leave once his part was done. Alarms would re-arm across the side and back but the front would remain clear. At that point we'd all be in with our emergency exit sorted.

I was sweating in the rubber mask, the smell beginning to nauseate me as Danny raised three fingers. We both knew the alarm should have been down three minutes ago. I patted him on the shoulder and took off, gut churning as I began running around the building.

Two minutes and I was at the front entrance. The darkness was empty. I glanced up to the camera, no flashing LED, and prayed as I reached out my hand and tested the main door. It opened.

No sign of Jazz, and Louis must have left, job done. I was off schedule by five minutes and in the wrong place. The gun felt hard as I drew it, my mouth dry, heart thudding faster than my feet as I ran through the still, black, corridor. Alone.

But I should've been with Danny. The plan was to set up together, and Terri and Wolf should be in place by now. I ran, knowing the internal stairs weren't alarmed. Two by two, up and up, no time to breathe, I half ran half threw myself onwards to the fourth floor.

The actual entrance to the vault was via a lift straight down directly to the centre. This lift was locked at night on the fifth floor, the management level. Sealed tight. Released at eight next morning. Security knew it was impenetrable. No one could use the lift. It was rigged with the ultimate electronic protection and immovable. And that lift was the only way into the vault. Which made Terri a fucking genius. The only other access point and entrance to that lift shaft was here via the fourth floor, the level where the dealer's shops were. Dealers used the lift to store the diamonds in the vault at night. Then it was sent to the fifth floor and locked.

Gasping I reached the fourth floor, hands on my

knees, bent forwards, recovery taking seconds I didn't have. I stood up. I had to get out. I pushed the door open. I was seven minutes late. But I was here and right in front of me, in the central square, were the team.

Terri waved her arms and shook her head pantomime style, as she pointed at her wristwatch. I had no chance to explain. No talking. Every fucking thing would be recorded. One Joker and one Batman were working simultaneously on the glass doors of the lift shaft. It had to be Danny and Jazz and then I realised, Danny wouldn't know Jazz wasn't me. We were similar build and wearing the same mask. I hadn't explained how we were going to get in, relief and adrenalin that Jazz was so fast on the uptake filled me.

In the half-light I saw the oil streaks gleaming on the glass. They were almost there, efficient and cleanly done. We were on schedule. Wolf and Terri simultaneously moved the suction pads in place as Danny and Jazz lowered glasscutters to the floor. There was a cracking sound and within the next second one huge circle of glass was being pulled free, I ran over as the four struggled to lower it to the floor, everyone bending beneath the weight.

The lift shaft doors now had a vast hole, middle to lower centre. Wolf and Terri moved as one, tying rope around a central pillar, securing it tight, double knotting and looping. Danny tugged hard, checking the rope was tight, as I did. Silently the five of us lined up.

After Terri had explained her plan yesterday we'd been abseiling at the management centre to get the practice, tackling outdoor drops. But this was inside a lift shaft, a totally different environment. It was the only chance we had. We were going to free fall abseil our way down to the vault. I looked at Terri, knowing she felt the same as me about heights. I wanted to reassure her, but there wasn't time. With rucksacks on their back, harnesses in place, torches in their mouths and ropes wrapped around their waist, Terri and Wolf lay down on the floor. Wolf lowered himself into the shaft. Terri lifted her head once, and joined him. I watched the gaping darkness swallow them.

At a minute and a half I felt a tug on the ropes. They were down.

Danny had repacked the glass kit tight into his rucksack. He nodded as I attached the rope to myself, thread the karabiner clip securely, turned, lay on the floor and pushed off without thinking.

It was endless, claustrophobic and black. Cables ran down the inside, the rope thick and fat between my gloved hands as I let go and dropped, stomach lurching. Too fast, jerking and clinging to the rope, I stopped. Letting go again, plummeting, swinging to one side, a chaotic pendulum, my feet narrowly missing the walls. I tried tucking my legs together, struggling with the images of Rae. Ropes meant Rae hanging helplessly and every second I had to fight against it, hands sweating. I saw her face, her body limp and swinging in front of me in the dark.

Then my feet hit the floor. Danny was down, slightly earlier slightly faster, unclipping himself as Terri and Wolf ran to him, taking the kit from his rucksack. They'd already oiled the glass doors. Danny got started on the cutter and I grabbed the other one. We were team handed when Jazz dropped down two minutes later. Danny was equipped with low key bang to get us in and deal with any unexpected problems, if needed we'd resort to a fast smash and grab.

But it didn't take long before we were pulling out the next circle. Sweating I checked my watch, the timing so tight it felt like a noose. Both Danny and I reached into our rucksacks, tugging out the portable screens to shield us from the infrared detectors. I took a deep breath and flexed up the screen, hiding myself behind it entirely. Jazz fitted next to me silent as a headstone.

Terri and Wolf bent down, knees tucked almost to the waist and then with their screen held up in front of them scooted through the glass cut-out and into the small square. This was the last hurdle, Danny next, then Jazz and me. The door to the vault was in front of us. We moved across the chamber like spiders, the screen preventing the sensor from picking up our body heat, protecting us from the alarms.

Wolf reached the security keypad on the door, tension souring the air. No one was sure if the door to the vault would simply open with the pass when the infrared alarm was on. Passes gave access during daytime when the sensors were off. This wasn't something we could try in advance.

Wolf slid his pass down and through the swipe magnet and keyed in the security code. The air was suffocating. Then as easy as a stick in water, the tonne heavy door clicked in response and swung open.

Lights were on in the vault. Every space was silver, oblong and ordered, layers of numbered boxes stacked from the ceiling to the floor.

I pulled out the reinforced sacks from my rucksack, throwing them to the team as relief jolted through me. Part one done. I glanced at my watch, we had less than one hour. Not much time. But we were in.

I started unlocking boxes, dragging them out one by one and tipping contents into the bag, bighting back the need to yell at Jazz.

'Why the fuck was Louis late with the signal?' almost burst out of my mouth every second, but I didn't dare break the silence. Terri and Wolf were working as a team, one unlocking boxes and the other pulling out, emptying contents into the sack as Danny trashed his way through his list one at a time.

Tug and pull, drag and empty. No time to think, no time to stop. When I looked up Jazz was on the other side of the vault breaking random safety deposits.

Light reflecting from the ceiling fell back onto silver. The vault was a dizzying white room limbo, the floor an obscene pirates cave, spewing money and paper bonds, as we crammed and jammed the stuff into the sacks, metal slamming as each empty box hit the floor.

The alarm on my watch went off. I shot up, startled even though I was waiting for it. Those nearest to me whirled round. I made circling movements with my hand and arm, wrap it up, 'Let's go come on' said as loudly as possible without words.

Joker-head Jazz was across the room. The pair wearing guard uniforms, Terri and Wolf dragged their sacks over to where I was standing. Danny easily lifted his and hugged it close to his chest, arms tight. Jazz ignored me.

I grabbed a box, aimed and threw it noisily to the floor to get Jazz's attention in the silence. It crashed and skidded near his feet, as I made huge 'get over here' movements even as I was at the door. We were all at the exit except for Jazz. I nodded at Danny who was by my side, then as one we twisted the handle, the two of us opening the solid exit door from the vault. The tunnel was a pit of darkness, the floodlit vault behind us.

My mind fixed on Spike. He had better be waiting as planned on that ground level past the gates. I stepped to the side. Terri and Wolf were out the door first, rucksacks on their backs and masks bobbing on their heads. Danny following them as Jazz pushed past, leaving me struggling to shut the door, which needed two people. In tiredness everything felt magnified, time exaggerated. Panic started to seep in, but the door closed leaving me in thick blackness.

The underground corridor to the car park was empty.

I couldn't hear the others and couldn't see anyone in the immediate square outside the vault. I knew once I turned that concrete corner and made it thirty paces, the lights would be on and I'd be on the stretch to the outside. All I had to do was run up the concrete slope past the sentry box and through the gates to the waiting van. It was going to take two minutes at most.

Renewed, I ran towards the corner. The exit was straight ahead now, I could see the others running out and up the slope. Terri and Wolf were in the lead. Adrenalin surged through me. I could taste it. Rae was free. Zara and Mum were fine. We were all going to make it.

Danny and Jazz were less than one minute ahead of me. They were more than half way towards the gates, already past the sentry box.

> "Arrete!" "Stop!"
> "Arrete!" "Stop!"

Shock blasted through me like shrapnel. Someone was there! My feet kept moving. I snapped a look back, and saw one guard backlit by the vault.

I kept going, my heart nearly bouncing out my ribs as the alarm hit, the noise piercing my head like steel jaws shutting on bone.

Chaos. The flood lights in the corridor were football-match bright, blinding and dazzling as the air screamed with sirens. This couldn't be happening. I couldn't believe it. We had less than eight minutes before the police arrived from the direct alarm.

Up ahead someone hesitated. Suddenly through the screech of the alarms, I could hear gunfire! They were fucking shooting at us! Instinct kicked in and instead of running directly to the exit at the T junction I doubled back and headed left at the last second. The corridor was slippery under foot as I ran hard, skidding fast and then slammed right again. It was a square. The lower corridor was a square. Vault central. If I could get up to the first floor I could get out through the main exit. My mind hit a loop, I kept repeating the plans: One access point via the lift and one exit through the vault to the underground corridor and car park. Stairs in each of the far corners.

Any staircase would take me back in to the building. Didn't matter about setting the alarm off if I broke open a fire door; it was ringing us all to hell now anyway. The guards had to chase me. I needed them to come after me to lead them away from the others. The team had to get away. If Erik got his stuff my family were going to be safe and that's all that mattered. I'd always known there was a chance I wasn't going to make it.

I ran right again at the next junction and taking the biggest fucking risk possible I headed back past the vault. I had never moved so fast in my life. I barely glimpsed it skidding past; the police would be here within six minutes. Fuck knows if the police were already here, already in, faster than we thought. But the corridor was empty. Gasping, I ran on. No guards running down the stairs to meet me as I pushed through the door, sweat running into my eyes, the mask raw against my face, breath trapped.

The loot sack dug in my back, as I scrambled up the tight flight of steps to the main floor. Ground level. I took one gulping deep breath. The door was heavy as I slammed into it, gun in position, as I pushed through, ready for the onslaught, waiting for the impact, as that door went swinging wide and open …

54

Jude - The Heist

Time suspended as I stepped out into the stillness and empty space of silence. No police, no guards, no one at all.

The entrance where I came in was directly ahead. And then I saw him clearly. Eyes wide open staring up at nothing. With no mask on his face Louis lay stone dead. I gagged as bile rose in my throat, and I started choking. The guards must have shot him.

He should have gone after the alarms went down. That was our deal. His skin was grey. I knelt down, pulled a glove off and touched his face, knowing the answer. He was cold. He couldn't have been shot just now. It wasn't possible. But the guards must have found him and shot him, so why didn't they find us earlier? Nothing made sense.

I ran out of the glass entrance, straight onto the concourse to the sound of police sirens and the night lit up with headlamps, as more gunshot followed. I glanced up and saw Wolf still dressed like a guard running towards me, no mask.

"Let's get out of here!" I screamed as Wolf swung round and opened fire on the nearest guard. The guard stared stunned and then crumpled, doubled over, releasing bullets as he fell. The police were on foot. I fired at the two running towards us, missing by a mile.

"What are you doing here?" I said, struggling to keep the gun steady.

"Never leave anyone behind!" Wolf said. "I jumped out, took the mask off. They thought I was one of them."

"Louis is dead," I hissed at him. A bullet whizzed past, Wolf cocked his rifle, took aim and fired back, his words getting lost in the sound.

"What? Fuck! We need to get out of here."

He nodded, "Over there, the coffee cart. On three, right? One, two, three."

He started running. It took me less than a second to catch up. We hid behind the cart and sheltered for another second. I scooted out, Wolf covering with me the rifle as I kicked the door, hard and the lock snapped.

Wolf leapt in after me, bent forwards, his hands on his knees, crouching, panting.

"Terri was right about you. Thanks for coming back … didn't plan … this shit," I said shaking my head between gasps. "We are completely fucked."

"No. We're not going down for this," Wolf peered at me. "Jude, is that you? What the fuck happened?"

"Yeah it's me. Don't have a fucking clue man," I said.

There was barely enough room to move in the coffee van, guards and police were swarming outside, shots ringing everywhere. "We can't stay here, they'll spring us."

"We'll make it," Wolf said. A couple of minutes passed, that was all but the brief respite was enough to get our breath back.

"What do you think happened to Louis?" I asked.

"I don't know. I wasn't there." Wolf said, shrugging. He stood by the hatch and peeled one tiny corner of the blind away from the cart's central window.

"See anything?" I asked. Wolf shook his head. The

shots had quietened down. "We should get the fuck out of here whilst it's quiet, they're distracted, won't be expecting us."

My phone buzzed interrupting me. A text. I flicked it open. "I hear things fucked up. Too bad for Rae and your little cousin."

"How the fuck? How does he know so fast?" I swore shoving the phone in my pocket, grabbing my gun, my mind scrambling.

"What's wrong?" Wolf snapped.

"There is no way he would know unless he has someone telling him. Someone is working for him directly. Or he's here. He is in Antwerp watching us." I said aloud staring at Wolf.

"Who? What are you talking about?" Wolf looked at me.

I grabbed him by the shoulders. "Have you been spying? Keeping him updated all this fucking time?"

Wolf's arms were up around mine in an instant. He was smaller than me but his strength uncoiled rattlesnake fast, forcing us both into the rows of coffee flavour optics, glass smashing and sticky liquids spilling everywhere as the car rocked dangerously.

"What the hell are you talking about?"

"Erik," I spat. "The bastard who sent you to the Bovine the other night, are you reporting back to him on the job?"

"What do you know about the Bovine?"

"Saw you in action!" I snarled.

He didn't miss a beat. "Yeah I owed him. That debt is now paid. Why would I spy on you? Jude, I have no idea what you are talking about. You're losing it," Wolf's eyes were wide, his face red, sweat smeared his skin.

The sirens broke, wailing and screaming split apart by the sound of shooting. The guns had started again.

"I believe you," I said. "I'm sorry man."

"There's no time for this bullshit now. We need to get out of here." Wolf said not waiting for an answer as he opened the door and shoved me out, jumping down next to me, gun cocked, already running.

I needed to keep it together, but Rae, Mum and Zara would all die today. I'd fucked up. Erik was going to kill them.

Someone had to be reporting back. How did Erik know? How the fuck did he know? My mind was reeling, couldn't take it in. It had to be Terri, all along. Or more likely it was Spike. It wasn't Danny. And it wasn't Wolf. My knees buckled and I went down.

Wolf's hand came towards me grabbing me by my wrist. He was pulling me up on my feet and wrenching my arm nearly out of its socket with the force as he was still running.

"Come on!" he yelled.

The shots were cracking past us, we were exposed, in a wide open space and then I heard the screaming engine as I saw the van. Spike was driving like a maniac roaring towards us, taking the bend on two wheels and mounting the pedestrian area heading straight at us. What the fuck? Shit! They were coming for us.

"Now!" Wolf yelled, as we doubled back on ourselves, racing towards the blue van.

The back doors flew open, Terri crouching and braced against the back of the door, reaching out to help us in, Wolf first. Terri had him by the hand, our bodies so close together, he and I pressed against each other scrambling, trying to get in the moving van as the bang went off. The explosion forced the breath out of my lungs, the shock-impact as the bullet hit blasting me backwards. I saw Wolf falling, away from Terri, and out of the van. Terri's screams were louder than the shots.

"No!" I shouted as he dropped.

Terri screamed again as I saw Jazz lift his rifle. He took aim and fired, hitting the guards and then four, five, six policemen with immaculate precision. One by one they went down as Wolf lay bleeding, blood seeping out, leaking on the floor, his life emptying. The concrete beneath him red and wet, his eyes staring open as I pressed my fingers against his neck. No pulse. Wolf was dead. Louis was dead. I shook my head in disbelief. They couldn't be dead.

Somehow all I could hear was Terri sobbing as I knelt with him on the floor, holding him. Numb.

The shooting stopped. Jazz looked down at me, his face lowering towards mine, his hand reaching out to help me up. And just when I was supposed to get in the van and we were supposed to escape, I stopped. No way in hell was I getting inside that van. Someone in that van was feeding Erik information.

Dropping Wolf, I spun the opposite direction and ran, pausing long enough to yank a helmet off one of the dead policeman and grab his gun. I launched myself onto an abandoned police motorbike, kicked it into life, felt the throttle surge beneath me and expelled relief as it roared forward.

I'd never seen Jazz on a job, I knew he could handle himself but I'd never seen anyone take out a row of human beings like that. That was live fucking target practice. But I knew Jazz. We were family.

My thoughts were hitting my brain like tennis balls as I

rode as fast as I dared over the dipping concourse, the bike tearing through the narrow diamond city streets. As I left the pedestrian area, one fast look in the mirror caught the van heading down one of the cobbled streets. As I flew past Spike cut in after me, wheels skidding. Why didn't they get out of here? Police sirens drenched the air as the van gorged on the space between us. Spike chasing me and being followed by the police who were hunting both of us. This was fucking stupid. We needed to split up.

It felt as if a razor blade was being dragged through my guts as my mind rattled through everything.

The heist had fucked up. Jazz was in that van because of me. Jazz was stuck with Spike, Danny and Terri, and one of those three had to be Erik's inside man. Louis and Wolf were dead. My head slammed against the helmet as the bike flew. I had one share of the loot in a rucksack, heavy against my back. Maybe it was enough.

The bike blasted out of the Old Town as I cannoned down the one-way system the wrong way. A lorry, horn blasting, approached as I leant in, knees swinging the weight to one side as I swerved. I accelerated, speeding into the bend, feeling the back wheel kick out slalom style, somehow managing to slide back on course with the G-force pushing me further ahead.

Spike, latched on by an invisible umbilical, racing behind in the van did the same. Fuck knows how there was enough room, but I glimpsed him scrape past in the mirror, almost veering sideways off the road but he made it. The police cars flooding towards the lorry began skidding, and in that split second I saw the lorry jack-knife. A moment later I heard the shattering ear-splitting noise of a collision, as my wing mirror reflected flames.

I had to concentrate. I was riding a straight line, racing west across Antwerp. The van never quite catching up, but I couldn't lose them.

I recognised where I was. Heading to the Grote Markt, a huge, simple space where Antwerp had its market. The city streets opened out, vast and wide. I flew the bike faster and faster, the air acrid as streetlights fused through my visor, fudging to a blur.

The market fair was on from midnight to 6am. People were everywhere. This was the last weekend of the Games. Police sirens were piercing, blaring blue fury in the near distance. The Ferris wheel surrounded by stands, hot dogs, candy floss and stalls loomed ahead. There were children on rides. It was a European fair, busy and sprawling. Speeding over the cobbles like a bowling ball missing skittles, I sliced through the chaos, taking a corner too fast. The wheel went from under me as I lost control, hitting the ground hard.

I shoved the bike off me and got up.

My leg hurt but I could stand, I could move. The rucksack was still strapped tight as I started walking. People scattered, stunned, staring, milling around in static groups. The pain was bad in my leg, but adrenalin pumped me through it. I tasted blood in my mouth as I merged into the claustrophobic crowd. Loud screams shredded my ears. I looked up and saw the van destroying stalls and crashing through people like plasticine dominos.

I ran past the mechanical swans, absurdly flying children into the air after 2.a.m, and families riding the horses on the merry-go-round. I kept going. My hotel wasn't far from here, down by the marina. I almost smiled through the agony and desperation. Maybe I should go to Lime and have a drink, sit and wait. I was running but there was nowhere to run. Rae would be dead by now.

My heart mirrored the agony in my body. I was at breaking point. I needed to get out of Antwerp. Leave. Somehow. But I couldn't just walk out of here.

A moment later the fog cleared. Why not? Why couldn't I just leave? The police didn't know me. I had no record. I had gloves on and was wearing a mask throughout the heist. They couldn't prove a thing. I needed to get rid of the rucksack, dispose of the jewels and the mask. Finally. I had a plan. I would dump the rucksack and pick my passport up from the train station locker before the police got the note. There was time. I was done here. The Chief of Police would have Erik's details in four hours.

Jazz would have to look out for himself. If our situations were reversed he would expect me to do the same. Gritting my teeth and trying to ignore the pain in my leg, I started walking.

55

Rae - Friday May 14th / Saturday May 15th

Manchester

Two take-away pizzas and two bottles of wine later, Auntie Lola and I were watching Game of Thrones when my mobile rang. I saw Scott's name and took a deep breath before I answered.

"You've taken your things. You've really gone haven't you?" he said.

I looked at Auntie Lola as I walked into the kitchen. "I had to. I couldn't stay. It wouldn't be fair. I've been … seeing someone else. I am sorry Scott, I feel shit about it," my words fell out in sharp gulps.

"Rae, whatever you've done, it doesn't mean anything, come home."

"Why? Because you've been fucking around on me for the past year and didn't say anything?" I heard my voice rise.

"Don't, please, I wanted to tell you …"

"But you thought you'd ask me to marry you instead."

"It … wasn't like that."

"Really? How was it like?"

"It wasn't important. It's you I want to marry …"

"You fucking idiot. You're having a laugh. You're not even denying it?" I shouted.

"I'm not denying it happened."

"So, you cheated on me, didn't tell me and then thought we could just get married as if nothing happened. That makes perfect fucking sense."

"We need to talk about this in person. Please come home Rae."

"No point. It isn't working, it isn't ever going to work, and you know it as well as I do."

"But if you love me, and I love you, we can fix it," he said, his voice breaking.

"Fuck you. It's over," I said.

The phone went silent and then I didn't know what to say, or what to do, and I was sobbing. My heart felt like it was breaking into tiny pieces. Scott and me were not getting married. We were over. I ran upstairs, crying so hard my chest hurt.

"Do you want some toast, Rae?" Auntie Lola asked, handing me a big mug of coffee.

My eyes still felt raw from the crying. "Thanks." I said, and started unpacking my few bits.

"If you don't want to talk about it, we don't have to," she said, hugging me and sitting on the bed.

"How come no one told me he was seeing someone? I mean, I know I was to blame too, for at least the past couple of weeks, but this thing with Scott ... You said you saw him about eight months ago? That's such a long time ago."

She sighed. "Miranda and I saw them both having dinner at a hotel, and they looked too close. He was with an Oriental woman and like Miranda said, what you don't know can't hurt you."

"How could you not say anything to me? I understand my mum has a fucked up sense of loyalty! But I thought you …"

Her hand felt warm on my arm. "Rae. We didn't want you to be hurt, that's all."

"How could you think everything was okay if he was seeing someone else?"

"I didn't think that, but I did believe it was better to leave it alone, and besides, you know how protective Alex and Jude are."

"What do you mean? It hasn't got anything to do with Alex or Jude!"

"Darling, you know them. If either would have heard about this, they would have taken matters into their own hands, blown it all up, and it is your life, not theirs. Look darling, if it was anything serious, then Scott would have told you himself. Not all relationships are monogamous Rae, you know that, it doesn't mean the feelings are invalid."

"I understand that, but we didn't have any kind of 'agreement.' So it's just plain old cheating. I loved Scott. I'm just not in love with him and I still didn't think we were going to break up." I felt my voice shake.

"Yet you've been seeing someone too?"

"Recently. At least I told him. He's a friend of Jude's."

Her eyebrows shot up in a silent question, but she didn't remark.

We went to bed early, I was exhausted and Auntie Lola seemed drained. I went to sleep in sheets of soft pastel blues, cocooned, surrounded by gentle colours, and dreaming of skies. And I woke up to a mobile ringing the life out of the room, shattering the perfect peace of early dawn. I looked at the display. Alex calling.

"What is it?" I managed.

"Rae, where the fuck are you? You're not at home, and your phone is dead. I just got this number off your mum. Are you all right?" Alex's voice sounded loud and brittle.

"What?"

"Where are you?" he yelled.

"Where are you?" I asked.

"I'm at your house. You're not here. What the fuck is going on?"

"What are you doing at my house? You just woke me up, what's going on?"

"I'm serious Rae, cut the shit. Are you okay?"

"No," I said.

"Fucking hell, this is going nowhere. Where are you?"

I was going to ask him what it was to him where I was. But his tone of voice and the fact he was violently awake and it was so early *and* he was calling me, all stopped me. I answered him straight.

"I'm at Jude's, I'm staying here for a while, I ... moved out of mine last night."

"See you in five minutes," Alex said.

A toothbrush, a fast black vest top, a pair of jeans later and Alex was calling, again.

"What?"

"Open up, I don't want to ring the bell."

As I let him in, he walked straight past me into the kitchen, waited and shut the door after me. He looked as rock star as ever, wearing sunglasses and biker's jacket, his car keys and mobile clanging in a pile as he junked them down on the kitchen counter along with a thick brown packet.

I'd not seen him since that horrible, blistering, row we'd had at the warehouse when he'd told me Jazz was a womanising whore. I hadn't spoken to him since he'd sacked me over the phone the next day and he'd told me to send my mum or Lola round for my wages.

"You're up early," I said looking at the floor.

It was a minute or more before he spoke. "I do get up early sometimes you know," he pulled a chair out, sat down and tugged at the one next to him for me. I stared. I wasn't used to Alex being considerate.

"I'm glad you're all right," he said. Then he got up and put the kettle on, fetched two clean mugs, tipped coffee in each and took the milk out the fridge. I was clearly hallucinating.

"You are … okay? I mean really okay? No one has done … Well, no one has … Fuck this is … You've not been …" his voice broke off as he looked at me from behind his shades, his gaze travelling straight through me.

"What are you doing here?" I asked.

"Checking you've not been … kidnapped … or … anything," he said as he poured water into mugs, making coffee.

"Alex, are you on drugs? What the fuck are you talking about?"

"Look Rae, I don't know how to say this to you, but, shit," Alex sighed, pushed his hair back from his face and took his sunglasses off.

"What in God's name are you doing going round to my house at six o' clock in the morning and why are you here asking me weirdo questions, looking at me like I don't know what?" I asked, arms tightly wrapped round my chest. "You're scaring me. What's going on?"

He shoved the chunky brown packet at me, "Special delivery, FedEx from Jude."

"Jude?" I asked.

Alex nodded. Curious, I picked the packet up. It was heavy. I opened it and tugged out a folder. On top was a note from Jude in his handwriting, yesterday's date.

Dear Alex,

I'm so fucking sorry to do this to you but a player named Erik has got Rae and I need your help. I saw Coco a month ago. She planted a packet of stolen ice on me, and vanished. I was furious, worried sick, so I went to find her. She never turned up. The ice is Erik's, and he thinks Rae is my sister so he took her to make sure I did a job as payment. It's personal. He knows us both. He's threatened your Zara and my mum next.

The job's tonight in Antwerp; By the time you get this it'll be over. I'll be dead, or as good as. If I make it through I'm going for Erik myself. I've sent a copy of this to the police in Antwerp. Do whatever's necessary to keep Zara safe, and protect my mum. Please. I know you'll do right by them. Jazz is over here with me, I needed his help on the job.

Find Rae, Alex, please, I don't know if he'll release her or it's already too late. Got nowhere else to turn, so it's on you. Sorry man.

Jude.

I dropped the envelope. This couldn't be real. This couldn't be happening. I wanted to be wrong, more than anything I wanted to be wrong but I knew what was in that package. I knew what I was going to find, and I didn't want to see. More than that, I desperately didn't want Alex to see. I stumbled backwards, knocking into the chair and the table.

Alex started speaking, "Look nothing matters as long as you're okay."

"You've seen them haven't you?"

"I saw the first one and …"

I couldn't breathe, asphyxiated, the same as if Jazz was holding a pillow over my head. Alex knew. He didn't have to say another word. Pity was wiped all over his face. Within a second I was jamming the key in the backdoor and shoving it open.

"Rae, wait," Alex grabbed my arm but I pulled free and was out the door before he could get near me again. I started running. Running in my bare feet. For one single moment I felt the gravel on the driveway as it drove into my skin, puncturing hard and I didn't care. I ran down the path to the front gate and out onto the pavement. The stinging sharp cuts hardly registered as pain next to what I was feeling inside.

Jazz had used me. He'd used me in a way I couldn't even comprehend. I'd been used so he could fuck Jude over. The things we'd done, all of it, just to get some stinking photographs? No. No way. How could he do this to me? How the fuck could he do this? He'd ripped my trust out and gutted me like a fish. I ended my fucking engagement over him. I blew my life apart because of him.

All that drama yesterday about me leaving, and him stopping me, I thought he cared! When all along it was only ever about Jude and some job? I was nothing to him.

Cars were on the road, the first of the early morning traffic jams and I kept running because I couldn't stop. It was never about me, none of it. When he hung me from the rope! I was sobbing so hard. All those things I'd let him do to me.

Kidnapped? I might as well have been. Any time he liked he could have kept me there, in that flat, or kept me anywhere he wanted!

Realisation soared through me. It wasn't all in my head! Everything I felt yesterday, all of it ... It wasn't in my head! He must have known I would go straight to Jude's house. I was so fucking obvious. How could he?

But how could I?

I hadn't had a single rational, sane, thought in my head since I'd met him. I'd treated Scott like dirt. Cheated on him when I could have been honest and I'd made that choice. My actions were nothing to do with Jazz, he played me all right, but he hadn't forced me. As much as I'd denied it, I'd wanted Jazz after the first bit of attention he showed me, when all along I knew that guys like Jazz *never* wanted girls like me. I'd been so fucking stupid. But what in hell had Jude been dragged into?

My heart was thudding so hard it hammered in my head, my nose was running, my eyes were streaming. I couldn't see where I was going, and I didn't care. Gardens flew past as my feet went on slamming into the concrete. Running was the only thing that made sense.

I missed the curb awkwardly and screamed as I fell. Crucifying pain shot through my ankle. Everything went dark.

"Rae! Thank fuck you're in one piece you fucking idiot," Alex was standing above me as I came round.

I was lying on the pavement and it was brutally hard. The pain was so bad in my ankle that I nearly blacked out again. "Alex," I started to sob and hid my face in my hands.

He crouched beside me, pulled my hands away and wiped the tears with his thumb.

"Listen, I only saw the first couple of pictures. I didn't look any further, honestly. I don't know what's going on here."

"You warned me. You said don't go near him," I felt like I was broken into a million fragments.

Alex stared at me, his face very pale. "Jazz?"

I nodded, burning, someplace beyond shame at Alex and Jude having seen me so exposed.

Alex hit his hand hard on the ground. "Christ Rae when I said stay away from him, I didn't think this. You have to believe me."

"What's he done to Jude?"

"Let's worry about Jude in a minute, are you all right?"

"Alex I am far from all right and my ankle is one hundred percent fucked."

He looked at me, "Can you stand on it if I hold you?" Alex stood up and wrapped his arms around me.

Trembling I put it down on the floor then lifted it straight back up as everything started to fade very fast. "No chance."

"We need to get you to a hospital," he said. "Come on, let me carry you?"

"Carry me?" I repeated at him.

"Either that or you stay here whilst I go back and get the car," Alex replied.

"Jude's in Antwerp, dead or arrested, and he's done some job cos he thinks I've been kidnapped and his ex girlfriend has disappeared. Jazz is actually some guy called Erik who got Jude into this by sending him a bunch of photos that I wish with my whole heart I could destroy off the face of the earth and my ankle is broken. Sure why don't you carry me, we'll go get your car and then we'll go to hospital. Why not? They fix everything there," I was choking on tears as they stuck in my throat.

Alex stared at me like I'd grown another head. "We have to get your ankle looked at," he said, still holding me up.

"What are we going to do about Jude? Don't you think we should call the police?" I asked the flood of panic making me feel sicker than the pain.

"No," Alex replied sharply.

"Why not? Have you heard from him?" I said.

"I got a text saying he was all right." Alex reached for his phone and opened it, skimmed down his inbox and showed me. It was a number I didn't recognise.

"Hi it's me. Hope you got the post. Sorry for everything. Jude."

"When did you get that text?" I asked, not convinced.

"Early," Alex replied shortly.

"But we don't know if he's okay," I said, crying again.

"If he sent the text he's okay. Trust me. He'll be in touch, got to give him time, Rae. If I've not heard anything by tomorrow night I'll deal with it, I promise."

It was all filtering in ever so slowly. One drip at a time until a pool gathered. The fall out from the explosion left me numb, shock settled like ash. Jazz had used me and he wasn't coming back, not next week, not ever. Jude was gone. Scott was a lying cheating bastard and now he was gone too.

Alex took advantage of my silence and scooped me up against his chest like I was made of air. I put an arm around his neck as he started walking back towards Jude's.

"Lola wasn't up when I left but I don't know if she's going to still be asleep now, do you want to go in?" Alex said as I saw his car parked in a hurry, slanting against the pavement by the house.

"Did you leave the photos on the table?"

"No of course not, I dropped them in the boot before I came after you."

I looked at the house and noticed that the downstairs curtains were open. I sighed, "Hospital?" I couldn't face Auntie Lola. Couldn't face anyone.

"Sure."

He set me down gently whilst he opened the car and then helped me swing in to the seat. Seconds later he was buckling up his seatbelt and we were merging into the morning traffic. The pain in my ankle obliterating almost everything else, I looked down and wished I hadn't, my foot was swollen and a nasty blue colour.

"So, have you really left Scott?" Alex asked concentrating on the traffic.

"Yep, it's over," I said.

"Even with Jazz gone?" he asked.

"Yes, even with Jazz gone," I said, shuddering.

"You sure?" he asked.

"He's been cheating on me for the past eight months, apparently."

"Oh shit. That's rough. I am really sorry."

I shrugged. "Yeah and I'm an idiot for not realising sooner."

"Sooner?"

"Thought something was up. But what can I do?" I coughed back a lump in my throat.

"Do you want me to have a word? I can …"

"Don't you dare! This is my crap!" I glared at him.

"Are you sure it's finished though?"

"Are you fucking kidding me? Everything is finished. I was engaged a whole five minutes and I ditched my lying cheating fiancé for a guy who is certifiably insane. Plus my cousin who I thought I knew better than myself is a complete fuckwit who goes off doing the kind of jobs I don't even want to think about."

Alex burst out laughing.

"You laughing at my life is not helping right now." I sniffed.

"So, you'll come out for dinner with me?" Alex said.

"What?" I felt my eyes launch out of their sockets towards him.

"Forget it." Alex said. "I'm sorry, it's a ridiculous idea."

I must have banged my head when I fell. "You are taking the piss, right?"

"No. I'm asking you out," Alex said smiling again.

"My life is in pieces and you're asking me out?"

"It'll take your mind off it," Alex said.

"So you feel sorry for me?"

"Yeah, kind of. How about tomorrow night?"

"If I'm not in hospital having surgery, I've got tickets for P. J. Harvey tomorrow night. Plus, since you haven't noticed it seems right to tell you that I have absolutely shit taste in men. I've screwed my entire life up and you're lethal where women are concerned. I'm not even your type."

"Fuck no way! You've got tickets?" Alex's jaw looked a little slack. "What do you mean you're not my type?" he turned his piercing blue gaze on me before he flickered back to the road and took the next turning for the hospital.

"You'd have said something years ago if you were ever interested," I mumbled blushing so hot that my face hurt almost as much as my foot. "Yes I have tickets. Scott was meant to be coming but he's not that into her and ..."

"They sold out so fast!" He shook his head.

"It's yours," I said.

"Great thanks," Alex replied.

"That's sorted then," I said trying really hard to pretend the rest of the conversation hadn't happened as we pulled up outside the hospital. But as the car stopped Alex turned to me, his eyes like the ocean.

"You're an idiot. I never went near you when you were younger because you needed someone who could give you ... what I couldn't," he said, looking down at his hands.

"Alex, please don't," I muttered, my eyes filling up.

"In a way, we're kind of similar, you and me," Alex continued, his fingers reaching for mine.

"What do you mean?" I asked.

He shrugged, "Maybe you settled for Scott because you were tired of looking for something else."

"But you don't settle at all. You're the opposite. Do you ever love anyone?" I asked, the words sticking a little.

"That's not fair Rae. I've been in love. Just easier to avoid, so maybe we both took ... the easy option, that's all I meant."

"Alex, my foot is killing me."

He looked down, "One step at a time."

Three hours later my leg was in a cast. I'd fractured the foot, not the ankle. The ankle was sprained and would heal without an op and the Doctor said I was extremely lucky.

As we pulled up to Auntie Lola's I turned to Alex. He'd been silent on the way home. I wasn't sure I could cope with him at the best of times and right now I was in pieces. Looking at him, I realised that I'd loved him for so long those feelings were part of my mental furniture.

But I didn't trust anything I thought or felt, other than knowing that love didn't mean a fucking thing. Love was bullshit. And although I couldn't go backwards, for one stupid second I really wished I had the safety of Scott to go home to and that we could just rewind this whole mess. Return to normality.

"Thanks for everything," I said, balancing crutches and seatbelt.

Alex was out in a flash and the door was open. "Let me take you to the gig tomorrow night, you'll need some help," he said, not quite meeting my eyes.

"So you've not changed your mind then?"

He shook his head, "Up to you."

"The ticket's got your name on it, pick it up later, but I'll go to the show myself … I can't … I'm not in a good place at the moment," I said, my voice cracking.

He nodded, and seemed very vulnerable for once, quite un-Alex like.

"Are we okay?" I asked.

He paused.

"You're not the only one who screws things up … There's a lot of stuff you don't know about me. Like Zara …"

"Like Zara's not actually your sister?" I finished, finally seeing the truth.

"Yep. She's my daughter. Her mum died when she was a year old, heroin overdose."

"Oh God. Am so sorry."

"Zara is the one good thing to come out of all that." He dropped his voice, "Now's not the right time."

"Rae! Alex! What's going on?" Auntie Lola was stood at the front door, pointing at the crutches.

"She'll be in – in a second." Alex said.

"Alex," I said, quietly and stood still.

"Yep?"

"It's just … 'not the right time' and I honestly don't know if it ever will be," I looked at him as the words fell out in a rush.

He squeezed my hand in reply and then pulled me close in a full body hug. I closed my eyes, tears falling into Alex's shoulder.

56

Jude 2.30 a.m.

Antwerp

There were police swarming everywhere, a navy moving blanket, spreading across the market as I left, head down, chin jammed into my jacket collar. The night wind was scathingly cold and I was limping. I kept going, following the wide-open roads towards the docks.

The statue of the Goddess of war and defender of trade, Minerva, stood to attention as I approached. Minerva invited ships into the harbour, offering a stern welcome, warning visitors that she was ready to defend Antwerp if the occasion needed. She was a fellow warrior, and I saluted her, hoping she would defend me. But I had just robbed her city and I didn't know if her protection would cover blowing a vault in exchange for our lives.

The breeze felt calmer by the docks. Sprawling, jagged, chunks of Antwerp were left unfinished, incomplete buildings, with roofs and walls missing. Skinny cranes jabbing upwards into the skies, standing next to potential apartment blocks, and I knew those half-built, leering, giants would fall to their knees should their rifle-like neighbours insist.

A mechanical screech startled me.

Police helicopters! For a second I couldn't believe it and then I laughed. We'd violated the World Diamond

Centre ninety minutes ago, what did I expect? The reality and enormity of what we'd done wasn't registering. Nothing was important other than getting Rae back. But suddenly the fear of getting caught burned through me as I heard the sirens again. My phone vibrated. Even that muffled sound was too huge in the night air. The water's edge was just ahead, not far now. I picked up the call and kept walking.

"It's me. Where the hell are you?" Terri sounded raw.

"What the fuck is going on?" I hissed, not raising my voice.

"It was chaos. Danny got out and Spike was pulled. Can't believe they took him," her voice dipped even lower.

"You okay?" I asked, instinctively.

"No. I'm not fucking okay," she snapped.

"But you got away," I said softly, standing still, staring at the water, dark and deep.

"Yes. I got away and Erik got away," Terri answered.

"Erik got away?" I repeated. I wasn't sure I heard right.

"Yeah …"

I killed the call. What the fuck did she mean? Erik got away? I rang her back.

"Sorry my phone cut out. Is Erik with you?" I asked.

"What?" she asked.

"Is he there?"

"No," Terri replied.

"We need to meet. Can you get the stuff back to him for me?"

"Are you fucking insane? There are pigs everywhere."

"We had masks on and you and Wolf were in uniform. They don't know who the fuck they're looking for."

Terri made an odd noise, "He was my brother. Wolf. He was my twin."

"Oh Jesus. I am so sorry baby, I didn't know. Forget it, you're right, let's leave it," I said, slipping off the rucksack even as I was speaking to her. There was no point. It was over. Done. I tightened up the bag, making sure the mask was in there before I lowered it down, soundlessly, into the water, watching as it sank.

"This is it," I said to her. "Take care of yourself."

"No. Look, I'm not far from your hotel," she said suddenly. "I want to see you ... Say goodbye in person."

"I'm not sure that's a sane idea." I said, staring into the water.

"You owe me that," she whispered.

"Okay. I'll meet you there," I relented. Despite myself I wanted to see her too, I owed it to Wolf to check on her for his effort in coming back for me.

The hotel was a five-minute walk from the harbour. I got there in three. Reception was empty as I walked through the hallway and caught the lift up to my room. The plastic key slid in to the metal slot and the door swung wide. I had never been so glad to see anywhere in my life. Even the air was welcoming and soothing, everything in this gently lit room was silent and still. Normal. Nothing had changed in here. But tonight had happened and should I have any doubt at all, there were plenty of physical reminders from coming off the bike. I was covered in bruises. My whole body hurt.

I poured myself a whisky from the mini bar and downed it. My head felt like a kettle bell and my neck was protesting. I tipped another whisky in the glass, drank hard and as the firewater hit my throat I threw the fucking glass, watching it splinter into a thousand pieces as it smashed into the wall.

It didn't help. I checked my watch, 2.46 a.m. I hoped Terri was going to be here soon. I needed to be gone. As if she knew my thoughts I heard knocking.

I opened the door to Terri's face, tearstained and small.

"Hi," I said.

"Jude I'm so sorry …"

"Quiet, bitch," said Jazz standing behind her, closing in tight.

"What the fuck's going on?" I said surprised to see him.

"It's been quite a night," Jazz said calmly as he pushed Terri inside and kicked the door shut. Then I saw the gun, pointed into her spine. Her wrists were taped together, arms pulled back.

"Talk to me bro, what's happening here?" I said backing away, slowly, hands up.

"Call it a debrief. Where's the loot Jude? What did you do with the stash?"

"I got rid. Nothing to tie us to this," I had my eyes on the gun, it was directed at me now.

"Oh man," he sighed. "You really fucked up."

"Jazz come on, it wasn't just down to me," I said.

Jazz loosened his shirt with one hand, pulled the neck open and smiled at me like we were going out for a drink, "Same old Jude, always someone else's fault. All you had to do was get out of there, well, get in and get out."

"What do you know about it?" I asked.

Jazz laughed, "I know plenty about lots of things. So, this is what my money bought you, a nice holiday for a few days. Did you enjoy yourself?"

"Your money? What the fuck are you talking about

Jazz? You're not making any sense."

"Neither are you!" Terri burst out. "Who the fuck is Jazz?"

"Didn't you two have time for introductions? That's Jazz." I said pointing at Jazz.

She looked first at me and then at him, "Jazz? He's not fucking Ja…"

"Shut. Up." Jazz said, casually slapping her with the back of his gun-hand. The weight of the blow knocking her sideways. She stumbled, falling onto her knees.

"I like a bitch on her knees. Don't you Jude? You know, your cousin loves being on her knees. She's not what you could call a 'nice Jewish' girl. But I had a lot of fun with her, and the fact she liked it made it all so much easier," he said laughing, moving as he was talking, pacing around the room. The gun still trained on me.

Terri was silent, a broken heap on the floor.

"I don't want to know what you did with Rae," I said, the words choking in my mouth.

"Jude, you're not shy. Tell me what you thought when you saw the pictures. You got hard didn't you? Looking at her like that. Wasn't she beautiful? Begging for it. She did beg for it. She loved it," he said.

I didn't think I'd heard him right, "What? What the fuck are you saying?"

He looked me in the eyes. "They're my photos. I took them all, every single shot. Man she tasted good," he kissed his fingers to his lips.

"Do you know what else?" he dropped his voice. "She really loves being fucked in the ass when she's tied up. Let me tell you Jude, Rae enjoyed every single one of those pictures. Ask her! There's no shame!"

I punched his face, square in the jaw, my fist smashing

upwards into the cheekbone even as I was grabbing him by the throat, shoving him against the wall, and diving into him with full bodyweight. I had one fist on his neck and the other on his wrist as I slammed his gun-arm hard into the wall. "What – have - you - done - to - her?" I said hitting him with each word.

"Nothing she didn't want me to," he said, spitting blood out.

My mind wasn't processing things well.

I was stuck somewhere on the fact that my best friend Jazz seemed to be telling me that he was Erik. And that Erik, the bastard who had taken Rae and done fuck knows what to Coco, was standing in front of me, looking and sounding exactly like Jazz. It didn't seem possible.

"No. I don't believe it. This wasn't you."

He didn't reply. But I knew, looking at his face, that it was true.

"How could you?"

He answered with his knee, aiming for my groin as I slammed his hand into the wall again, until finally he dropped the gun. Lunging after the weapon, we both hit the floor on top of one another, rolling into the side of the bed, and then hitting the desk. My fist thudded into bone and somehow I sat astride him, knees in his chest and stopped raining blows.

"Why?"

The question enraged him. He broke free. Then both of us were tearing our souls out for the gun, both of us, but only him getting it.

Jazz stood upright, aiming the barrel at me, as he mopped at his face, wiping the blood. "I didn't want it to come to this Jude. But I told her two years ago you were useless."

"Rae?"

"No!"

"Who?"

"Coco."

"My Coco?" I asked.

"No. My Coco," Jazz laughed.

"You and her?" I said, my voice sounded tight.

"I forgot there's so much you don't know," Jazz laughed. "You were always getting into things that didn't concern you in London. Our upstairs club … and there you were, nosing around causing problems. So, Alex suggested Amsterdam and I told Coco to keep you occupied," he stepped towards the window, the gun pointing on me the whole time.

My eyes followed him. It was dawn. The sky was alight with streaks of yellow as the sun began to rise. I was numb.

"You're lying."

Jazz shrugged. "Believe whatever you want Jude, the real lies you tell yourself or the fake truth you think you're hearing now."

My head was spinning. "You're making no sense. You said Alex knows everything?"

"No. That's the fucking point, Alex is a stupid cunt. But you and a woman like that. Laughable."

"I fucking loved her!"

"You're fucking spineless! That bitch tried to cross me, get the ice to Alex, and it's not the first time she's done that. The two of them have been cutting me out of my own jobs," Jazz waved the gun.

"That's got nothing to do with me or Rae!"

"Alex is in love with your little cousin, he told me about it years ago," Jazz laughed. "Coco chose you! You could have kept the stuff, sold it, or anything. Man, the irony when you came directly to me. I could have taken it off you whenever I wanted. Instead, when the time was right I took the guy out and gave you the biggest opportunity you'll ever have! All your life you've been following me around like a puppy. Antwerp was set up a long while ago and I welcome you to the game with open arms! What happens? You fuck it up. Man do I ever hate fuck ups. That alarm guy tonight fucked up. If I hadn't been there we never would have got in. Not that it did us much good. But the world's a better place without idiots," Jazz said.

"You're fucking insane! You think you did me a favour? You set me up! You made me think you'd kidnapped Rae and you killed Louis."

"He was a fucking idiot!"

"And you're an asshole! You played me and I trusted you with my fucking life."

Jazz / Erik laughed, "This is my life Jude and I trusted you. We're the same you and me. Look at what you did to him, that alarm guy; you threatened his family didn't you? He told me! He begged for his grandkid's life, told me to take his instead. Jude you used anything you could, we both know that you'd have taken that kid out if I had told you to. You'd play anyone given the chance, use anyone, you'd do anything to get what you want. You're just like me. You'd like to think you're different but you're not."

"I'm nothing like you."

"Sure you're nothing like me. You're going straight now." Jazz / Erik laughed again, waving his arm in a huge circle. "How many jobs have you had since you went straight? How many decent girlfriends? Do you even know their fucking names? The women you take back to your flat night after night and get rid of in the morning?"

I was silent.

"So I'm wrong and corporate business loves you? They welcome you to their golf clubs and their gyms with open arms?" Jazz / Erik shook his head. "Jude, don't make the mistake of thinking you're like them, you're not. You'll never be anything other than who you are. Only you couldn't even get this right." Jazz raised the gun and aimed it at me.

"Yeah, you may as well fucking kill me. I loved you like you were my fucking brother. You and me, man we were brothers," I said staring at the barrel and looking over at Terri behind Jazz.

I stared at him, and nodded at her. "Do it, if you're going to do it. Just do it! Cos I've had enough of this shit, I don't give a fuck any more. Get it over with. Do it now!"

I heard a strangled noise. Terri was up, running hard and fast, straight into Jazz, her head bowed, head butting his stomach, pure force taking over, as she drove into him pushing him. The gun cracked. The shot sent fear drilling through me as I dived and hit the floor. Two more bangs as the gun fired upwards into the glass, the window shattering as the bullets blew it apart. They both went straight through, gravity and momentum forcing them out the gaping hole, smashing five floors down into the harbour. They'd missed the balcony and gone straight through an ordinary window.

My heart skipped. Terri's hands were still tied. She could drown if she even survived the glass and the impact. If Jazz was alive he was going to kill her. I stood up and looked around, the gun wasn't here. He must have still had it when he fell. I grabbed at the phone and called reception. "Accident, fifth floor east, two people have broken ... fallen through a window."

I slammed the handset down and started running. If the hotel called the police they wouldn't know who'd carried out the heist. But it wouldn't be a far stretch to guess. A fight in a local hotel, with guests falling through the window and a gun going off? They'd know it was us as soon as the call went through. Who the fuck was I kidding?

I prayed Terri was going to be okay, grabbed my stuff and left. Two solid security guards were on their way out of the lift opposite in the hallway. I hung back, chest thudding, as another minute was lost and I stood waiting behind the corner until they'd gone. Then I snuck down the stairs. As fast I could, one foot in front of another, not even walking was automatic anymore. I had to concentrate as one by one each white step took me further and further down, my leg ached like lead as I went side by side with the metal railings, past each red number.

I took the steps all the way down to the pool level and hovered for a second near the small square glass window in the door. Outside the window was chaos, it had been a matter of minutes and already people jammed my vision. I knew there was no way I could go through that door full of blood and bruises, looking like this. I wouldn't get out again. Too many questions would be asked.

Feeling sick and torn apart with guilt I turned and left the woman who had saved my life. I denied every impulse to run and dive into that pool and drag her out. I wouldn't be able to save us both. But I wasn't going through all this for nothing, Terri couldn't be my problem. I needed to survive. I slipped back through the door and round the fire exit to the side of the hotel and then out.

57

Jude – dawn

Antwerp

It was almost 5 a.m. The sun lay hidden beneath golden milky clouds. Ribbons of pink and smears of lilac suffused the morning sky as I made my way down to the harbour. Limping past the orange cranes piercing the skyline, and along the open, wide, brick walkway, exhaustion threatened to overwhelm. But the construction site was just ahead. The early morning smell of the water, a mixture of fish and oil clung to the air and lingered.

I checked my watch.

Stopping when I reached two minutes walking time, I looked carefully for the marker I'd left earlier. The entire place was deserted. I sank to my knees and very quickly twisted together the two cheap metal coat hangers that I'd brought with me. I leant forwards, and with one movement pulled out the rucksack. The water released it, slick, wet and unharmed.

The ice was settled safely where I'd left it. Using the letter opener from the hotel I slashed the mask into pieces. Wiping my mouth, I gulped down nausea and worry about Terri but there was nothing I could do. I took another deep breath, dropped the rubbish into the cleansing water and walked briskly to the train station. Alex would have the packet I'd sent him and would do right by Zara, Rae and my mum. I needed to vanish.

At the station I switched on my old mobile. It took a moment to check for any missed calls and quickly copy any last numbers I needed. I snapped the sim card in two pieces and dropped it in the nearest bin, smiling.

A text had come through at some time during the job last night. It was a picture message, from an unknown number. My breath caught as I'd opened it, and saw three red mice in the palm of a familiar hand.

The adventure continues . . .
Stay in touch with the author via:

Website: www.rachealbloom.com

Facebook: www.facebook.com/rachealbloom

Twitter: http://twitter.com/Vixen_

If you liked RED MiCE, please post a review at Amazon, or visit her website. Let your friends know about the RED MiCE series. Thank you.

Printed in Poland
by Amazon Fulfillment
Poland Sp. z o.o., Wrocław